Abo

Eamonn Griffin was born ⸱   ... Lincolnshire, though these days he lives in north-east Wales.

He has worked as a stonemason, a strawberry picker, in plastics factories, in agricultural and industrial laboratories, in a computer games shop, and latterly in further and higher education.

He has taught and lectured in subjects as diverse as leisure and tourism, uniformed public services, English studies, creative writing, film studies, TV and film production, and media theory. He doesn't do any of that any more. Instead he writes full time, either as a freelancer, or else on fiction.

Eamonn has a PhD in creative writing with the University of Lancaster, specialising in historical fiction, having previously completed both an MA in popular film and a BSc in sociology and politics via the Open University. He really likes biltong, and has recently returned to learning to play piano, something he abandoned when he was about seven and has regretted since.

EAST OF ENGLAND

EAST OF ENGLAND

EAMONN GRIFFIN

Unbound Digital

This edition first published in 2019

Unbound

6th Floor Mutual House, 70 Conduit Street, London W1S 2GF

www.unbound.com

All rights reserved

© Eamonn Griffin, 2019

ISBN (eBook): 978-1-78965-015-0
ISBN (Paperback): 978-1-78965-014-3

Cover design by Mecob

Printed and bound in Great Britain by Clays Ltd, Elcograf S.p.A.

This is for Joanne

Dear Reader,

The book you are holding came about in a rather different way to most others. It was funded directly by readers through a new website: Unbound.

Unbound is the creation of three writers. We started the company because we believed there had to be a better deal for both writers and readers. On the Unbound website, authors share the ideas for the books they want to write directly with readers. If enough of you support the book by pledging for it in advance, we produce a beautifully bound special subscribers' edition and distribute a regular edition and e-book wherever books are sold, in shops and online.

This new way of publishing is actually a very old idea (Samuel Johnson funded his dictionary this way). We're just using the internet to build each writer a network of patrons. Here, at the back of this book, you'll find the names of all the people who made it happen.

Publishing in this way means readers are no longer just passive consumers of the books they buy, and authors are free to write the books they really want. They get a much fairer return too – half the profits their books generate, rather than a tiny percentage of the cover price.

If you're not yet a subscriber, we hope that you'll want to join our publishing revolution and have your name listed in one of our books in the future. To get you started, here is a £5 discount on your first pledge. Just visit unbound.com, make your pledge and type GRIFFIN19 in the promo code box when you check out.

Thank you for your support,

Dan, Justin and John
Founders, Unbound

Super Patrons

Graeme Oxby
Mr B Runo AKA Bruno Pearce
George Pearce and Sasha Pearce
Joanne Pearce
Mark Randall
Paul Roberts
Tony Roberts
Anne Russell
Michael T A Smith
John Smyth
Anita Squires
David Stapleton
Jakki Stemp
John Tarrow
Diane Thompson
Adam Tinworth
Martin Togher
Paul Verrico
Julie Warren
Philip Whiteley
Howard Wix
Lucy Yvart

I am a debtor both to the Greeks, and to the Barbarians; both to the wise and to the unwise.
    – *Romans* 1:14

Monday

Dan Matlock stepped out into the real world again. Somewhere behind him, the guard who had opened the door shouted 'See you soon', but Matlock was already walking away from jail.

There was no one waiting for him.

Okay then.

He wasn't expecting Joe to be there. Not really. But it might have been nice. Would have made things simpler.

Lincoln County Hospital is opposite the city's prison.

Matlock crossed the road without looking left or right. It was early. He'd have heard something if there was any traffic.

The car park on the far side of the road was a third full. Six-to-two workers, spouses on overnight bedside vigils, keen-bean office suits.

Scant remnants of a hedge led to a muddy incline down to the tarmac. Matlock scanned till he found the right kind of car. Something old, something uncomplicated.

A once-red hatchback, its paint faded to a blush. No one around. Matlock put the bag with his belongings from the prison tight up to the driver's side window. He punched through the bag to quell the noise and to not get cut.

The glass gave way like it wanted to.

Matlock chucked the bag onto the passenger front seat. He swept away the worst of the glass into the footwell, then wound what was left of the window right down. It'd pass a glancing inspection.

He snapped the plastic trim away from under the steering column, and found the right wires. Some tricks you never unlearn. The car coughed into life. The radio lit up; local-news chatter.

Okay. Deep breath. It had been two years since Matlock had sat behind the wheel of a motor. Last time he'd done so, he had killed the wrong man.

Matlock pulled off towards the car park exit. An early-morning smoker – IV stand and dressing gown – lurked far enough from the sliding main doors to deter a jobsworth from coming out to grumble

1

something about keeping that shit in the shelters. Matlock passed the patient, turned right towards the main road.

He slowed to give way at the car park exit, even though there was no road traffic coming in either direction.

He could turn right. Back to where it had all gone wrong.

Where it might be worse than ever, and waiting for him, fists balled.

Or he could turn left, make his way through Lincoln city centre, and be out of the county within half an hour. Put the last two years and more behind him. Family, lost loves, the lot of it. Head west, as if chased by the racing sun. Make up a name. Fall into something or other somewhere else. Shed his old skin.

But not without his dad saying that it was okay to do your own thing. That he understood.

Joe was supposed to be here.

Promises had been made.

Something was wrong.

Joe was meant to be here.

Okay.

Matlock didn't indicate. He turned to head east.

A recess between the front seats. Loose change and the stubby roll ends of mints. Three, maybe four quid there in coins. Enough for a coffee. There was a McDonald's on the way out of town.

Most of a tank of fuel. He'd be getting rid of the car sooner rather than later, plus he wasn't going far. Less than thirty miles. And just one stop on the way. Two, if you counted picking up the hot drink.

*

Matlock pulled off the A158 onto a side road. Then onto a farm track; tilled land on one side, thickish woodland on the other. He parked. Got out of the car, bringing his coffee with him. Was glad of its warmth.

A rummage in the glove compartment had yielded a screwdriver. The kind with multiple changeable ends fitted into the handle. The sort of tool an amateur would buy. Nevertheless, Matlock selected a flat blade and clicked it into the shaft of the driver. It locked into place with a pleasing magnetic snap.

Matlock turned to the rear of the vehicle. He slipped the blade into the lock of the hatchback and gave a shove and a twist. The lock surrendered.

He'd hoped for a toolbox, maybe a snow shovel. An ice scraper even. It was that time of year. Something to dig with. The boot space felt like it had scarcely ever been troubled. Clean carpet. A plastic tub of detergents and cloths. The distant tang of cleanliness. No wheel brace with the spare tyre though. That would have done nicely. Matlock shut the boot, and took the screwdriver and the coffee into the woods.

It was still dark under the canopy. Matlock gave it a few minutes for his eyes to adjust. There was a path, marked periodically with wooden signs for ramblers, that he followed for fifty yards or so. Twice there had been signs of activity: a stamped-out fire circle; a little clearing, the trees thereabouts garlanded with used condoms and cigarette ends. He carried on until he found the right spot. A turn into the thicker undergrowth.

His secret stash. An insurance policy. Sometimes it pays to be cautious.

An all but imperceptible bump in the ground. That was where Matlock started working. First with the screwdriver to loosen the compacted earth, and then with his hands.

It took less time to dig it up than it had to bury it in the first place.

Matlock lifted it out. A freezer bag; the sort with a ziplock. Inside the bag, a metal tin. It had held toffees originally, some ill-advised holiday gift from a previous life. Still, the box had turned out useful more than once.

Deep breath. The container popped its lid on demand. Another ziplock bag. The money was all there inside, as it had been when he had buried it. And under the money, the other thing. This, Matlock slipped into a pocket without checking.

Matlock had done his research, and had chosen the denomination which had most recently been updated, design-wise. This gave the notes the longest storage life possible. There was enough here to get started again. Not Caribbean island-style, but enough.

White sands weren't what Matlock had in mind.

He poured away the last of the now-cold coffee. He dropped the takeaway beaker into the hole he'd scraped out, and kicked the mound of loose soil back over. He pressed the earth back into place with his shoe, and headed back to the car.

Safe in the vehicle, Matlock retrieved the unchecked packet. He unwrapped it. A revolver. A .38 Ruger Speed Six.

The Ruger is a small firearm with a short barrel, designed for concealment. A back-up gun. A throwdown.

There were five live cartridges left.

If it came to it, Matlock reckoned, five would be plenty.

*

The A158 runs west to east from Lincoln. Bland agricultural land, commuter villages bisected by the main road, lay-bys with shipping containers converted into lock-up cafes.

At Wragglesby, Matlock took the left-hand spur onto the A157. To stay on the main road would see him curve southwards through Baincaster, then diagonally across the Wolds to the coast. To Skegthorpe. Skeg Vegas.

The A157 keeps a truer course east.

Matlock flipped the sun visor down. It was early enough to make driving into the sun a matter of squinting in places. Where the road slalomed, sunlight spasmed through bare trees.

A sign. Area of Outstanding Natural Beauty. Not quite a national park, this bit of Lincolnshire. Hills that roll, but land which is worked. High points are spattered with remnants of Cold War defence early-warning installations and Iron Age hill forts. The Romans were here once. Nineteen hundred years later, the Royal Air Force. In between, Viking settlements, Civil War skirmishes. Rust and blood on the workmen's tools. The harvest demands its due. There, to the right, the red dots of the aircraft warning lights on the county's tallest structure, Melmarsh television transmitter mast.

The road passed not far away. There was enough wind to let Matlock hear the support cables on the mast sing their metal song.

The dashboard clock couldn't be read. The LED readouts had corrupted; each line of every digit was as intermittent as its neighbour. Seven-something, Matlock reckoned. He was making good enough time.

A series of hamlets. A newsagent's shop, a jumble of bikes outside. A boarded-up pub. An estate agent sign offering the opportunity to run your own establishment.

Five miles to the right, signs claimed, the county's racing circuit. The mini-Nürburgring: Rushwell Park. Mostly bike meets; some vintage car stuff. Track days. Matlock kept pure east.

Then he saw it. Peeping over then dipping under the horizon with the undulation of the road. St Herefrith's church. Loweth was only a few miles away.

The last proper village before the town came up fast. The habitation proper was down the hill to the left, but up here on the main road there was a bus stop, a brace of blocky houses and the garage.

There was a light on in the office. Matlock pulled in.

The kind of place that still had pumps but didn't sell petrol any more. A padlocked compound, pallets stacked high on one side. Pallets bought and sold. All sizes wanted. Cash waiting.

The car bumped over a hose; once upon a time it might have sounded a bell for service. Now it lay silent; a snake waiting for the sun.

Matlock got out.

It was colder here than in the city. No frost, but not far off it being cold enough. A degree or two over freezing.

The office door opened.

Mark hadn't changed much. Hair more salt than pepper swept back into a loose ponytail. A perpetual week's worth of stubble. Rigger boots and overalls. He'd not be far off sixty.

'Back, then?'

Matlock nodded.

'Been anywhere nice?'

'Not really.'

Mark pulled out a baccy tin. Made himself a smoke. Lit it. Smoked. 'Where'd you get the car?'

'Borrowed it.'

'Right.'

'Could do with a swap.'

Mark came up close. Oil and grease and tobacco smell. He grinned. He'd lost a few more teeth since Matlock had last seen him. 'Pop the lid.'

Matlock leaned in and found the lever. The bonnet quivered.

Eventually: 'Looks sound enough.' Mark checked the steering column. Tsked. Glanced at the number plates. 'I've got a van,' he said.

'Anything's good.'

'Worth a bit more than this though. What with its… provenance.'

'How much more?'

'Couple of hundred should do it.'

Matlock nodded.

Mark took out a ring of keys. He unlocked the compound. Left the gate open and disappeared into the pallets.

A vee of geese crossed the sky. A bus – double-decker – rumbled past, headed back towards Lincoln.

An engine started up. It sounded far away. The compound went back further than it looked. Matlock took two hundred from his stash. Put another hundred in a pocket. The rest went into the bag from the prison. Matlock covered his possessions with clothes. Made it look like laundry.

A white Transit-type van. Nowhere near new, but solid enough. Bird shit and wet leaves on the windscreen; it had been standing a while. Mark got out. 'Two hundred and it's yours.'

Matlock handed over the money.

Mark swapped the cash for his baccy tin. Rolled another smoke. 'You staying around then?'

'Not sure yet.'

'Well, if you are, don't be causing no trouble.'

'As if.'

'Yeah. As if.' Mark lit his fresh cig. Thought about something.

Decided what to do with the thought. 'Got a phone call the other day,' he said.

'Oh yeah?'

'Big Christine.'

'Oh?'

'Said you might be passing through soon. Says that if you need a job and somewhere to stay, then it can be sorted.'

'Chris still in the usual place?'

'Usually. New number though. She says you'll know how to look her up.'

'I'll maybe drop in.' Chris changed her phone number often.

'You do that.' Mark handed over a set of keys.

Matlock put his bag in the cab, then got in. The van was musty. He wasn't sure if it was damp inside, or only cold. The engine started first time. That was what was important.

Matlock held a hand up. Thanks.

Mark held one up in response. The nub of his cigarette glowed, then faded to grey. Matlock pulled out of the forecourt and back onto the road. The faraway noise of a phone ringing. Too loud for a house phone. An extension through to a workshop; an additional bell so it could be heard from the forecourt.

He checked the mirrors.

Mark was standing there, watching the van drive away.

The phone kept ringing.

He stayed in the mirrors until Matlock cleared the road through the village. Then the road fell away towards the town Matlock hadn't been in since he'd killed.

*

Mondays are quiet in Loweth. Market days are the busiest: Wednesday, Friday and Saturday. But busy is relative these days. An outsider might mistake what the locals think is bustle for rural tranquillity.

That strange sensation that's not quite déjà vu. A place you've not seen for years, but which has refused to change. Streets that hadn't altered in four decades, let alone two years.

Matlock took Westgate towards the church, went right around

the hulking mass of St Herefrith's, then second left into Haberdasher Row. He parked up where it opened into Market Square.

The old market-hall clock said it was quarter past eight. The convenience store on the corner was doing a steady enough trade. It had changed branding since he'd last been here. Folk on their way to work. Three kids in school uniform gooning around. A single taxi at the rank outside the Oxfam shop.

Matlock got out of the van. He stretched. The movement caught one of the kids. They smirked, said something to their mates, who laughed in turn.

Little shits.

He'd have said something, but the kids shushed and got out of his way as he went into what was now the Spar shop. The layout hadn't changed. Matlock strode to the back wall, past the long run of magazines and fridge snacks. A carousel of cards: birthdays and valentines. Past the dairy section. He picked up a pint. Gold top. Treat yourself.

Next to the door through to the back office – number-pad entry, what looked like two-way glass above the handle – a noticeboard. Community notices. Small ads handwritten on postcards for a quid a fortnight.

Ironing services. Handyman. Caravan for sale.

There it was. Matlock pulled the card he was looking for out of the corkboard. A tack popped out, skittered across the floor somewhere. Matlock slid the card into a pocket and paid for the milk.

The kids had gone from outside the shop. Opposite, a big guy was fussing with the padlock on a metal door-sized gate that led to the recessed entrance of a jeweller's shop. A car pulled up by the Oxfam; a woman got out and placed a bin-liner stuffed with soft things by the front door.

Matlock finished his milk. The bottle went into the bin. He retrieved the card. Read it back through a couple of times. Smiled. Fetched out some change, and went over to the twin phone boxes.

*

Matlock let the phone ring five times, then he cut the call. He did the same again. The call was picked up on the first ring third time around.

8

'I'm ringing about the lawnmower,' Matlock said.

'You best come and have look at it.' Big Chris's flat tone hadn't changed in two years. 'It's in the shed, so you come around back.'

'Now okay?'

'As good as any other time.'

*

Matlock parked by the railway line. Not that there'd been an actual train through here for years. Cuts had seen to that in the '60s. The route was a pleasant-enough walk across town nowadays, the track-way overgrown enough to make it feel you were in the countryside, but the path the council had put down was solid and wide enough for pushchairs and kids on cycles on Sundays. Chris's house backed onto the railway line. A desire line up the embankment to a high fence with a gate.

The gate was unlocked. Chris must have done this. Matlock let himself in, then slid home the two bolts he found on the garden side. There was a light on in the garage. Low-wattage orange through spiders' webs and accumulated dust. The garage was old. Wooden double doors that opened up at the front, not the overhead metal kind. Matlock went in through the secondary side door.

Chris was sitting on a tall stool at the far end of the workbench which ran the length of the garage. Room enough for a couple of bikes in here, but not for a car. Not really. The usual assortment of tools. Kids' summer garden toys. Boxes stacked in an ungainly ziggurat.

Chris nodded hello.

A nod back. Matlock tried to ignore the shotgun close by Chris's right hand. He held his hands out. Nothing to see here.

'Sorry I didn't visit.'

Matlock shrugged. 'Wasn't expecting you to.'

Chris opened her fist. A set of keys. 'You get a car?'

'Yeah. Thanks.'

'Caravan,' Chris said. She put the keys on the bench. Pushed them forwards like she was a croupier shifting chips.

Matlock waited until Chris had withdrawn her hand. Chris didn't like to be touched.

A pink fob with a paper insert on the keyring. An address and a number in Chris's handwriting: a miniature version of the contact card from the shop. 'Thanks.'

'You know I owe you.'

'That was a long time ago.'

Chris shrugged.

'This is it then. You don't owe me anything any more.'

'No. You don't know what I owe. The worth of what you did. So I'll decide when my account's paid.'

There was no arguing with that.

'You got money?'

'Yeah. Some.'

'I've got work if you need it.'

'Okay.'

'You staying around here long?'

'Dunno yet.'

'Couple of things to sort out?'

'Yeah.'

'You going to see your dad?'

'He was meant to meet me in Lincoln.'

'Not like him not to be where he said he'd be.'

'No.'

'So what do you think it means?'

Now it was Matlock's turn to shrug.

'Go to the caravan then. Get prison showered off your skin. Ring me later.'

'Yeah.'

'And Daniel?'

'Yeah?'

'Low profile. Word'll get out fast enough. So don't do anything that'll paint an even larger target on your back.'

*

Loweth is fifteen miles west of the coast, but there's been a steady flow of tourist money since the Victorians put the railway through the town. The town trades a little off weekend bed-and-breakfasters, race fans camping out at the Rushwell Park track, cottage self-catering rentals. There are caravan parks too. Not as many as there are further east out towards the resorts, but there are some. A mix of residential parks and holiday camps. This time of year, the latter are quiet.

Horsley Green Park was half and half. Boxy static caravans for year-round residents. Hardstanding for tourers; none of the spaces were taken. A toilet-and-shower block. Another building, low and wooden like a village hall. Office all year round, something of a bar and shop in the high season.

Chris's caravan was second from the far end. Its neighbour looked unoccupied, so Matlock parked up on the far side of that one so the car was not visible from the road. Chris rented the static out over the summer. Easter to October half-term was the season. Chocolate eggs to toffee apples.

Matlock didn't like caravans. Flimsy structures. Loud in the rain, hot in the sun, cold in the winter. This one was okay as far as it went. Clean and neutral inside, but fusty. No one had been in here since it had got its November deep clean.

Four berths. Some loo roll in the toilet. Portable TV. Radio in the kitchen area. A fridge. Matlock opened the refrigerator. No hum. No light.

Outside there was cabling for a power supply. A locked housing covered the stand where the power was sourced. Doubtless there'd be a fee to pay. That could wait.

Matlock finished his recce. Cleaning products under the sink. A shelf of holiday reading left behind. James Herbert. Leon Uris. A run of slim romances. Stephen King.

This would more than do.

'Hello!'

A shadow at the doorway. The gun was in the van.

'Hello, neighbour!' Two raps on the door. Politeness and insistence.

Matlock opened the door.

The man was maybe seventy. Sideburns and a tumbledown quiff. A pipe – the curved sort – in one hand. A flammable-looking shirt and polyester slacks.

'Ah, hello, yes. Couldn't help noticing we'd had a new arrival. Frank. Frank Bird. I'm next one over. Settling in alright?'

'Yeah, yes.'

'Good-o. Well, if you need anything, knock. I'm usually around and about. When Mr Jarvis isn't on site, I'm usually the go-to person to, er, go to.'

'Thanks.'

'Well that's it. Call any time. If the light's on then I'm open for business...'

'Dan.'

'Dan. Lovely. Well, catch up later, Dan. I'll let you get unpacked.' Frank strode off, pipe stem raised.

Matlock gave him five minutes, then went back to the van to fetch his stuff. He spread out his belongings on the fold-out kitchen table. Made a list in his head for what he'd need. Recounted his money.

It was time to get to work.

*

There was a phone box at the entrance to the caravan park. Matlock went through the pantomime so that Chris would know the call was friendly.

'Yes.'

'All settled in.'

'Okay. Call in at the office if you can. Best show yourself to Jarvis. He's alright. Knows not to ask questions. Watch the neighbours though.'

'Already met one.'

'There you go.'

'I need that work you said you had.'

A pause. 'Okay.'

Why the gap for thought? Chris had brought up the idea in the first place. 'The offer still open?'

'Yeah.'

'Look. You're doing enough already. I won't be here long. I don't have to bother you.'

'No.'

'So…'

'There's work. The usual. Not much, but I can go to thirty per cent.'

'Anything's fine.' Matlock had enough to start again somewhere else. If he could earn enough to not have to break into his stashed savings, then that was all he needed. A few quid a day. It would only be for a week, after all.

'Come by after school. I'll have a list for you.'

'Thanks, Chris.'

The phone went dead in response.

It wasn't even eleven o'clock yet.

Time to rattle a cage.

*

Having two years to think about something was more of a curse than a boon. Two years of lying on the bottom bunk, staring up at the slats supporting the upper bed's mattress. Two years of counting the bricks in the exercise yard walls. Two years of weak tea, indifferent carbohydrates three times a day and no visitors. Two years of not rising to the baiting of the screws, facing down thugs, not getting involved.

No visitors. That had been his choice. He'd been adamant.

That wasn't to say it didn't hurt.

The first week was important. Matlock let a big kid pick a fight just so he could best him in public.

It wasn't the kid's fault. He didn't know any better. A head full of lies about what it was to be a man inside. Set up to prove himself, so he could attach himself to some clique or other.

Pale skin, cropped hair on the ginger side of blond. Sunken cheeks. Six inches taller but three stone lighter than Matlock. He had reach but no power. And as it turned out, no heart.

Matlock took the first punch so the kid would have something to show. Maybe it would be enough for his lieutenant to take him on anyway. A hard blow, but nothing special. Deep under the ribs, intended to make him buckle.

A jab into the face broke the kid's nose. A fast left, round onto the ear, took his knees away. Before he could buckle over, a right. Piledriver into the eye socket. There was no way that the bone didn't break.

The kid went to his knees. Some idiot shouted something about finishing him off. Later, someone else tried to start a meal queue conversation about how he'd have grasped the kid by his ears and kneed him in the face until his jaw broke.

Two years. Prison was all talk. Big plans and schemes, lies about innocence.

Matlock was left alone after that.

Two years and one idea. Over time, that idea took form. Grit in an oyster slowly becoming a pearl.

*

The new graves were at the lower end of the cemetery, furthest away from the main gates and the chapels. The land must have been a later acquisition to accommodate the town's slow growth since the mid-Victorian opening of the cemetery. Matlock was no historian, but he knew Gothic when he saw it. A superintendent's home, an arched fantasy of turrets and slit windows over the archway of the main drive-in entrance. The monuments up at that end were ornate, bulky, intimidating. Weathered angels and replicas of Cleopatra's Needle. Hand-carved protestations of civic worthiness and of fealty to the Lord.

Down here, memorials tended to the modest. Slim white marble or York stone headstones with letters painted black; little gilded or leaded. More than a few had wooden crosses with brass nameplates or else flower holders but no stone.

Anthony Corrigan's was different. Grey granite. Gold inscription. A kerb set marking out the dimensions of his resting place. Stone chippings within. No weeds poking through. Fresh flowers; a day or two old at most.

Matlock crouched. Read the inscription. The usual platitudes. A date of death, two and a bit years ago.

The memorial did not give when Matlock pushed. The upright headstone was adhered to a base, which in turn was attached to a flat concrete mount which acted as a foundation. There'd be glued or cemented dowels drilled up inside the stone, holding the pieces together.

But it was top-heavy. Matlock stepped into the grave space and seized the polished top of the stone. He gave it full force. The stone quivered. Again. A tearing sensation where the upright stone came free from the base it had been adhered to. A third shove, and the granite cantilevered over. It fell back.

Matlock pulled the flowers out of their holder and threw them aside.

That would more than do.

For now.

*

Prison is good for one thing. It teaches you patience. Not everyone learns the lesson, but for those who are open to its wisdom, prison is there to help you learn. Two years. Five years. Ten. You can learn your place in the cosmos in jail.

Years ago, back when he had a normal life, Matlock had answered the door. An ordinary sunny Saturday morning. A man and a woman, dressed too smart for the weekend, but not as smart as they'd be for church the following day. They had leaflets about the apocalypse, about Satan's sure grasp on the world and about the long game Christ Jesus was playing until His Second Coming.

These ordinary people with their unfashionable message. Performing what they saw as their Christian obligation. Facing doors being slammed in their faces, their knocks being ignored when there plainly were folk in. Matlock let them talk for a minute or so, took their leaflet. Thought no more about them.

It wasn't until later – in prison – that they came back to mind. This pedestrian couple, doing their duty. Playing their own long game. They could do no other.

That made sense to Matlock.

He could now do no other either.

And so he had waited, had made his course of action plain and had waited some more.

Within the week it would all be over, one way or another.

*

Matlock was eating a pear. It tasted fresh. The first truly fresh thing he'd eaten for two years. He lingered over the fruit. He ate it the way his dad used to, core and all. He flicked the stalk away when the fruit was gone. It wasn't as good as he'd remembered as a child, but it was still pretty good. There were others in the bag for later.

Lunchtime. Matlock was back in the town centre, sitting on one of the benches that framed the market area. Schoolkids with trays of chips, cans of Coke. Office workers running errands. A delivery vehicle, its tailgate down. Two guys handballing boxes off the back of the lorry. Watching them work was a pleasure. The easy routine of skilled labour.

That was a form of meditation too, Matlock supposed. To be lost in the rhythm of muscle memory-supported motion. Bend, pick, swing, down, let go. Work that didn't feel like it.

The guys were soon done, a pallet-sized stack of boxes ready to be taken away. Forms were signed; someone came through with a hand truck and wheeled the pallet into a side alley that looked scarcely wide enough for the task.

You'd have thought that the boxes were stock for a shop. Shoes or chocolates or dog biscuits.

Matlock knew better.

That was the downside of routine. The underbelly of meditation. You got used to the everyday, became so accustomed to the persistence of the usual that habits were impossible to shake. Even when changes were imposed, it was all too easy to slide back into the groove of the familiar.

Two years and more, and the Monday noontime drop hadn't changed one iota.

The lorry pulled away. Followed the road around. Paused to let a slick of school uniforms cross the road, and was gone.

Matlock picked up his bag of pears and followed the pallet into the alley.

*

The alleyway ran the length of the building it shadowed, and then opened into a small courtyard. Matlock watched from the street end of the cut-through. Two more guys, stacking the boxes onto a sack barrow. When the barrow was full, one of them would wheel it away through a workshop door. It took four trips to clear the delivery.

The empty pallet was carried in after the boxes. The unloaders came out of the workshop, with one of the boxes. A roller-shutter was dropped, then bolted tight. There was a housing for a padlock to be inserted, but they didn't seem to have one. The guys went through a side door.

Matlock followed. The side door led to a set of stairs. Plain wood, smoothed and polished by time and use. Matlock took the steps in twos, careful not to put pressure on the middle of each tread where any squeak was liable to be loudest.

Two doors off the first-floor landing. A lavatory and a kitchen area. No one around. The stairs continued up.

Voices overhead. Everyday chatter. Business as usual. An undercurrent of something else; something light and perhaps mechanical. A radio. The burble of local news and views.

One voice now louder. Someone coming down.

Matlock ducked into the kitchen. He stood behind the door. Something cold behind him. Something that jabbed into his back. He breathed lightly, through his mouth. Readied himself for the attack he'd need to make.

Footsteps down and away. The toilet door opening. Matlock let the tension out of his balled right fist.

Weapons check. Chopping board, blunt knives, toaster, kettle. Nothing useful presented itself. A glance behind. Matlock had backed into a wall-mounted fire extinguisher.

Toilet flush. Door. Steps across the landing. A pause. They were outside the open kitchen door. Ingrained nicotine smell. A shirt not changed since before the weekend.

Motion blur through the crack in the door by the hinges. The footsteps carried on up.

Matlock gave it until the footfall changed from stairway to landing. He put the fruit down, and unhooked the extinguisher. Checked the type. Dry powder, discharged through a short hose. It was heavy; maybe a stone. The size of a deep-sea diver's air tank.

The stairs up hadn't complained when the tobacco-smelling guy had gone up, so Matlock took them fast and light, but careful.

There was one door off the second-floor landing. It was open about a foot. Matlock kicked it wide, and went in fast, extinguisher raised.

Three men sat around an oval table. Blink. Little other furniture in the room; filing cabinet, typewriter on top. A padlock and keys. A phone on a stack of directories in one corner. One window, facing back into the courtyard.

Blink. The box, opened. Money; notes bundled together with thick rubber bands. A counting machine; the source of the mechanical noise heard from below. A calculator. The chunky desk type that would print out your sums if you wanted. A ledger, pens. Bags for loose change. A set of scales. Radio sound but no sign of the device.

Blink. The three guys. The two who had shifted the boxes, and some office-looking bloke. Dark blue suit and coordinating tie. Crisp white shirt accentuating even skin tones. He moisturised. Trimmed his goatee daily. Maybe forty, in a took-some-exercise way. Matlock dredged up a name. Kayode. Joe Kayode. Matlock had never met him, but had heard prison tales. Of the smart-looking fella come up from London to work the numbers for the Mintons a few years earlier. Was good with money, and in making it disappear.

The other two rose. Tobacco Man was nearest. It was a pleasure to drop him with the butt of the fire extinguisher. The metal rim thumped off his temple; a sideswipe with the metal tank toppled him over, a thin red moon of blood forming across the man's temple and ear.

The second was halfway around the table. The suit hadn't shifted. He'd be no trouble.

The other guy wasn't yet past the obstruction of the table. Matlock pulled the hose out of its retaining clip and flicked out the pin that prevented accidental discharge of the extinguisher. He brought the hose tip up as the man roared something and made to grab Matlock.

The man's face filled with a fast white jet of powder. He collapsed, his hands now to his throat. Matlock kept squeezing the trigger till he keeled over on the floor, coughing, gasping for free air.

The other guy had sat himself up on the floor. He wasn't going to re-engage though.

'Sit on your hands,' Matlock said. Tobacco Guy complied.

Powdery dust spread across the room, billowing in low clouds. Kayode stayed in his seat. The white-faced man was still struggling to breathe right, but had got himself sitting, his back to the filing cabinet.

'Hands under your arse too,' Matlock said. The guy did as he was told, spittle flecking his albino chin.

Kayode had resolve. Firmness in his eyes, like an egg being cooked to solid.

'I don't want your money,' Matlock said. 'But I know it's what you want, so I'm going to take some anyway.' He put the extinguisher on the table, then took two of the bundles. One each of fives and tens. He tucked these into trouser back pockets.

'You,' Matlock said to Tobacco Guy. 'Matches, lighter. Whatever you've got.'

Matches were handed over.

'Appreciate it.'

Matlock hit the trigger again, firing the extinguisher first into Tobacco Guy's face and then into the room until it was filled with choking white dust. He got out of the room fast, closing the door behind him, leaving the empty extinguisher on the landing.

He ran, rounding the last of the stairs and into the courtyard. He should have taken the padlock with him. No matter now.

Above, a yell. Someone stumbling over the fire extinguisher. Collapsing. Falling down the stairs until their trip was halted by the first dog-leg. Good.

In the yard, Matlock opened the roller-shutter. He struck a handful of matches in one go, then put the new flames to the boxes. Shutter back down behind him, he ran back through the alley to the street.

He must have been half covered in the fire-retardant powder. Would have been streaming a vapour trail behind him. Couldn't be helped.

He got to the far side of the van by the time the first of the men charged out into the road. No movement; that was crucial. They were looking for someone running; a getaway car pulling off, tyres yelping. Don't give them that.

Two of them now. Kayode and Tobacco. Must have been the New Albino left crumpled on the stairwell. They checked left and right. Ahead. Nothing.

Kayode nudged Tobacco, and they went back down the cut-through.

Matlock got into his van, and drove back to the caravan site.

*

Matlock brushed off the bulk of the fire-retardant powder. Now it looked like brick dust. Like he'd been working. Good. He needed some clothes anyway. There was an army surplus place on the outskirts of town. He'd pick up something there to tide him over.

He counted the money. Each bundle held a hundred notes. Five hundred in fives, a thousand in tens. He didn't think that the pallet would have been all money. And not all of it would have been in notes; coin was important too. The cash would have been on the bottom of the stack in the van, so when it was handballed off in town, it would have been on top. That way, if the van had been stopped for whatever reason, the chances of the money being found were minimal.

Still. Fifteen hundred in two stacks. Judging by the size of the boxes, a full one would have held thousands. Enough money for people to get serious about.

*

That the office had been back there wasn't much of a secret. Matlock had known about it for over two years, after all. And they'd not thought to change it, or else get some additional security measures put in place. That was sloppy. Condescending. Lazy. A dozen words.

He doubted they'd make such mistakes again.

He had a couple of hours before meeting Chris. Even with taking thirty minutes off for picking up some new clothes, that still left plenty of time to do one more thing this afternoon.

Keep bringing the fight to them. Then wait for their response. Then move behind that response, and strike.

Matlock knew exactly what to do.

He drove out to the phone box by the park entrance. No point walking back again for the vehicle, and it'd avoid another meeting with his curiosity-infected neighbour.

It took three calls and most of his spare coins to find the right nursing home.

'Hi, can you tell me what time visiting is, please?'

'Oh, you can come any time between two and eight, love. As long as you sign in and out of the visitors' book. Who are you coming to see?'

Matlock gave the woman on the other end of the line the name.

'Oh, that'll be lovely. I take it you're not a regular visitor?'

'I'm afraid not. I don't get over to this side of the country that often, even for family occasions. So while I'm here, I need to make the most of it. It's been years since I've seen her.'

'Well, pet, don't be disappointed if she's asleep, or not quite all there. She's quite distant at times I'm afraid.'

'Thanks for letting me know.'

*

Matlock called in at the army surplus store first. The place had been here since he was a kid. A small front sales room was decked out with the best stock. Helmets, dress uniforms, a cabinet full of sew-on badges, campaign medals. Shelves of second-hand books. Most of them were about the Nazis.

A guy behind the counter. He'd been reading when Matlock entered. He left the book open, face down on the countertop. *Edged Weapons of the Third Reich.* Cropped hair, steel-rimmed aviator glasses.

Maybe five foot five and ten stone when fully clothed and wet through. A fascistic jockey.

'Sizes,' the man murmured, as much to himself as to Matlock. 'Let me see. Five eleven, twelve stone, so that's a thirty-two waist and a ten in a shoe.'

You get used to the gaze when in prison. Perpetual eyes on you, wardens and cons alike. Contempt, threat awareness, lust. The pre-historic bit of the brain that tingled a warning when you were being watched spiked on its readout. Matlock refocused while the measure-ments were being checked. More books behind the counter. World Wars, Vietnam. Mostly second-hand, arranged in date-of-conflict order. To the right, new stock. Accounts of the recent Falklands war, of the US invasion of Grenada a year or so back.

Matlock told the guy what he wanted. He was shown through into the larger storeroom beyond. Racks of folded shirts, trousers, thick sweaters with padded elbows and epaulettes. Matlock picked out two sets of clothing: nondescript greens and browns. Extra tees and under-wear. A pair of worn-in but still-sturdy boots. A rucksack to put his purchases in. A jacket.

He asked to try a set on. The guy showed him to a booth with a drawstring curtain. Matlock changed. The guy hung around, a little too near for proper privacy.

Creep.

The clothes were fine. Matlock kept them on, put his old clothes and the spare new ones in the bag and paid the man. The clothes were cheap. The guy said something about the wastefulness of the Ministry of Defence, and the pittance he paid for nearly-new stuff at specialist auctions, allowing him to pass on bargains to working men like you in turn.

On his way out, Matlock asked if there was a florist nearby.

*

As soon as he said it, Matlock realised he didn't need to pick up any flowers. He drove back to the cemetery. The headstone was as he'd left it. The contents of the vase were where he'd thrown them. Mat-lock went down onto his haunches and picked the flowers up one by one. They were in good-enough nick. A regular weekend grave-site visitor. He wondered who.

He shook off a couple of loose petals. Wondered what kinds of flowers they were. A mix. None of the obvious sorts: not roses, daffodils, tulips. Matlock didn't know the names of many plants.

There was a rubber band in the little well in front of the gearstick in the van. Matlock bound the stems into a bunch, then laid them on the double-width passenger seat.

*

Ashburn House must have been a grand pile when it was first built. Built between the World Wars, Matlock reckoned. A grand statement of new money. At some point those fortunes had been lost though. It had been a nursing and residential home for as long as Matlock could remember.

He had been here once before. An aunt – a former nurse herself – had ended up here. For a while. The place always had a reputation for being on the expensive side. Aunt Angelina had been here maybe a year, and then had moved to more affordable accommodation. There had been one last move after that, to somewhere that was basic, but clean. By that stage Aunt Angelina was in no mind of her own, and worked on the ongoing assumption that she was twenty-one and fresh off the boat over from Dublin to Liverpool.

The grounds were well maintained. A private ambulance with a recent licence plate and a fresh wax. Entry was by a buzzer system. A bright-looking woman in an outfit made to look like she was a nurse activated the door mechanism with the press of a button.

'Hi,' Matlock said. 'Signing in. For Mrs Minton.'

The almost-nurse beamed. She indicated the signing-in register. 'Room 112,' she said. 'Up the stairs, and down the right-hand side corridor.'

These places all had the same smell. The fine tiling on the floors and the ornate woodwork on the stairwell were all well and good, but looks and a smear of sophistication were nothing against the warm odour of faeces masked with bleach.

There was a nurses' station at the end of the corridor off the landing. Matlock stuck his head around the corner, waved the flowers. 'Visiting in twelve,' he said. The woman behind the desk barely looked up from her word search.

The calm after lunch. Residents were sedated by food and their noontime meds. An orderly nodded as Matlock passed him and his trolley loaded with trays and dirty cutlery. Some of it was plastic. Thick; the reusable kind.

112 was open. Matlock entered. A bed in the centre of the room. The hospital sort, with raised sides. A chart hung off the foot of the bed.

Mrs Minton was asleep. A foetal comma under one of those blankets with a satin edge and holes in its weave. The kind Matlock associated with babies.

Her breathing was light. Skin as grey as her hair. Matlock watched her.

Eventually, he found a tall glass to place the flowers in. He bent the stems over so that they'd fit in tight and wouldn't topple over. Gave them a drink from a jug of water.

A last glance at the old woman. Matlock wondered what she knew.

*

On his way out, Matlock printed his name rather than scribble a signature. From signing in to his time out he had been there less than ten minutes.

'Sleeping?' The bright-faced not-nurse said.

'Yeah.'

'See you again maybe.' A spasm of interest.

Two years is a long time. 'I'll try again another day.'

'Tomorrow maybe. I'm on days all week.' A smile.

A smile in return. 'You never know.' She had a name tag, but Matlock couldn't catch what it said without staring. He left it.

She buzzed him out.

*

Part of him wanted to do more, but Matlock had a schedule. A plan to keep to. The elements fitted together in only one way, and not only was the sequencing an aspect of the design, but their timing too. There was nothing left on the list for Monday.

Matlock had been out of prison for less than ten hours.

He had no idea where his dad was.

*

'So. What's the job?'

'Collections. A small list.'

'Let me see.'

Big Chris slid a sheet of paper across. The sheet had a neat tear down its left-hand edge. The sort you'd get if you'd used a ruler to help remove it from the exercise book it had come from. The paper was printed with little squares. Mathematics.

Three columns. Names, with addresses underneath. Amounts. Dates. Who and where, how much and how late they were.

Big Chris had come into money a while back. Insurance payout after her husband's death. She had put the cash to work on the street. Small loans, quick turnaround. Terms strictly twenty per cent. Sometimes per week, sometimes per month. Details depended on Chris, and of her appraisal of you.

She kept it low-key. Nothing to mess with the area's big moneylenders.

Matlock checked the list again. The dates indicated these debts were stale. Lent money is odd stuff. It never quite feels real. Too easy to begrudge the service of the loan. Too easy to rationalise not paying what was due.

Chris didn't use strong-arm tactics. Not her way. Persuasion and guilt were her forte. The shotgun was pragmatic; self-defence.

That wasn't to say she'd let a debt slide. Bad for trade.

'Who do you normally use?'

'Gnat Jackson.'

Matlock didn't know the name.

'Bodybuilder. He's away. Some story about a competition and training.'

These debts were old. This Gnat couldn't have been much use. Matlock had an impression of some huge but slow oaf. Someone who was listened to because of their size, not their seriousness. Gnat was probably at home. Pushing weights and drinking raw eggs and wondering why the phone didn't ring as often as it used to.

Money on the street at twenty per cent meant that you dealt in volume of small transactions, not in big gains. Turnover and quick payment were key. Twenty was no threat to any big operators, who wouldn't see the benefit in working either with small sums lent or in the modest return. But non-payers were bad for any business. It wasn't unheard for a major moneylender have some proxy take out a large loan from a rival purely to corrupt their money supply. Non-payment had repercussions.

Matlock doubted that was the case with these amounts. Just people who considered themselves above their obligations. He could deal with that.

'Any tips for these three?'

Chris said no.

'Leave it with. Usual commission?'

'Yeah.'

Matlock nodded. Money wasn't an immediate issue for him since his lunchtime windfall. He folded the list of names away. 'I'll get this sorted.'

'And what about you?'

'Me?'

'Yes. You.'

'You know there's unfinished business.'

'I'd hoped you might have learned something when you were away. Some things can't be helped.'

'You still knew I'd come back.'

'Yeah. You never were any good at cutting your losses.'

'Says the loan shark.'

'You know what I mean.'

'This is family.'

'He made his own decisions. He knew what he was getting into.'

Chris sighed. 'And?'

'And I'm going to make it right.'

'You killed a man. The wrong man.'

'That was unintentional.'

'It's never "unintentional" to family. You know that better than anyone.'

Matlock thought about what to say next. 'I'm not going to do anything stupid.'

'Really?'

'Yes. Really.'

'And what if the Mintons decide to do something stupid once word's round – if it isn't already – that you're back?'

Matlock didn't have anything to say to that.

'They've left you alone for a reason. Don't forget that.'

*

Keeping busy was the best way. Don't dwell. Do. A pebble had started rolling from the summit. It wasn't too late to stop it from running all the way down the mountainside, picking up speed, urgency and partners along the way. Becoming a landslide. Crushing the villagers in the valley.

Matlock knew himself. Prison had been the best thing for him. Two years to make a plan. To commit utterly.

He could still back out. Take that van and the money and drive until he ran out of fuel. And then start walking from there until he didn't know where he was. Never turn back. Never look back. And never go back.

Easier said, though. Another of jail's life lessons. There's no getting away from yourself.

Matlock retrieved Chris's list of names. Picked the middle of the three.

Keep busy. Hold focus.

*

Michael Charlton's home was a standard ex-council semi-detached. Wheelie bins and a kid's trike in the scrubby front yard. The houses to either side had newish double glazing, cars between five and ten years old parked in their drives. Matlock didn't doubt that there'd be laminate flooring, a decent-sized telly and the bulk of the week's grocery shop in the cupboards and fridge. Charlton's looked different. No carpet on the stairs, but no fancy restoration job being undertaken either. An empty kitchen. A sofa that doubled as a bed most nights.

The curtains were drawn. Matlock didn't doubt that they were seldom open.

A kid on a bike at the far end of the street. Lazy orbits of the turning circle of the cul-de-sac.

There were fixings, but no gate. The driveway was empty. A garage. The concrete kind; a boxy prefab, its door part-raised. A whisper of a washing line, flags flying, sizes small to large.

Okay. Wife and kids were out in the car. A supermarket run after pickup from school maybe.

Matlock walked down the road a bit. Beckoned the kid on the bike over.

'What you want with number six?'

'I'm an old friend. Just got out.'

'From nick?' The kid, perhaps ten, scrawny. A stud earring and plasticky sports gear. He looked impressed.

'Yeah.'

'What were you in for?'

'Vehicular manslaughter.'

'Fuck off.'

Matlock stared. The kid blushed.

'Fiver for you. All you need to do is wait till I'm round the back of the house, then you roll up and do a knock and run. I'll let myself in the back. Surprise him, like.' The money appeared in Matlock's palm.

'That's all?'

'It's easy money.'

The kid got off his bike. Took the cash. Tagged along with Matlock.

Matlock walked down the driveway of the Charlton house. Nodded back to the kid. Disappeared around the corner. A few seconds later he heard the rattling bang of knuckles on glass. Shave-and-a-haircut.

Now there was movement in the house. The kitchen was at the back of the building. A rear window and a door leading to the indifferent lawn. Matlock could see all the way down the hallway to the front door. A head from one side; living room. Charlton was half expecting the family to be arriving home. Maybe they were earlier than he'd anticipated. Caught mid-wank.

A second set of knocks. The kid, occluded through dirty windows and the frosting on the front-door glass.

Matlock found the back door unlocked. He stepped in, leaving the door open behind him.

The kid-shaped shadow faded. Now Charlton was in the hallway. Part of him wanted to peek out front, see who it was. He owed money after all; maybe had kept it a secret from his other half. Men often did.

The kitchen smelled like other people's houses.

Charlton was six foot tall. Shaved head. Bulky rather than muscular. A football shirt several seasons old. Jeans. Barefoot. A new set of smells: weed and farts.

Matlock walked up behind the man. Stood firm. 'Hey.'

Charlton turned, a puzzled expression forming. Matlock hit him in the gut.

'Fu–' Charlton wheezed. He looked up, half crouched into the blow.

Matlock showed him he was ready with another.

'Wait.'

Matlock let him get his breath.

'Sneaky fuck,' Charlton said. As much to himself as to Matlock.

'You know why I'm here.'

A nod. 'Thought I had a few days' grace. Word was her gorilla was out of town.'

Don't let them ever get you talking. You have the advantage. Keep it. Matlock told Charlton what was owed. Like Charlton wouldn't know.

'I've got it. I can get it.'

'Which is it?'

'The first one. Both. It's upstairs.'

Why keep it then? Why not pay it back?

'I'll need to go up and fetch it.'

'I'll come with you.'

Charlton led the way. Tried talking again. About how he didn't usually borrow money. But this was a special thing. He'd overheard something. Man-in-a-pub stuff. A fix at the greyhound racing at Skegthorpe Stadium. He couldn't not win.

And the dog had come in as well. But the bet had attracted attention. He was known as a small-timer. Fiver here, a quid there. An easy mark, and no real harm. So to win that amount in one go. On a race that was rigged. That was trouble. That's why he hadn't answered the door. Why he'd rung in sick for the last week and a half; had even got himself signed off with his back.

Matlock listened as the guy counted out the money on an unmade bed. It had come from a jewellery box from a drawer. The sort of box with a pop-up clockwork ballerina. Charlton folded the last note in half as a makeshift binding, and then handed the wad over.

Matlock took the cash.

The sound of a car pulling up. Charlton tucked the box with the rest of the money away quick. 'Out the back,' he said. 'She doesn't know.'

Matlock left him to it. Down the stairs and out the back door to the approaching sounds of kids being hauled out of the car and bags being taken from the boot. He ducked under the kitchen window. Hung back until he heard the front door close again, and then strode to the van.

One down.

Keep busy.

You've done what you set out to do today. Get the Mintons' attention. Leave traces everywhere. Let them know you're back.

Start the war tomorrow.

Two names on the list. It was something to do.

*

The next address – the one at the top of the list – was a flat. A once-good street of three-storey Victorian town houses long since subdivided into apartments.

Six buzzers. Six slips with names. Matlock pressed his hand over the plate of buttons. Someone let him in.

A shelf inside the front door loaded with fliers and uncollected post. Most of a bicycle, locked to a radiator.

The flat he wanted was on the top floor. He knocked. No answer.

Sometimes you can feel when a home is occupied. When it isn't. This felt empty.

The door gave in on the second kick.

Matlock checked the flat fast. People usually kept their business to themselves in these buildings and seldom got involved in the lives of others, but a boot-print on an entry could arouse hitherto dormant neighbourly instincts. A tiny hallway, scarcely worth the second door into the flat proper. Shoes on a rack, tidy and neat. Two coats hanging; both for males. One lightweight, one good for foul weather. The flat opened into a combined living room and kitchen area. Again, clean and looked-after. Modernist prints on the walls. Thriving potted plants. If there was a smell, it was of leather polish.

A bedroom off, then a shower room with lavatory. The flat was as empty as Matlock had expected to find it. He started his search in the bathroom.

Usual places first. Nothing in the cistern. No loose ceiling tiles. Nothing in the toiletries cabinet above the washbasin. Nothing taped behind the pedestal. If there'd been a bath, he'd have checked the panels for scratches on the screws indicating they'd been frequently removed. The flooring was vinyl; no need to worry about loose tiles or floorboards concealing hidey-holes.

The bedroom was next. The carcass of the bedside cabinet was clear. Inside, nothing more than a stack of magazines. Gay pornography. European. Leather and cowboy fetishes. No money.

Nothing of interest in the drawer. The same in the wardrobe and chest of drawers opposite. Old but good-quality clothing. Some suits, two still in their wrappers from their last dry-cleaning.

Nothing under the bed.

Kitchen next. Again, Matlock started with the obvious. Matter out of place. The freezer was clean. Same with the fridge. The cupboards told the same tale; someone with perhaps limited cash flow but with what they considered to be good taste. Living the echo of a finer life. Baked beans and saffron.

Living room. A bookcase. Again, you look for what shouldn't be there.

Rows of paperbacks. Green Viragos. White Picadors. Orange Penguins. Many novelists Matlock hadn't heard of. Some he had, thanks to the randomness of the prison library stock. Virginia Woolf to Edmund White. Nothing here before *Dracula*, and nothing that would get made into a movie with car chases.

Apart from a Bible.

Hardbacked.

Gilt-lettered.

Anomalous.

The book had been hollowed out inside. A money clip with £460. Not the full debt, but a start. And two bags of pills. Clear sandwich bags, each with a couple of dozen tablets. Matlock pocketed these.

Footsteps. Up to the top of the stairs. Huffing. Someone unfit, or carrying something. Then silence.

Take the initiative. Matlock called out. 'Come in. No point running. I'm not here to hurt you.'

A sigh. Rustling. Unwilling movement, then a shadow at the door to the kitchen/living space.

He – Barry de Graff, according to Chris's bit of paper – was as Matlock expected. Balding, puffy. But well kept in a gentleman's club manner. Tweed jacket and slacks. Brown Oxfords. Only a neckerchief was lacking to complete the ensemble. A bulging jute bag. Shopping; fresh bread and wine were evident.

That look of being caught. Apprehension and uncertainty, but also relaxation. Tension was already lifting. Capture can be a relief.

'You really shouldn't have,' de Graff said, indicating back to the boot-print on the hallway door. 'The flat was hard enough to get as it was.'

'I'm sure you talked your way into it quite nicely. What with your qualifications, doctor.'

'How–?'

A shrug. Move the conversation on. Forward momentum.

Matlock saw the man's life in a moment. Locum post to locum post. Stealing to feed his own addiction, and a little more on top to pay for life's little luxuries. He'd probably had some kind of professional set-back which meant he needed money fast, hence the loan. Probably came across the other kind of drug dealers.

And then the reluctance to pay. Some class issue, maybe. Why should he pay some oik back what was rightfully his, and which had been stolen by other peasants? Maybe that was overly harsh.

'There's four hundred-odd here. You need to pay the rest. Today.'

'I've... I've got it. Here. I was going to pay, I was, it's just I had some additional shifts and I'm not in a position to turn the work down. I should have phoned. If I could extend my apologies. Another three-forty. That's right, isn't it?' De Graff reached into an inside jacket pocket. Hands, trembling, passed a wallet across.

Matlock took the notes out, counted off the sum in twenties and tens. He did it with care, to show no sleight of hand was extracting extra. Handed the wallet back.

'Thank you.'

'Don't be late in future.'

'No.'

Matlock thought. 'What's your phone number?'

De Graff couldn't write it down fast enough.

'Appreciate it. I might call on you. Professional services. There'd be a fee payable to you.'

De Graff nodded. 'I've done, er, out-of-hours work before.'

'Okay then. Here. Hands out.'

The man had soft hands. Scrupulous nails. Matlock placed the bags of pills into the nest they made.

'That's a kindness.'

Matlock left Dr de Graff to his cheese and wine. To his opiates.

*

Third and last on the list. Sarah Parker. Matlock drove to the address given. Terraced housing on a side road; front doors direct onto the pavement. There was no one in.

Matlock tried the houses either side. The second one answered.

A small woman wearing a bushy wig. Skin like papier mâché over her bones. Walking stick in her left hand. A blast of central heating from behind. Medical smells. Cats. Cancer. 'Yes love?'

'I'm looking for the lady who lives next door.'

'Oh, she's not there, I don't think.'

'Do you reckon she'll be back later?'

'Oh, that's not what I meant. She's not there at all. Got into a car with a bag of clothes and her little one last week sometime, the moment that man of hers had left for work. Wednesday. It might have been Wednesday.'

'I see. That's a shame. I had some money for her.'

The woman was thinking about what to do for the best. Matlock didn't want her standing there too long.

'I tell you what,' Matlock said. 'I'll try again later. Any idea what time this man of hers gets home?'

'Six-ish usually, but then he goes out. Drinking. With her not being here there's no telling, is there? He was out till all hours over the weekend. Makes you wonder where they get the money from for it all.'

'Maybe I'll swing back later on. Thanks for your time.'

'No problem, pet.'

*

His stomach gurgled. He had barely eaten all day. A coffee, some milk and a pear. Hardly a welcome-home feast.

Matlock bought some basics at a corner shop. There was a chippy not far off. Matlock got in line. The queue moved fast.

Being near food made him all the hungrier. He ordered for a couple, down to two cans of soft drink and two buttered buns to go with the wrapped-up parcels and the twin pots of mushy peas. He made one last stop on the way back to the caravan.

*

Matlock ate fast with his hands. Chunks of crisp haddock, handfuls of chips. The way that the chips had wilted from the extra steaming they'd had being wrapped in paper for the few minutes on the way back reminded him of childhood. Of late-night bags of post-pub chips sneaked into his room by his dad. Half squashed from being in under his coat. The paper a mix of frying oil and tobacco smoke on the outside, vinegar tang and hot salt within.

He drank the first pot of peas from the polystyrene tub. Necked a can of shandy in three gulps.

The drink both cleansed his mouth for the second course and scolded him for how full he now was.

Matlock got a fork for the second meal. He took this slow, pouring half of the peas onto the chips, eating mouthful-sized scoops of fish and potato alternated with more of the pop. He knew he wouldn't be able to finish it all. The haddock was picked from its batter and consumed; Matlock left a fair amount of the chips. He put the lid back on the peas, wrapped the leftover takeaway up. He might go back to it, he might not.

He rinsed his hands in the sink. Cold water and washing-up liquid. The flow wasn't good. Maybe the water tank was nearing empty. He'd check it in the morning.

Matlock squared away the few groceries and toiletries he'd picked up from the shop. Then he found a glass in one of the overhead cupboards. An octagonal tumbler, the same sort he'd had water from during school lunches nearly thirty years previously. The glasses had writing on the underside. A maker's mark and a number. A school ritual was to check the number under the glass. Highest number got pudding first.

He checked. A three.

Fair enough.

Matlock went to what he'd bought from his third and final stop on the way here. The shop assistant had wrapped the bottle in crêpe paper before putting it into the bag.

The bottle and glass stood on the little table where Matlock was now sat. Scotch. Talisker. He had been surprised to see it on sale in a small place. Leftover Christmas stock, the assistant said. The new owners' fault. Newcomers with ideas above their customers' station. People wanted telly-advertised beers, wines, cheap branded spirits, cigarettes, sweets, crisps, fizzy drinks. They didn't have money for expensive whiskies. Not even at Christmas time.

Two years and more since his last drink. Last time he'd drunk he had killed a man. The wrong man. The brother of the man he was aiming for.

It had all got hushed up. As much as it could have. That was the way of things out here. You dealt with your own troubles. Sorted out your own business. Only involved the cops when it suited you to, and as often as not that was when you were paying them off to not enquire into your private dealings.

It could have gone another way. But they knew they were in the wrong. Couldn't have the cops involved. Some things even the greediest of pigs will refuse. Like they had a shred of honour deep inside them. Hidden, all along. Waiting for the right moment to be revealed.

It was all bullshit.

The ritual of it. That's what they talked about inside, whenever Matlock had cared to listen. Never the thing itself, but the things that went alongside. The whisper of silk over skin. The moment of resistance before she opened fully for you. The gasp of a bottle opening.

He'd heard tell of drunks who'd only got through the first year sober through having ice melting in a beaker, so they could have the homeopathic hit of booze that wasn't there. Of gamblers who'd played eternal games of Monopoly so they could handle cash they didn't have. Sex cases who'd pleaded to have their balls smashed in, hoping to be rid of their terrible cravings.

Nothing worked. That was what they had told him inside. The therapist who'd tried to engage him in weekly circle sessions. You could deal with it and carry on, or not deal with it and go on making the same mistakes. But it never went away. It was always there.

All golden behind glass.

Patient.

Matlock upended the glass and put it over the top of the bottle. He closed his eyes. Eventually, it would be morning.

Eventually, it was.

Tuesday

Matlock washed as best he could, there being no hot water and no way that he could figure to get any heated besides boiling a kettle and bollocks to that at this time of day.

He stashed the whisky bottle at the back of the same cupboard he'd found the glass in.

He sorted the money out. Two piles for Chris. One for him.

One name still on the list.

It was early. If he'd come home last night, there'd be no way he wasn't still in.

Matlock got in the van.

Pulling out, a light came on in a neighbouring caravan. Frank, Matlock assumed. He was the only resident he'd seen thus far. He wondered if he'd woken the old man up. Felt bad about it if he had. He'd make it up to him somehow. Yeah, he was nosey. But nosey could work in your favour as much as against.

*

Matlock parked around the corner from the last address on the list. Delivery vans and kids on paper rounds had been the bulk of the traffic. Here, it was quiet. No lights, no noise.

He went around the rear of the terrace. Back yards with high walls. Some of them still had the old outside loos in place, or at least their shells. Matlock counted the gates till he got to the right one. It was locked, but a finger poked through the gap snicked the latch up. Matlock wedged the gate open with a brick seemingly propped to one side for that purpose.

The windows were old. The original early-Victorian ones. Once-fine woodworking lines layered to vagueness with generations of paint. Most of the glass had been replaced over the years, but at least one pane bore the imperfections of age.

It was this one Matlock pressed. He checked each of the corners;

sometimes the putty held itself there only out of habit, the last two coats of gloss providing the only chemical-adhesion bond.

He was right. The pane gave at the bottom right. Gentle now, so that the paint line tore along the bottom of the rectangle of glass as Matlock pushed more. The window now had a hinge like a cat flap. Matlock took the underside of the glass and pushed upwards, careful not to put too much tension on the pane. Again, it tore just right. A small twist, and the glass came free.

Matlock laid it down quietly, and reached in and unlocked the window.

He paused when the window was open. No sound. No movement. Okay.

The window opened into the kitchen. A sink and drainer, empty. She had washed and dried up the breakfast things in the morning before she'd left with the kid.

The kitchen was nothing special. Cheaper appliances; Matlock didn't recognise the brands. Mismatched chairs crowded under a too-small table. Folded piles of washing to be ironed. Not enough room for everything. The table was a shanty town of beer cans and foil Chinese takeaway cartons, one of them used as an ashtray. One mug, stained with unrinsed reuse.

If there was any money in the house, then she'd have taken it with her. Either that or he'd have it hidden somewhere she couldn't get to it. A locker at work. An account she knew nothing of. Notes stuffed into an old tea caddy at his mother's house. Anywhere but here.

But that wasn't why Matlock had come.

Snoring above. Eight pints and a beef in black bean sauce with special fried rice weighed heavy.

A single family photograph in the hall. Kid, Dad, Mum. The boy and the man were in suits. Sarah was in a light green summer dress. It looked like a professional picture taken at a wedding.

Sarah. She'd scarcely aged. The hair at the top of her spine, soft as angel pubes.

Shit.

Shit.

Another snore brought him back.

Matlock walked up the stairs. No need for creeping. He checked the kid's room to be sure it was empty – it was – and so was the bathroom. He found something useful there.

Cologne. Acrid stuff. He'd seen it advertised on TV in the years before prison. Boxers and footballers swore by it, if you believed the commercials. Matlock unscrewed the spray diffuser. The bottle was nigh full.

The bedroom door was open. He was sleeping in tee shirt and underpants. He had kicked the covers off in the night. Matlock pulled them back over him. This was important.

He tucked them in on each side of the bed, making sure they would not come loose easily. Then he poured a little of the aftershave on the man's face.

He spluttered, bringing a hand to his eyes to rub whatever it was away. Then he screamed as the sharp cologne hit his eyes.

Then Matlock hit him.

It's not easy to hit a man who's lying down.

Matlock got better with each blow until the nose gave way with a crack of cartilage.

Blood, tears and the remnants of the aftershave ran down the man's face, staining the bedding pink.

He tried to say something, but Matlock cut through the man's attempted bluster with a raised hand.

'Listen. She's gone. She'll stay gone. Try to mess and you'll get more of this. Do you understand?'

Matlock poured the rest of the bottle onto the bedding. He made sure that the fresh aftershave didn't go too near the man's face and hands. Then he picked up the man's lighter from the bedside table.

'Yes. Jesus. Yes. I get it.'

Still pinned by the tucked-in bedding, he had nowhere to go. If he'd lit the cologne, then the alcohol would have burned off pretty harmlessly before any real fire took. But those aren't the kind of things you think about when woken by a broken nose the night after a skinful.

You can tell when the fight's gone out of a man. Wife-beaters were the easiest of all. Cowards. Taught from an early age to respect a fist, and to be in awe of the power it can wield. Not smart enough to see that there are alternatives in life.

Matlock wiped the bottle clean of prints and let it drop. He kept the lighter. He let himself out the front door. By the time he left, he'd heard nothing to indicate that the man who'd been fucking his ex had got himself out of the bed.

*

Matlock drove around by the industrial estate. An asphalt labyrinth of corrugated units; every size represented from epic to sole trader. The bigger ones housed the town's newer commercial focuses. Plastic. Cardboard. Agriculture had given way to food processing. Folk had their fruit and veg tinned or frozen as often as fresh; if not now, then when they consumed it in ready meals or takeaways. This all meant cans and bottles, polyethylene sacks, cardboard boxes and Styrofoam cartons.

That meant there was work for the generation that wouldn't have laboured in the fields their grandfathers had even if automation and migrant labour hadn't conspired to take their jobs. That was the way they told it, anyway.

Matlock had heard the tale a dozen ways inside. How the Poles and the Latvians had stolen the work, and what's a man to do to raise his family? Deal a little, that's what.

It was horseshit, of course. A comforting lie. Still, here was where you'd find the town's workers. Extrusion operatives in the plastics factories, turning milky pellets into carrier bags for the supermarkets. Or else flexographic printing: rubbery printing plates adding logos to reels of film that'd get palleted up and forklifted across the way to the converter. Pellet to packaging in a shift.

It meant you'd get breakfast. That was what Matlock was here for. The industrial estate was far enough out of town to make walking into the town centre to get something to eat prohibitive. And foil-wrapped sandwiches get boring.

The van was parked up where it had always been. Flinttstones; the extra 't' presumably some gesture towards appreciation of copyright infringement laws. Still the same rock-face font as used by the cartoon cavemen though.

A fold-out A-board: teas, coffees, minerals. An off-white patio table supporting squirty refillable bottles. Red, brown, yellow. A washed-out ice-cream tub half-full of clumped sugar. A scattering of white plastic spoons. Dead tea bags that hadn't made it to the bin.

Woody hadn't changed. Ancient apron over a sweater thinning at the elbows. The brittle remnants of a pompadour. Chunky hands studded with the pastel blue of youthful tattoo experiments.

Woody flipped a spatula of onions over. Didn't look up from the flat griddle. 'What'll it be?'

'Bacon and sausage. Black coffee.'

'Bacon'll be a couple of minutes.'

Woody reached into a fridge. Peeled off two rashers from a slab of bacon. Laid the meat down, nearest end first, like he must have been taught in the army catering corps forty years previously.

A polystyrene beaker appeared. 'Thought I'd lost a customer,' Woody murmured. A spoonful of granules went into the beaker. He filled the cup with water from the urn. Gave it a stir.

'Been away.'

'So I gather.' Woody turned the bacon. Selected two already-cook-ing sausages and split them lengthwise with the sharp side of the spat-ula. Laid them innards sides down. 'Working?'

'Got some things lined up.'

'That's good. Not much around these days.'

'No.'

Woody sliced open a bread roll, and flicked margarine over both halves. The bacon went in first, then the sausages. He folded a paper napkin around the food. 'Want a bag to go?'

'Thanks. I'll eat it here.'

No sauce. The bap was rich and hot. It didn't last long. Matlock slurped the now-cooled coffee. That wasn't great. Warm and wet though.

'Aye,' Woody said. 'Shame about the work. Desperate men'll do anything to make ends meet. Even turn grass.'

'That's low.'

'As long as it isn't to the cops, folk can justify it.'

'Money.'

'Yeah. Word is, reports of your precise whereabouts would be very much appreciated in certain quarters.'

'Oh.'

'You might want to buy a hat or something. The sums being talked about would keep someone in bacon and sausage for a while.'

'Thanks.'

'No bother. It'd be a shame to lose you so soon after you becoming a customer again.'

*

Matlock bought another roll. Sausage, bacon, egg, onions. Slice of plastic cheese. Red and brown sauces. This one to go. He found a phone box and rang Big Chris.

Chris met Matlock in the shed. She'd made him a coffee. The mug celebrated Prince Charles and Lady Diana Spencer, faded but still yet to be married. Her own mug displayed a riot of kittens.

'Here you go.' Matlock laid out three piles of notes, each held in place with the last tenner folded over, a name written in capitals over Her Majesty's face.

'That's treason, that is.' She took the money anyway. Made squirrely notes in a journal. Closed the book with a fat rubber band; the kind postmen drop on their rounds. Stuck her biro along the top edge of the notebook so it'd be held in place by the elastic. 'Prison,' she said.

She knew. That Matlock had made up the money from the last of the debtors out of his own pocket. That the woman – Parker, Sarah – had given him a sob story.

Unless she guessed something else.

That Sarah hadn't always had the surname Parker. That once upon a time her last name had been Wright, and had very nearly been Matlock.

A long time ago.

No time at all.

Matlock sipped his coffee. If anything, it was worse than the stuff Woody sold. More chicory than arabica.

Chris drank from her own brew. 'You always were cake-hearted.'
Another sip.

Chris moved on. Good. 'Been busy.' She'd put the money away.
She didn't mean that. This was about yesterday.

Matlock shrugged.

'Hope you know what you're doing. And why.'

He shouldn't tell her. Not really. Some things it's better not to
share. You're only saying this because you're trying to convince yourself that it's okay to do that. 'It's Joe.'

'What about him?'

'He didn't visit.'

Chris's eyes flickered up and away. Then back. 'I've not heard anything.'

'You wouldn't though, would you?'

A shrug. 'Did he say he would?'

'Yeah.'

'Oh.'

'Yeah.'

'And you told him not to, but you thought he might anyway.'

'Yeah.'

'And that was what yesterday was all about.'

Matlock nodded.

'What are you going to do about it?'

'About Joe?'

'It's family, isn't it?'

'Yeah.'

'Job's done then. You could have walked away.'

'Not from Joe.'

'No. You tried his house?'

'Not yet. He's not there. If he was then everything would be
alright. He would have met me. I'd have stayed there last night. Telly
and crumpets and listening to his National Service and British Rail
stories.'

'Okay. So?'

'So something's happened. Either he's been warned away from me,
sent off, or else something else.'

'There'd have been word. Someone would have told you.'

'That's what I thought. So he's somewhere.'

'And you want him back.'

'He's the only dad I've got.'

'Yeah.' Chris was going to say something. Then she stopped. Started again. 'Check the house anyway. You can't not. Then–'

Matlock waited.

'You know the egg place on the A16?'

'Course.'

'Try there.'

'Thanks.'

*

Joe's house gave off that empty feeling. A two-bed end terrace. Maybe late Victorian. A little courtyard at the back; a shed that had once been an outside toilet. Dusty windows with the curtains pulled closed inside.

Matlock didn't have a front door key. It didn't matter. The back door had never had a working lock. There was a mechanism there, but it was coated in layers of brilliant white gloss faded to nicotine custard. At some point a bolt had been screwed into the door frame to keep it shut from the inside.

Matlock checked up and down the alley between the backs of the runs of houses. Midweek daytime quiet. He went in the back gate and gave the door an exploratory shove. It gave on the third attempt.

The kitchen was how it had always been. Faded, decades-old table and chairs. Well ordered though. The RAF had instilled a sense of routine and systematic working which had never left Joe. Everything in its place.

Milk in the fridge. Fresh enough to drink.

The kettle was cold.

Joe's coat was hanging in the hall. His walking stick was hooked over the banister at the bottom of the stairs. 'Joe?'

The lack of echo of an uninhabited house.

Nothing out of place in the front room. This week's TV listings magazine, the pages folded over to Saturday. Three days ago. Joe liked to tick what he planned to see, then put a cross through the tick when he'd watched it. Saturday was planned for an afternoon Western, the football scores. A gap, then a new film Matlock hadn't heard of. Football highlights late on.

There was a cross through the tick of the Western. *Winchester '73*. James Stewart, Shelley Winters. Black and white.

The rest of the day's viewing was uncrossed.

Shit.

Upstairs. Nothing. The bedroom was ordered as ever. The bathroom tidy enough. The back bedroom held some of Matlock's stuff in boxes. A single bed, stripped back to the mattress. A wardrobe, empty except for mismatched hangers.

A creak from downstairs. The back door swinging on its hinges. Then footsteps. Heavy and fast.

Matlock left the wardrobe half open. A mirror – near enough full length – was on the inside of the door. He ducked inside the bathroom.

The footsteps were at the bottom of the stairs. And now up. Another sound, almost metallic. Something clattering against the spindles on the staircase moving upwards.

Motion outside the bathroom door. Someone swept past, making for the bedrooms.

Mistake. They should have waited downstairs. Outside would have been better.

A man on the landing. Silhouetted; one arm comically longer than the other.

No. Baseball bat.

That changed things. But only a little. The bat would give the stranger confidence. But there was barely room to make effective use of it unless it was used for forward jabbing or else as a defensive tool to parry attacks.

Still. The bat meant preparedness. The stranger's presence meant that the house had been watched. Or Matlock had been. Some combination of the two. Maybe he'd picked up a tail; from Big Chris's place would have been the logical point to start. Then again, Matlock was always going to come here at some point.

Matlock waited until the shadow moved. Let him check the rooms. Bedroom. Then spare. The longer you search the less likely it feels you're going to find what you're looking for.

There was nowhere to hide in the bathroom. Matlock stood his ground.

Two taps; more echoey than you'd credit. The tip of the baseball bat on the landing railing. A prison guard fantasy: rattling the bars with your nightstick, because you could.

He'd use the bat to open the door. Prod it open, then step in, bringing the bat back up to the shoulder.

Matlock cradled the bathroom door handle. Waited for contact.

Tap. The sensation of pressure. The door, opening.

Matlock yanked the door open, grabbing and pulling the end of the baseball bat in a single liquid move. He tugged to exert dominance. The bat came out of the stranger's hand. A grunt. Surprise. Annoyance. Puzzlement.

Matlock rammed the handle end of the bat back into the stranger's gut. It caught him right above the belt buckle.

'Fuck.' More a statement than an exclamation. The man stepped back under the shock of the blow, arms opening wide.

Centre of gravity.

Matlock went low, sweeping the bat across the man's shins. He yelped. A higher pitch than you might expect. Another step back, twisting now to try to avoid what might be coming.

Matlock's third move came down from above. A forty-five-degree angle at speed onto the collarbone. An unmistakable snap. The man slumped. His eyelids flickered a Morse code emergency signal to his central nervous system. There was little response.

The man was perhaps thirty-five. Hard to judge. Shaven-headed goateed guys all look the same. A tee shirt advertising bourbon. The belt buckle likewise. Pub giveaways. Motorbike trade show freebies. Tan lines around the face indicated a baseball cap was often worn. But not today.

No tattoos. Tired jeans, rigger boots.

He was breathing.

One pocket yielded a wallet. Some notes, a bank card. Matlock took the cash. Bent the card in two, flexed it until it began to feel warm, then tore it along the white scar through the bank's logo.

R. Jackson, according to the card. Matlock didn't know any R's. Robert. Ronald. Ralph. Rex. Rover. Dog names.

Enough.

Matlock crouched, inspecting the distortion under the tee shirt between arm and neck. Something under there wasn't right. He pressed. An exploratory squeeze.

The dog-named man grunted. His eyes stopped their stuttering.

Another squeeze.

'Fuck. Christ. Jesus. Stop it.'

Matlock gave him a count of ten to compose himself.

'My shoulder's fucked.'

Eye contact. No point going on about it.

The guy breathed through whatever pain he was feeling. 'Fuck. Okay. Okay.'

Let him speak. If you ask questions, you'll get answers only to the questions you've been asking. Allow him to talk though and there might be information Matlock wouldn't have thought was available. Directions he'd never have travelled.

Plus, Matlock had the bat. He wasn't inclined to use it, but the guy didn't know that. He made a show of flexing his grip on the handle to make the possibility self-evident.

'Shit. Fuck.' The hand on his good side now raised in submission. 'Only meant to be a warning. That you've made your point, now fuck off out the county. That this ain't your home any more.' Two deep breaths. Matlock imagined pain breaking like waves on a shoreline. 'Was meant to be easy.'

'Easy.'

'Rough you up, send you on your way. No broken bones. My arm's fucked. I'll not work for weeks. Jesus.'

'Why?'

Confusion. 'For the hundred. Five minutes' work. Knock you on your arse and give you your walking orders.'

'Why?'

Realisation now. 'I don't know. You don't think she says anything

47

about *why* to me, do you? I just do what I'm told. I don't need to know wh–'

'She?'

'Yeah.' An 'I've-said-too-much' grimace.

'Who?'

'I can't.'

'Client privilege?'

'What?'

Matlock raised the bat.

'Jesus, no.'

Matlock rested the bat where the shoulder met the arm socket. There was a medical name for the collarbone. Clavicle? Clavicle. The lump under the tee shirt looked worse than before. Bigger. More wrongly shaped.

Eye contact.

'Jesus. Fuck. She calls me up. Offers a hundred. In and out. Give you the message. Make sure you act on it.'

'Well. Give me the message.'

'To get out of the county. To not come back. To not look behind. There's nothing and no one for you here any more.'

'That's it?'

'Word for word. I swear.'

'Then you've made your point. One last question. Who?'

'Big Chris.'

*

Sometimes you can't help yourself. You hear something and you break inside. And you take that broken feeling and you pass it on. You lash out. And whoever's there at that point in time bears the brunt, whether it's their fault or not.

This is the folly of men. Matlock had seen it no end of times.

He had seen it in himself.

And he saw it again now.

He didn't kill the guy. But he left him in a mess. Then he dragged that mess downstairs, out into the back garden and out again into the alley behind.

Then Matlock went back into the house. If Joe had ever installed a shower he'd have had one, but Joe had always sworn by baths, which Matlock didn't like. Instead, he washed his hands until the throbbing from the beating they'd administered was replaced by a different kind of pulsation, one from the heat of the water he washed his hands in, and then he made himself a cup of tea.

*

This time Matlock went through the house with a forensic zeal, until he was satisfied there was nothing odd, weird, extraordinary or otherwise problematic. Part of this was delaying an inevitability, but it had to be done nevertheless.

Now he was done. He felt that he should take something. A keepsake. A memento.

The listings magazine. Date and time of Joe's vanishing, as close as he could make out.

He would have to go and see Chris.

It was inevitable.

On the way out, Matlock checked the alley. The guy wasn't there. Some Samaritan had come along, or else the council had shovelled him up and dumped him into a bin. Maybe they found out that he had a dog name after all and had taken him to the pound.

*

Chris could wait. Would have to. Matlock wasn't sure what to do about this. What did it mean?

He needed time.

Not necessarily to think, but to let his brain process the information. Sometimes problem solving was like roasting a joint. You put the stuff in the oven and a few hours later the raw ingredients would have transformed themselves into a satisfying whole.

There had to be an answer. But Matlock couldn't see how it could be a logical one.

So now what?

Keep going. Distract yourself. Searching the house had provided some respite, but more was needed. Forward motion. Kick over more rocks. See what came crawling out.

He kept the baseball bat. You never knew.

*

Matlock parked by the caravan. The van juddered when he shut the engine off. Something shifted in the cargo section behind him. Some junk left behind by its previous owner, or else stashed by Mark and forgotten about. Matlock told himself he'd clear out whatever it was at some point. Not right now, though. It was hardly a priority.

Matlock got his stuff out of the caravan. The gun, the whisky, everything. It all fitted into a bag. He laid the TV magazine on top. He dumped the bag on the wide passenger seat in the cab of the van.

Then he went back into the caravan. Drew the curtains closed. Left a light on. When it got dark it would look like someone was in.

'Now then.'

Matlock turned.

Frank from next door. 'How's you settling in? Your light's on.'

Shit. Actually, not so shit. Matlock asked a few questions. Frank was glad to help. Sorted him out with the wherewithal about water supply, how the heating worked, the payment for electricity usage. Gave a rundown on who was who in the other caravans. Mail came to the vans if the postie knew you, otherwise it went to the office.

The old boy wasn't so bad. Living on the site had shrunk his world, that was all. Not so different from prison.

*

Chris had said something about the egg place on the A16. To try there after Joe's house. Of course, the plan was for Matlock to have been moved off by then, and so he would never have gone there. Which meant to Matlock that maybe the deception was enveloped in the truth. That the egg place had something to do with this after all.

There were two options, both on the same road.

The A16 is a vertical scar through Lincolnshire, joining Loweth with Grimsby above and Boston below. If someone here says 'A16', then they mean to go north. The same road south is known only as 'the London road'.

North it was. The big egg place was a series of low factory-like buildings about five miles out of town; battery-like production for the supermarkets. The second one was Tom Coton's roadside market. That was where Matlock headed first.

Coton had run a smallholding since before the war. The Cotons had worked the same land for as long as anyone could recall. Some of the produce went to the family market stall in Loweth; the rest was sold at the farm gate. The perpetual display, the honesty box and the quality and variety of the goods available was a constant low-level source of admiration and wonder. At Christmas time, part of the stand became an Advent display. At Halloween, there were carved turnips. At Easter, a melange of eggs, bunnies and crosses.

This was the second egg place. Always fresh, and often as not double-yolkers, there was always a stack of boxed half-dozens of eggs besides the home-made chutneys, marmalades and fresh seasonal fruit and veg. A taped-up airtight tin, the kind a miner might have taken his lunch to the coalface in, stood in as shopkeeper.

Matlock pulled up on the grass verge. Put a couple of quid into the slot that'd been cut into the lid of the tin and took a jar of blackberry jam. Then he got back into the van, hit the horn and waited.

Tom Coton eventually made an appearance. Cap and overalls; washed so many times they'd gone from navy to aquamarine. Ruddy and creased. He carried a basket lined with straw. Fresh eggs, ready for boxing.

Matlock got out of the van. 'Now then.'

'Now then.' An amused tone.

'I'm Joe Matlock's boy.'

'You are as well. I see him in you.'

'I'm looking for Joe.'

'He's not here lad. Not seen Joe for I don't know how long. Couple of years.'

'Me neither.'

'Well you've been away. Lincoln. Nasty place. Went there once. Jury duty, of all things. Guilty, he was.' Still, a sense of comic detachment. 'Argument over a vehicle repair gone wrong. Bus garage, it was. Went for someone with one of those torches. The big ones with rubber grips. Anyway. Turned out he had previous for assault so he ended up with a handful of years behind bars. That's Lincoln for you, I reckon. Now, what's all this got to do with Joe Matlock?'

'He's missing.'

'Oh. How long?'

'Three days.'

Tom Coton put the basket down. 'Like I said, I've not seen Joe for years. Used to, mind. Useful chap, Joe. Good with his hands. A mind for mechanicals. Helped me with a few things over the years. Still, not much call for the old skills these days, unless you're one of those enthusiast types. Rail preservation. Traction engines. That mob. Only get their hands dirty on Sundays, them. No harm in them, mind. It's a shame, that's all.'

'What is?'

'The way life changes. You'll be too young for this, but in my day – and in your dad's day too – we had our paths laid out. You'd enter the family business, like me, and work the land or run the shop or the pub or whatever. Or you'd be apprenticed and you'd learn a trade. Seven years. Leave school at fourteen and a man at twenty-one. Keys to the door and getting time-served all at the same time.'

'Joe worked the railways.'

'He did.'

'Mechie fitter.'

'That's the one.'

'But…' Matlock let the unasked question trail. He didn't mind the old boy taking his time. He'd always liked the way they talked. And besides, it put off dealing with Chris.

'But not now. You're, what, thirties? And how many jobs have you had?'

A shrug.

'See? How can anyone expect to get good at something when they're spending their time doing anything and everything? I've worked this same land since I could toddle between the furrows. Every stone, every twig I know. What to tend and what to leave, what to feed the chucks, how to keep vermin respectful. It's all I know, mind, but it is *all* that I know.

'You can drive, you've got your van. But can you turn a lathe, preserve greengages or medlars, wire an electric fence and churn butter all on the same day? I daresay not. These days, we buy everything, know nothing and worry about money all the time because we rely on it, and not on ourselves.

'Listen to me,' Tom said. 'Going on. Where I was trying to get to was that your Joe knows engines. Better than that, he knows steam. Coal and coke, as well as petrol and diesel. And there's not many who do. Expertise. That's the key. Specialisms. Mine, for what it's worth, is the soil behind the house and the life I can raise from it. I'm not keeping you, am I?'

'No,' Matlock said.

'Then indulge an old man. Let me show you what Joe's done for me.'

*

Tom insisted on making tea first. While the kettle came up to the boil, he cut thick slices from a home-made loaf and buttered them. With the brew steeping in the pot, Tom produced a hunk of cheese and a hock of boiled ham on the bone. He made a pair of hefty sandwiches, and slid them from the chopping board onto enamel plates.

'Thanks.'

Tom grunted. 'I'll be mother,' he said. He poured red-brown tea into mugs matching the plates, then set one in front of Matlock. There was milk already on the table. Sugar in a bag with the sides rolled down, a tannin-darkened spoon sticking out like Excalibur.

They ate. The ticking of an unfamiliar house. The electric shiver of an elderly refrigerator. The kitchen smelled of oil and of abrasive cleaner, of leather and yeast. Of honey and butter and hot, sweet tea. And something ancient, a carbolic cleanliness. Tom kept his house shipshape.

Tom cut in before Matlock could offer further praise or thanks. 'Alright,' he said. 'Top up your brew, and we'll go have a look-see.'

Matlock was led out back. A line of trees led to a series of outbuildings. 'Half of these are full of junk I should really get sorted out, but the older you get the harder it is to part with things,' Tom said. 'The rest is all for the business, such as it is. My niece, she's the one who runs the market stall in town, she looks after much of this. I don't go into town these days unless I need to. And I find as I get older it's easier not to. I like it here.'

Tom rummaged. Produced a set of keys looped together on a metal ring. He undid the padlock on a shed door. Reached around the jamb. An electric light came on. 'C'mon on,' Tom said, stepping back to allow Matlock to enter.

The shed smelled of metal and of grease. Of parts rubbed and oiled. Of iron and copper and brass. Of age.

There was a long workbench. Tools. Gear for cutting metal, for welding. There were sheets of steel propped up against a wall. What looked first like an oil drum, but on second glance more like a homemade boiler. Maybe a petrol tank. Perhaps a still. The county grew enough beets and potatoes to make moonshining an inevitability.

Then there was the machine.

At a respectful distance from the working clutter. A tarpaulin, which Tom pulled back to expose the device.

It was beautiful.

'What it is?' Matlock asked at last.

'That is a Stanley Steamer. American. Steam-powered automobile. 1905 or thereabouts. Fully restored and working. All it needs is water in the boiler and a fire under it and you can drive out if you've a mind to.'

'And Joe did this?'

'Well, I did the basics. The surface work. Cleaning and polishing and so on. But it was Joe made her safe, got her ready to run. Without him it'd still be a bundle of parts under a cobwebbed drop cloth. There'll come a day when the back goes, or arthritis claims my hands, or my lungs won't push me around all day. My niece has the house and land promised to her; that's her inheritance and she's that and more. I've no real money in the bank or under my bed. And I'll need something to keep me, whether it's with nursing here or those bloody homes they have.

'Joe might have been tinkering with old machinery as the kind of favour you might do to an old friend, but what he's given me is something else. A pension. Security.'

'It's a lovely thing.'

'It is. And was a good thing your dad did for me. It's not forgotten. I'm sorry you don't know where he is. What's your thinking on it? And why did you think to call on me?'

Matlock summarised the information about the 'egg place'. That he'd had no contact for two years, but it looked as though Joe had been in his house until as recently as Saturday afternoon.

'And you think this is all about you? Your return to town and after what you did to get sent away?'

'After what happened, yes.'

'And?'

'And that maybe I've been going about things the wrong way.'

'How so?'

Matlock felt the pull of the question. Tom Coton knew what he was doing. Patient and gentle, like drawing a splinter out of a child's hand. 'That I might have made it worse.'

Tom made a face. A thoughtful screwing up of his lips. 'Kettle back on first. Then let's get this sorted out. There'll be some sense to be found.'

'Maybe.'

*

Tom made two more teas. He turned on a radio. The device was old. Big press-down buttons on its top; a flurry of tiny diamond-shaped stickers along the frequency display to mark where stations had changed their positions over time. It came onto the local BBC station. Traffic news from familiar places. Music that was neither pop nor country. Avuncular chatter about last night's television.

'Here you go.' The same mugs, reused.

'Ta.'

Tom indicated a square tin. Christmas characters danced along its sides. The printing on the metal had faded where it had been held for opening and closing. Festive reds turned pastel from years of contact with the incoming sun. 'Something sweet. The niece's shortbread.'

'I'm good, thanks.'

'I'm not. The older I get the more I need something every couple of hours, else my guts play up merry hell.' Tom put a handful of irregularly shaped biscuits onto one of the plates he'd used earlier.

The blether from the radio made the kitchen feel conspiratorial. Like they were having a secret conversation in the midst of bustle. It made it easier to talk. Matlock ran through the last day and a bit. Everything from crossing the road to the car park through to putting his money in Tom Coton's honesty box.

By the time he'd finished, Tom had eaten all but one of the biscuits on the plate. Matlock took the last bit of shortbread. Snapped it in half. Ate. A butter–sugar hit; the biscuit fell apart in his mouth. He ate the rest. Didn't have a sweet tooth, but regretted not having taken another earlier.

'Things come together,' Tom said at last. 'Coincidences do happen. But I'm not sure I believe that here. Whatever happened two years ago is messed up with this right enough. You might not have done for the best in bringing the fight to them yesterday, though. Messing with their money.

'Then again,' Tom continued. 'If your dad was home until the beginning of the weekend, but disappeared then, well. That's something different. He went – or was taken – on Saturday. You got out on Monday, so why not wait until then? There's two things working together somehow. That's what I reckon.'

'So what do I do next?'

'You're thinking your Joe's been got by the Mintons. To do with the Corrigan boy you ran over. Payback. That they're letting you stew about it. Course, the authorities'd never get involved. Not the Lincolnshire way, is it?'

No.

'Stands to reason, I reckon. Unfinished business on both sides. The Corrigan boy in the middle.'

And then there was Big Chris. What was she doing? Playing both sides? Had she been paid off to organise the welcoming committee at Joe's place? The one person left in this town that Matlock thought he could have relied on, Joe aside.

And what of Joe? They'd taken Matlock's entire family. So he'd take theirs, then be gone from the county forever, west through Nottinghamshire, or south via Hookland, either under his own steam or else bundled into the same dark hole as Joe.

The Mintons had to have him. Holding him to use as leverage. Or to propose a swap. Matlock senior for junior.

'What are you thinking?' Tom murmured. The radio had turned to news headlines. Two o'clock bulletin.

'The Mintons have Joe. They'll contact me to say so. There'll be a meet.'

'A meet you won't walk away from.'

'That'll be their plan.'

'And so?'

'So Joe's got value to them. They'll not harm him because of that. All they want is me.'

'That's my reckoning. Sounds like you've got something in mind.'

'Something, yeah.'

*

Tom Coton walked Matlock back to his gate. 'If there's something I can do, let me know.'

'I will. Thanks.'

'Another thing.'

'Yes?'

'Your friend Chris.'

'What about her?'

'She knows things. She sent you here, didn't she?'

And sent some goon around to rearrange my face and send me on my way. 'I suppose.'

'So, remember there's more than one egg place.' Tom didn't wait for a reply to that, but headed back towards his house.

Matlock got into the van. Not long past two. That meant visiting hours were open.

The reception desk was empty at the nursing home. Matlock buzzed a handful of times before a harassed-looking orderly came to the door. Ice-black hair, a plastic apron over her uniform. Must have been the tail end of lunchtime. Matlock made a hopeful face. Held up the jar of jam like it was self-explanatory. He was buzzed in; the orderly scuttled off before Matlock could give any thanks.

He signed in. No one had visited room 112 since he'd been here the day before. Or at least, no one had recorded their presence.

The room was open as it had been yesterday. And old Mrs Minton asleep once more. Her hair had been recently brushed, her nightdress changed from the one she had been wearing the last time Matlock had been here.

He put the jam jar down on a side table. The sort with wheels that could be pushed to overhang a hospital bed.

A tube slithered out from the bottom of the bedclothes to a stand on the floor. She'd been catheterised.

Matlock watched her sleep. Frail, shallow, rapid breathing. Eyes dancing under their fragile closed lids. He wondered if she was dreaming.

A pillow would do it.

She'd never know.

All the doors on the corridor were open. No real privacy here. Then he got it. You could patrol up and down; a turn of the head to either side could confirm that everything was okay. The rooms would have push-button alarms, but if the other residents in this part of the place were like old Mrs Minton, then they'd either be oblivious to their condition, or else they'd cry out for assistance, or they'd be in comfort because they'd been visited again by the ghosts of whomever they were soon to join.

The doors were held open by magnetic closures that looked like doorstops. Matlock guessed that if the fire alarm went off, then that cut an electric circuit and the doors swung closed automatically. A fire door bought you half an hour.

He gave it ten minutes. Then went down to sign out.

'I thought you'd be back.'

'Can't stay away.'

'Evidently.' She had the same bright look she had yesterday. Summery freckles, clear skin, hair in a ponytail exposing the ways that tendons flexed under the skin when she shifted. 'How is she?'

Matlock caught what the name tag said. L. Sullivan. 'Asleep again. I'll try once more tomorrow.'

'Aw.'

Matlock wasn't sure if the sentiment was meant for the cuteness of the old sleeping lady, or for this relative's diligence. 'Maybe see you then, then.'

'It's entirely possible, Dan Matlock.'

'You peeked, L. Sullivan.'

'L, which is short for Lucy, which is short for Lucifer.'

'See you tomorrow, Lucy.'

'Missing you already, Dan.'

*

Chris was next. Matlock couldn't put it off any more. He didn't ring ahead. He thought about the Ruger, but that felt a step too far. Just talk. A threat with a gun would have been empty, and she'd know that. And besides, it would have made Matlock no better than other men she'd known.

The back of the van rumbled when Matlock pulled up by the walkway to the railway line which led to Chris's back garden. Whatever it was was loose. Had space to roll around in an otherwise empty cargo compartment. He'd get to it. Wasn't a priority.

He'd walked this line a dozen times with his dad as a kid. Shaky early-learning independence bike rides. The line cut through the town north to south; there'd been talk about rerouting the A16 down the line after the railways withdrew, but that never came to pass. Save for the couple of miles of track still in place where the rail enthusiasts did their hobby thing halfway between Loweth and Grimsby, you could pretty much walk the culvert clear from the Humber to the Wash. Maybe fifty miles. Some of it had been turned into official walking routes marked out redundantly by arrowed signs with the county logo, the ecstatic imp figure modelled on a carving in Lincoln cathedral.

Joe had pointed out bits and bobs of railway arcana. Had held him steady as he got his balance, the bike a new one out of the catalogue. Him being an only child and with no mother around, they'd been forced to spend time together. Found their own ways to be close and to keep space for themselves.

Still, he had learned to ride up and down this track.

Chris wasn't in her shed. Matlock turned the light on and waited. It didn't take long. Maybe she'd linked the light switch to a doorbell mechanism. Perhaps one of her kids kept watch.

The baggy top over the loose trousers she was wearing didn't hide the sawn-off which rode in a deep side pocket.

Matlock opened the shed door to show that it was him. He moved slow and with care. No sudden moves. Open hands.

Chris shook her head. Sadness, resignation maybe. At least she hadn't pointed her gun at him. 'You're not meant to be here.'

'But here I am.'

'Yeah. Here you are. Back in the shed with you. Good a place to talk as any.'

*

Chris rested the shotgun on the workbench. Within her reach, but not on her person. 'He's a mess.'

'That was Gnat Jackson, I suppose.'

'Broken collarbone. Couple of ribs smashed. A long list. I could barely keep up.'

'What were you thinking, sending someone after me?'

'What do you think? Trying to save your hide. Shame. I thought Gnat was harder than you. Than this. That prison would have softened you up even more.'

'Yeah. Well.'

'Didn't think you'd take a hint from me. Or a request.'

'So you sent a one-man heavy mob?'

'He's never let me down before. He's not a thinker like you. Does what he's told.'

'It wasn't his fault.'

'So what am I going to do with you? The Mintons are going to come down on you hard and fast.'

'They've got Joe.'

'See? This is only the beginning. They want you for the Corrigan boy.'

'He shouldn't have been there.'

'You think I don't know that? It wasn't his debt. He had no reason to be involved.'

'The Corrigans should never have dealt with you.'

'I should have never have dealt with them.'

Matlock shrugged. 'They came to you.'

'Even so.'

*

This was how it had played out. The Corrigans and the Mintons were kin. Unpicking precisely how was a fool's errand. Their family trees were a rat king, forever entangled and with a hundred desperate sets of jaws.

Of the two families, the Mintons always held the upper position, having the land, the money, the building contracts and the business contacts. Councillors, planning officials, the farming associations, the Rotary Club, Round Table, masonic lodge and golf club connections.

The Corrigans were meat and muscle. Labourers and cleaners, farmhands and funfair operators. Amusement arcades down the coast. Launderettes; a couple of betting shops in the resorts.

They were self-sufficient as a unit. All their needs could be satisfied by someone else in the clan. That was the problem. You didn't deal with outsiders unless you had to. Unless it had been cleared.

So when Liam Corrigan came to Big Chris he came with a promise. That he'd had permission to borrow money from outside the family. The way Chris told it, young Corrigan had disgraced himself – there was a tale about a bridesmaid at a wedding being got pregnant and a private abortion to be paid for, and that Liam had been told to sort his own mess out, with no support from the family – and so he'd had dispensation to come to someone like Chris.

It turned out that wasn't quite true. No bridesmaid, no private hospital. Liam Corrigan wanted to borrow money for some get-rich-quick scheme he'd been sweet-talked into fronting the money for. He'd been told not to get involved. Repeatedly. But he'd been seduced by London connections: sharp suits and elegant patter far further away from Lincolnshire than the hundred and fifty miles' distance would suggest. The London link made Matlock think that Kayode might have had something to do with this. Not as a favour; as a set-up for some slight.

It was big money. But Chris put it up because there was the assurance that this was treading on no one's toes.

For a while it had been fine. Liam had been canny enough to borrow more than he needed, so he could make the first repayments out of what he'd been loaned. It took six months for the wheels to fall off.

First of the month, and Matlock had gone to pick up the instalment that had come due. Liam held court in a town-centre place that fancied itself a wine bar. Jerry's. The licence was in another's name but half the town understood that this was one of the Mintons' businesses.

Liam had been at his usual stool at the dark end of the bar. A weekday lunchtime. No market today; custom was sparse.

Matlock nodded at the kid behind the pumps. He looked barely old enough to know what a pint tasted like, let alone pull one. The kid glanced down and away. Something between guilt and embarrassment. Complicity.

'Liam.'

'Dan.'

Corrigan had a drink on the go. Clear. Bubbles. Ice. Vodka and tonic. His face was pinker than it ought to be. He was on his third at least.

'You don't have an envelope for me.'

'For Chris. No. Not right now. Maybe later.'

'"Later"?'

A sip. A palate cleanser for the lie fresh told. And now a swig; to lubricate the next.

'Tonight. Tomorrow, latest. Tops.'

'Chris won't like it.'

Arms wide; submissive and open. A gesture meant to show that no harm was meant. 'It's simply a cashflow thing. Short term. A misunderstanding in London. There's someone on their way up this afternoon, isn't there, our Ant?'

The younger Corrigan nodded. Blustered something about a phone call a few minutes ago.

'See. It's all under control. Come back tomorrow, yeah. Same time?'

'Noon.'

'Twelve, yeah. Same time, same place. We'll be here, won't we, our Ant?'

Another heads-down nod.

'I'll need to talk to Chris.'

'Sure, yeah, use the house phone. Ant, hand it over, will you?'

The phone was on a cord long enough to run the length of the bar. Matlock took it as far as it could go. Dialled. 'Chris?'

'Go on.'

'Corrigan wants twenty-four hours.'

Chris told him a few things, and Matlock put the phone down. Left it trailing along the bar.

'We good?' Corrigan's glass was empty save for slivers of ice.

'Twenty-four hours.'

'See?' Corrigan was salmon-faced. 'We're all good. You want a drink? I want a drink. Ant, get the man what he wants. And another for me.'

'Nothing for me.'

'Just me then.'

'There's something else.'

'And what's that?'

'Another ten per cent. For the delay.'

'Ten?'

'Ten.'

It's called vigorish. Vig for short. The word has different meanings in different contexts, so it's useful to be clear. In some situations the vig is the interest on a loan. In others, it's the house charge or the bookie's cut for the placing of a bet win or lose; like an auction-eer's commission on a sale. There's an element of professional services being paid for. In yet other versions, only the winner pays vig. Like a sales tax.

Here, it was a late fee. A surcharge over and above the original rate because of the nuisance. A reminder not to do it again. Chris kept her books simple to make matters easy for herself and for her clients. Compound interest made little sense to many; that was often how they ended up using moneylenders in the first place.

Sometimes, a real shark gets their teeth into you by allowing you to only pay back the vig. The principal remains unpaid. So you owe forever, and the debt is always due on the first of the month.

Corrigan was going to say something, but his brother put another drink in front of him, cutting short the thought.

Probably a good thing, too.

He was in his own place, but Liam Corrigan was out on a limb. He'd been cut loose by the Mintons to sort out his mess himself for a change; he couldn't go back to them. If he welshed on the loan, then all it would take would be a phone call from Chris to Roy Minton. Chris would be reimbursed in full and with apologies. And Liam would be dealt with in-house. Pride, you see.

The point had been made. Matlock nodded goodbye to the brother on the way out and that was that.

Except it wasn't.

Matlock did two kinds of work for Chris. Receipts and collections. Receipts were simply the taking of monies due. Today with Corrigan was a receipt job. Collections were simply that. The taking of what had been owed and not repaid in a timely manner. Collections came with a thirty per cent cut to the collector. That meant that the money-lender was still out of pocket but seventy per cent was better than nothing, and failing that, the hiding the defaulter got stood as both an encouragement to the others as well as free advertising for loanshark-ing services. Plus, if you were collecting, you got to take out your frustrations on the mark.

Rule one of lending money. They've always got the money to

make the repayment. They might not know it, but there's always a way.

Chris had told Matlock to watch the place. The top two floors of the building with Jerry's on the street level were flats. One was Liam's; the other Anthony's. No one really expected Liam to skip, but you had to be sure. Matlock checked at midnight. The bar had closed a few minutes earlier; week nights were quiet. There were the blue lights of televisions on in both flats.

*

Matlock came back at six. He'd considered making a drive out into the country first. He had a gun stashed, far out of town, for those better-safe-than-sorry situations. He decided against it; too much for a small-town loudmouth. Besides, it was an early enough start as it was.

Matlock parked in the marketplace. He picked up a full milk bottle on the way from a bank's doorstep, and used it to break one of the Corrigans' windows. Then a second. This set off an alarm in the wine bar. Matlock threw the milk in after the shattered glass.

The flats had a separate entrance; it took less than a minute for Liam to make an appearance. A hooded dressing gown like he was a prize-fighter on his way to the ring. Slippers that might have been Christmas presents.

He came out, saw the damage, swore. Found the right key. Went inside the bar. Matlock followed.

The alarm dropped out of hearing; Matlock's ears shivered in the fresh silence. Corrigan had his back to him; resetting something in a cabinet at the same end of the bar he'd been sitting at the day before. Muttering, cursing as he worked.

Matlock came up behind Corrigan. Tapped him on his right shoulder. A schoolboy trick.

Corrigan was right-handed, like most people. Matlock saw this when he was drinking at the bar. So if he turned to the right it took his leading hand out of action. Any response would be with his weaker left. Boxing robe or no, Matlock didn't think Corrigan was either a southpaw or a switch-hitter.

Corrigan swivelled like he was meant to – was opening his mouth to snap something – and stepped into Matlock's oncoming fist.

Nothing serious; that might have dislocated his jaw. A tap to disorientate. To show this was business. To get some answers swift.

Corrigan flailed, lurching over a stool. He didn't hit the ground but it was a close thing. 'Fuck. Can't you knock like a decent person?'

'The envelope.'

'Think you loosened a tooth or something.'

'The envelope.'

'Jesus. Fuck. First you smash the place up, throw fucking gold top everywhere, and then you expect me to pull your precious envelope out of my arse before dawn.'

Matlock raised his fist. Let him see it tighten.

'Nine. Fuck. You can have it at nine. Alright? Jesus.'

'Where is it?'

'In the bank. You think I keep that kind of money here? Mixed in with the takings? You think I'm going to pay you out of the till like you're the window cleaner?'

'How come it's in the bank?'

'Because that's where you keep your money. Why they call it a bank. Envelope got here eight-ish last night. It went straight in the night safe. Bank opens at nine. You get your money at nine.' The fight had gone out of him. 'Look at this place. Fuck. You know how much windows cost?'

Matlock stayed with Corrigan till almost nine. Watched him make a couple of calls to find a glazier who'd come out. Another to get his brother out of bed. Anthony was wide-eyed, but knew not to say anything. He went to work with a mop and bucket on the milk, then swept up the remaining glass.

Anthony stayed downstairs to wait for the window replacement fella. Matlock went upstairs with Liam to his flat. Gave it the once-over. A wall display of touristy-looking samurai swords aside, there was nothing troubling. He supposed that there were drugs here somewhere, but that was no concern of his. After checking the bathroom, he told Liam to find a set of clothes and get himself showered and dressed.

While the shower ran, Matlock made a sandwich. Cheese and pickle. That was about all there was in the fridge. Couple of bottles of lager. Milk. The freezer compartment above the top shelf ballooned with ice.

Corrigan came back through. Wet hair, skin pink from hot water this time. Poured a bowl of cereal. Three cap-wearing elves capered on the box. The cereal rustled when the milk hit it. Matlock wasn't offered anything.

Two hours passed slowly. Anthony came up once to say that the glazier had arrived.

Eventually, it was time. Twenty-five to nine.

'Grab your coat.'

'Don't need one.'

Token defiance, but it was there nevertheless. Matlock shoved Corrigan towards the exit.

*

'We'll need Ant.'

'What for?'

'For the night safe. It's in his name. I'm not an account holder.'

'Right.'

The glazier had been and gone. Two new windows. They were cleaner than those surrounding them. 'Lock up behind us, our Ant. You'll need to come with,' Liam said.

'One sec.'

The point of a night safe is to deposit takings after hours. There's a locked slot on the wall of the bank; a chute leads to a holding strongbox. They give you a key to the slot and a handful of cloth paying-in bags. Your money and a deposit slip go into the bag. Tradition demands the bag is folded over and secured with a rubber band. The bundle goes into the slot. There's the distant sound of impact from within. The next working day, the strongbox gets opened up and the contents deposited into the appropriate accounts.

There's usually some boilerplate text on the night safe agreement that the monies aren't to be considered as deposited until trading hours begin. Until then, the cash is held for safekeeping only.

Things can get a little lax in small towns though. Unorthodox custom and practice sneak in. Here, the trick was simple. The night safe acted as an informal safety deposit box. You could drop something in at night, and retrieve it first thing. As long as you were there for the bank's opening, and had the requisite ID, then you got your own bag back, no questions asked.

With the night safe only being opened by the bank once a day, this little service can prove useful if repeated. Of course, there's a fee for such services. And a little cash in hand is always welcome.

It was barely a two-minute walk along the side street where Jerry's stood then out into the marketplace to the bank. Two cashiers were standing outside, waiting for a keyholder to arrive. They were tutting about the milkman. He'd left them a pint short, apparently. Either that or one of those thieving paper boys had nicked one.

The manager was there by quarter-to.

Matlock glanced at Liam, who passed the look onto his little brother. Ant shuffled forwards and had a brief conversation with the manager. Nods were exchanged. 'You'll need to wait until nine when we open for custom. But you'll be first in. It won't take a second to sort out.' The manager unlocked the door, having been joined by his deputy; the required number of keyholders now being present, the staff went in.

Ten to.

Earlier, Matlock had parked only a few paces away. He'd never been a petrolhead. A succession of functional vehicles. Sometimes ordinary saloons, sometimes small vans. Practical, cheap to run, anonymous. Nothing fancy, nothing remarkable. He didn't draw attention to his car now. Besides, the elder Corrigan was killing time by pronouncing on what was being driven by.

'Piece of shit,' Liam said. Another car went past. 'Piece of shit.' And a third. 'Utter dog-egg.'

Five to.

Shops were opening up. Mums dropping into town after the school run; a small parade of buggies and pushchairs. Delivery vehicles.

Two minutes to.

Liam Corrigan's hair was wet. It'd been dry long before they'd left his flat. He had his hair short. He'd messed it up with some ointment or other, but this was nothing to do with that. The gel had given him a spiky look. That was starting to wilt. His neck was red. Raw tuna rather than salmon. A smear of sweat along the collar.

Something wasn't right with him.

Matlock had learned a long time ago about the difference between what you could and what you couldn't personally affect. There was a prayer about it. Know the difference, and act upon that knowledge. This prevents that gut-twisting lurch of apprehension. Action or there being no need to engage.

Whatever the problem with Liam Corrigan was, it resided within him. The branching alternatives of what might happen next were mapped out as far as Matlock was concerned. Either he'd get the money for Chris, or he wouldn't. If yes, all well and good. If not, then that was up to Chris.

He was only a representative. An emissary.

The bank opened up. The manager popped his head out. Found Ant. 'In you come, son.'

Liam shuffled. Left foot, right foot. Hay foot, straw foot. Where had that come from?

Other customers went inside. The sun came out from what had been banks of oppressive grey clouds. Starting to look like a decent day for the time of year.

The younger Corrigan reappeared. A muslin bag in his hand, folded over a couple of times. The bank's logo stuttered across the package. 'Here y'go.'

Liam snatched the packet. Found an envelope inside. Manila. A5. Opened it. Handed it to Matlock. 'Here. Plus your precious extra ten per cent.'

Matlock wasn't going to count it out here in the open. 'Back to the bar,' he said.

'Jesus,' Liam hissed. 'You've got your fucking blood money. Now fuck off with it. I don't owe you any more.'

'Not until the First comes around again.'

Liam headed off back the way they'd come. Matlock followed, Ant in tow. Let him storm off. It didn't mean anything.

Liam went back up into his flat. Ant let Matlock into the bar. With the premises otherwise silent, hearing Liam stamp around upstairs was simple enough. Fretting to himself that he'd lost control. Pride, messing with him.

Ant turned some lights on. Didn't help the gloom much, but Matlock appreciated the touch, and the cup of coffee which soon followed.

You count the money twice. Once for them, and once for yourself to be sure. It was all there, first time around. Miscounts were common enough. It paid to be careful.

Matlock noticed it on the recount. Not the quantity. The quality of the money. You handle something all day every day, and it's perhaps surprising how nuanced you can be. Matlock knew of guys working in the plastics factories whose touch was accurate within ten microns. Men who could tell if a job intended to be running at fifty thousandths of a centimetre thickness felt right or not.

This money was wrong.

Corrigan stomped about upstairs.

The paper wasn't right.

The notes were counterfeit. 'Ant?'

'Yeah?'

'Call your brother down, would you?'

'Sure.' He dialled. Waited for the pickup.

The movement upstairs ceased.

Ant spoke, quiet into the receiver. While he was still on the phone, Matlock stacked the notes. Put them back into order. He had a feeling the money had been bundled. Genuine currency sandwiching the duds within.

Sneaky little fucker.

'He'll be down in a minute,' Ant said.

'Good.'

'I'm getting some crisps from the back room.'

'Don't mind me.' Matlock stood. Tucked the envelope away. Wondered which way this would go.

Ant came back through with a stack of cartons of snacks. Picked out a perforated hole in the side of each box. Fished out the remaining packets from the flavours he was replenishing, stuck them into the new box and slid that into position under the bar's back counter.

Silence from upstairs. Matlock faced the entrance.

You can feel it when they're going to bolt. Electric discharge from the fight-or-flight response. Matlock had a sense for this when a punch was going to be thrown at him; a scintilla of foresight. He stood.

The kid gabbled something behind him, but Matlock wasn't listening. He made for the door. Still nothing physical from above. The static build-up intensified. The kid tried again; a higher, more urgent pitch meant to communicate urgency and attention, but which simply signalled a desperate attempt at distraction. He'd been told by his brother to stick a wrench in his gears.

Matlock was almost at the door. Then the rumble came. Feet on wood, downstairs, fast.

Too fast. Matlock had an even chance of being lucky; if Corrigan broke right then he'd come into his path and it'd all be over. If he went left, though – back towards town – then anything was possible.

Turned out Liam was lucky. Two, three paces ahead of Matlock, and already running fast towards town, propelled by the impetus of racing downstairs.

No point shouting. Run. Get within a yard, then tackle him down.

The side street was slick. Not with moisture, but with the rounded heels of cobblestones. Tricky to maintain pace on. Corrigan seemed used to it; more so than Matlock. He was getting away. He broke out into the main street, Haberdasher Row, and had already doubled his lead.

Shit.

Something in his hand. Running towards the bank now; Corrigan had something bunched in a fist. Might have been a knife. A duster. No; too small.

Car keys.

There were cars scattered across the marketplace. Some on-street parking too. Corrigan didn't seem the type to concern himself overmuch with one-hour no-return parking regulations.

He'd never get to his mark before he was inside his vehicle. Or would he? Matlock's future branched. One: he followed his man, grabbing him by his shiny lapels before he was inside his car. Two: he got inside the car, but Matlock pile-drove his fist through the driver-side front window, getting his man but shredding his arm up to the elbow. Three: he went for his own car.

Corrigan stopped by a red car. Sporty but underpowered. The kind other men might sneeringly refer to as a hairdresser's car. He glanced at Matlock's position. Did his own maths. Went to get in.

He was right. Matlock diverted to his wheels. Fumbled the keys. Found the right one.

The red car revved. Screeched from standing.

Matlock got in, started up. The curve of the road meant that he had a straight line of sight towards where Corrigan was going to be in about five seconds' time. He could cut him off. The car bucked into life.

Afterwards, Matlock revisited the next five seconds seven hundred different ways. One for each night he'd spent in prison. No matter how he went back to those moments, he never once saw quite how Ant Corrigan got to where he was when he was hit.

*

'Even so,' Chris said again. 'Should never have come to anything like this.'

'But here we are.'

'Here we are.'

Aircraft came over low. Probably some military exercise ongoing somewhere. Lincolnshire still bristled with air force bases; had made a tourist thing of its Bomber County status. Lancasters and Welling-tons running sorties against the Hun. Half the villages in these parts ran charity 1940s weekends; an excuse to dress up and reminisce, even if they were far too young to have any meaningful connection with rationing or Churchill. The sky's rumble faded.

Chris picked the firearm up from the bench. She did it slowly – forefinger and thumb only – to show no harm intended, then opened the breech. Took out the two shells.

The left-hand shell was packed with rock salt. The right-hand shell was filled with shot.

Chris was never less than fair. Or at least she had been up until today. 'So you're going to stay?'

'Just to put this right. To find Joe and make sure he's settled. And that he won't get any trouble on my account again. And then I'm gone.'

'So what's really going on?'

'I was expecting something from the Mintons. For them to come for me.'

'They've got your dad it seems.'

'This has nothing to do with him.'

'But that's not how they think. Mintons. Corrigans. It's all family. You mess with one of theirs, they mess with one of yours. That's how they're wired.'

'And Joe?'

'He's bait.'

'And I suppose I've got to bite down hard on the hook to release him.'

'I reckon.'

'How?'

'Did you go to the egg place?' Chris asked.

'Tom Coton's? Yes.'

'No. Didn't think of Tom. He's a buddy of your old man's, isn't he?'

'Steam engines,' Matlock said. 'Double-yolkers. A mutual interest in pottering in sheds.'

'I meant the other place. The egg factory.'

'What about it?'

'Nothing. A Corrigan place; packers and drivers for Minton goods. I was hoping that someone there'd give you a hiding if you hadn't already got the message.'

'I'm not receiving messages much these days. Broadcast only.'

'It's not gone unnoticed.' Chris looked thoughtful. 'What do you want to do?'

'I'll need a meeting. A sit-down with Roy Minton. It's the only way this'll get cleared up.'

Chris nodded. 'There'll be no guarantees for your safety.'

Matlock shrugged. 'As long as I get Joe back. Anything else? That's a bonus.'

'It'll take a little time. Can you keep clear of trouble till the morning?'

'I'll try.'

Chris picked up the broken sawn-off. Thumbed the shells back into their respective chambers. 'Do so.'

*

Matlock drove for a while. Laps of the town. Let muscle memory do its thing. Up and down the gears. Mirrors, signals, pedals. The town had expanded to the east. The floodplain out towards the coast was being nibbled at. An estate here, a development there. Growth to the west was prohibited by geography; the town's main parks and then the Wolds got in the way. North was the industrial estate. South was the cemetery, the cattle market, the council landfill site, allotments. East was what was left.

Matlock parked up eventually. Let the van and its old cargo settle. The engine's tick slowed.

Drizzle spattered the windscreen. Matlock got out. Felt the flicked water. Two years since his last proper rain. It felt good; fresh, vital. High walls around the exercise yard had shielded him from the worst of the weather. He stood there until he was wet. Until his hair was slicked to his scalp, and until water ran off into his eyes.

Cars came by. Lorries. Livestock transporters. Beasts off to the abattoir. Then an ambulance; neither lights nor sirens.

Matlock walked along the grass verge. A sign ahead. A wonky little hand-painted thing; the kind that might have been stuck into the ground by church worthies advertising their flower festival. 'Open 10 to 4. Teas and cake available.'

No. It wasn't a notice.

A cross. Perhaps a foot high, with the cross-brace made of a wider piece of wood, so that the name could be more easily read. Matlock had to walk around the spot to face it. There were flowers here; a rubber-banded bunch, the crêpe paper and plastic wrapping dappled with age and wear. The flowers had gone from brown to grey. Dust would be next for them.

RIP Mazzie. No other message.

This was no place for a road accident. Not a fast stretch, no obvious hazards. Simply one of those hinterland stretches of minor road on the very edges of a smallish town. There wasn't much out here except trees, irregularly spaced houses and the final fading to farmland.

Mazzie. No idea. Sounded young. A nickname for a kid. A family name for a beloved daughter. Daddy's little angel, now always youthful.

Matlock righted the cross. Angled it so that it could be read more easily by passers-by. He had nothing to leave, but he arranged the dead flowers so that they looked like a recent offering. Then he went back to the van.

From the cab, the cross looked alright. He supposed that the memorial had been supplanted by a more permanent construction in the cemetery. But Matlock reckoned also that there was at least one person in this town who either avoided this route for their own reasons, or who took every chance they could to come this way, always slowing down at this point in the road, in case there was a sign of the person they'd lost.

Matlock tugged a piece of clothing out from the bag on his passenger seat. Wiped his face dry enough. Smeared the worst from his hair. Chucked the tee shirt he'd used onto the bag. Started up again.

He was back at the cemetery in minutes. The place was empty; dull weather would do that to a graveyard. Anthony Corrigan's headstone was how he'd left it the previous day. Maybe the vandalism had been reported, maybe not.

This wouldn't be easy. The rain had all but stopped, but even so. Matlock wiped down the sides of the granite headstone. The memorial was polished on all of its faces. That was more expensive, and made handling the stone a bastard. Granite was slippery at the best of times. Add damp and polished surfaces. Not ideal.

Plus it was heavy. This was a two-man job. But it could be done. If you took it in stages.

The inscription faced upwards. The grey of the low clouds was a decent match for the stone. Matlock stood at the head end, went down on his haunches. Pushed his fingers into the grass at either side. Found purchase on the stone. Lifted.

It was greasy, but nevertheless. Matlock held on, pivoting the top end of the headstone upwards. He stepped into the job, now crouching. His right hand squeaked; it was slipping. He needed to adjust his grip, but couldn't do so without letting go first. Matlock rested the lip of the stone on his bent knees. Made the finger-shift. Christ, but it was heavy. He lifted again, this time bringing the headstone upright.

Now, rest. Matlock leaned on the standing stone. Stubby dowels poked from the base. Not a good job. They needed to have been longer to have offered better support. The stone might have toppled anyway.

Grabbing it by the top corners, Matlock walked the headstone up to its base, pivoting it on alternate corners to shuffle it forwards. To get it back onto its stand. That was another thing. Again, Matlock walked it forwards, this time at an exaggerated angle so that the bottom corner of the stone would rise over the lip of the base. The first side was straightforward enough; the second was trickier. It took three attempts to get it right. On each go, the granite complained where the bottom corner of the headstone ground against the slick surface of the base. The contact point would be scuffed, but it was far enough into the base for the headstone to cover it when put right.

Matlock rested again. This was the lower, newest part of the cemetery. The stones around here glistened with their newness in the aftermath of the rain. Granite greys and blacks. White marble. A smattering of wooden crosses either as placeholders or else as modest statements of life and death. There were two grave spaces fresh from funerals: mounded earth covered with replaced turf. A further hole had been dug, the soil beside it covered in a square of the kind of artificial lawn material Matlock associated with display tables outside greengrocers' shops. Cut turf was stacked nearby, soil to soil, green to green.

Those dowels were token efforts only. Matlock tugged to see if they'd come away, but they were cemented in firm. They protruded only a couple of inches. It was doable. Matlock shuffled the headstone into place, first over one and then over the other dowel. It now stood upright, back where it had been on Monday. It would need fixing into place, but it was good enough for now.

Better.

Up the hill, where the chapels and the old headstones stood – still-impressive sarcophagi, lichened praying angels – there was movement. Shadows against shadows in the tree-lined walkways. One of the groundskeepers. A wheelbarrow loaded with shovels.

Matlock made that he'd not seen the observer. Wiped his hands on his thighs. Stamped the ground back into shape where handling the headstone had corrupted the soil. Then, hands in pockets, he went looking. Down and back up the rows of grave markers.

He found her after a few minutes. A modest white marble headstone, a flower container offset to one side of the base. Lisa 'Mazzie' Webster. Dates; she'd been twenty-one. Had died a little over a year ago. A further inscription. *You were always amazing.*

Amazing. Mazzie.

A child's mispronunciation which had stuck as a family name. A lisping toddler repeating the same word, pointing at whatever.

The flowers were new enough. Glistened with the afternoon's rainfall. The grass around the headstone was well trodden enough to be patchy, mud breaking through. Someone came here often. Said their prayers. Spoke to the stone as if it might hear them.

Being here felt intrusive. Matlock went back to the van. From inside, he checked the treeline. There was no sign of the groundskeeper.

Matlock drove out of the cemetery.

*

The plan was to stay at Joe's. But first Matlock wanted to check on the caravan; see if anyone had been poking around.

The old boy was outside, picking up turds after his dog. He raised his filled bag in welcome. 'Alright?'

'Not bad.'

'Jarvis has been looking for you.'

'Right.' There were lights on in the building.

'Said for you to go to the office if or when you ever got here.'

'Ta.'

'Pop over when you're done. I'll have the kettle on.' A pause. 'If you like.'

'Yeah, sure. Back in a minute then.' The dog snuffled around Matlock's feet, then went back to its master.

*

Matlock knocked and entered the site office door. A man sat behind a desk. Typewriter, phone, in and out trays. A wall planner on a corkboard behind him. Little stickers bearing information in some personal code. The room was the smallest of three in the block: single-storey, pitch-roofed. The others looked like a site shop and a makeshift bar. Not much more than chipboard and plain windows. Might have been a converted outbuilding. Something temporarily knocked up that had outlived its original usefulness.

The man behind the desk wore a knitted tie. A short-sleeved shirt with epaulettes. Moustache. Hair that was either pubic curls cropped and then tamed further with lotion to ward off unruliness, or else had been deliberately styled that way. Matlock suspected the latter. Maybe this had been the fashion when this Jarvis had done his military service. He gave off other smells. Pipe tobacco, sweet tea. Body odour.

'Ah, yes. You're Chris's... guest.'

'Yes.'

'Bit irregular, this time of year. Still, she pays her fees. Usually only residents onsite until Easter. Did try a couple of years back with contractors when the water board was replacing pipelines through the county, but it was more trouble than it was worth.

'Anyway. Yes. Message for you. Not that this is the Horsley Green Farm Post Office.' Jarvis pushed a slip of paper forward on the desk. The paper was folded over as though that made the contents somehow private.

'Thanks.' Matlock didn't look at what was inside.

'Staying... long? Not that it's any bother, or any business of mine, but it's good to know who's about and who's not. For security reasons.'

'Of course. Not long. Maybe until the weekend.'

'Good. That is good.' Jarvis's voice tailed away. He retrieved a pipe from an ashtray. Found a small knife in a pocket and began to clear out the bowl. 'That's it. I'd be obliged, though, if… whoever it is… respects the office in future. There's a payphone by the roadside, after all.'

'I'll see what I can do.'

I'd appreciate that.' Jarvis tapped the bowl of the pipe into the ashtray. Once-impacted grey dust fell into the container. He took a speculative draw on the pipe. A nod. Opened a pouch, took a pinch of shredded tobacco. Tamped it into the pipe with the boss of the knife he'd used earlier.

Matlock closed the door behind him without saying anything further. A sigh of relaxation from the office as the latch clicked tight.

*

'Staying long, then?' Frank Bird had been waiting. Had ushered Matlock into his caravan with promises of tea and a slice of something home-made. Now he was serving up a pair of brews. He'd lied about the home-made. Four slices of Jamaica Ginger Cake sat between them on a saucer. 'Dig in.'

'Only till the weekend.'

'Shame. Be good to have some company around here. Gets quiet out of season. And Mr Jarvis and I don't have much in common except this–' indicating his pipe '–and a patchy service history in Her Majesty's armed forces.'

'Oh?'

'Me? Missile technician. Sounds fancier than it was. Still, I could tell you some stories about nukes that nearly went off. Signed the Act. Official Secrets. We all did. Live weapons loaded when they oughtn't have been. Planes gone down in training missions. We were bribed and threatened at the same time. Money and menaces. Not like nowadays. One or the other. That's what you get.'

Matlock took a bit of cake. A memory hit. This stuff, covered in warmed-through tinned custard. A regular childhood thing. Couldn't remember if that was a school dinners recollection or if it was a memory from home. Kak, they called it in the playground. Custard and cake. Kak. Funny when you were small. 'Cheers.'

Matlock let Frank talk. Interjected every now and again to show he was paying attention, and to orient the conversation back towards Frank and away from him wherever possible. He was in no particular rush. Small-town waffle; a bit of background. Detours into football and television.

'So, what was Jarvis after you for then?'

'Ah, he'd taken a phone message for me, he said. Didn't seem too pleased about it.'

'Well, he wouldn't. Likes the quiet life, does our Mr Jarvis. No mess, no fuss. No one runs a caravan site if they're looking for adventure.'

'I suppose not.'

'Was it important?'

'The message? Not sure. Haven't read it yet.'

'Oh. There were others here today. Poking around your digs.'

'Really?'

'Two of them. They went in the office afterwards. I pointed out you weren't in. They asked me how I knew, and I said that your van wasn't there.'

'That'd do it. I hadn't realised they'd called in person.' Jarvis had put the mention of the payphone in only to give that impression, he now realised. Matlock took a second slice of the cake. Broke it in two. Ate the first half, enjoying its gooey ginger topping. 'What did they look like, these two?'

Frank told him. The descriptions matched Tobacco Man and Joe Kayode; two of the three Matlock had bested in the money-counting room the previous morning. Part of him was impressed that they'd managed to track him down so quickly. He wondered if they'd had help with that.

Matlock finished his cake. Swigged his now-cooling tea. 'Cheers Frank.'

'Any time. It's nice to have someone to talk with. Chatting with the dog gets a bit one-sided.'

'I'm nipping into town. Probably getting something to eat on the way back. I'll pick you up a fish supper if you like.'

'No need. I was going to open a tin of oxtail.'

'You sure?'

'Well. If you insist.'

'Give me an hour.'

'I'll have some plates warmed up.'

'Good man.'

*

Matlock drove into town. Found a phone box. Waited until it was free. Then got out of the van.

He didn't read the message given to him by Jarvis until he was inside the phone box. Urine and dog-end smell. Occluded windows where glass panes had been replaced by perspex. One of these additions had a smiley face cigarette-burned into it.

The message was simple. A phone number. And two words, in capitals: FROM YESTERDAY.

Matlock guessed what that was all about.

And figured out a way that it might be useful to him.

He dialled Chris's number. 'Yes?'

'Chris? Me.'

'I'm waiting on a reply from Minton.'

'When do you think you'll hear?'

'Any minute. Get off the phone. I'll call you back.'

'I'm in town. Hang on.' Matlock gave her the number for the phone box. 'Got an errand to run. I'll be back here in, oh, fifteen minutes. Okay?'

'Okay.'

*

Matlock picked up haddock, chips and peas for Frank. A couple of buttered rolls as well. Chicken and mushroom pie, chips and curry sauce for himself. Went back to the phone box. Felt self-conscious hanging around, so waited in the box. A woman came up, change in her hand. He mimed being on a call; gestured that it'd take some time. She nodded, moved on.

'Matlock?'

'Here.'

'You know Mabo?'

'A bit. Why?'

'Central Boulevard. Golden Mile amusements.'

'I'm sure I can find it.'

'Tomorrow morning. Nine, sharp.'

'Just me and Roy Minton?'

'That's what he says.'

'You believe him. Don't you?'

Chris's breathing was heavy. Deliberate. Measured. 'Yes. I think I do.'

'Okay then.'

'Ring me after, alright?'

'Will do.'

Chris cut the call off.

Matlock dialled the number on the handwritten message. The call was picked up on the first ring. 'You took your bloody–'

Matlock hung up. The phone started ringing almost immediately.

Fuck 'em. He had chips to eat.

*

The pie wasn't bad, but the chips were great. Frank took the tail end of his fish and gave it to his dog on the same saucer he'd served up ginger cake earlier that afternoon.

They ate, more or less in silence, except for Frank making the odd comment on the excellence of this or that mouthful. Frank used a lot of ketchup. Asked to taste the curry sauce. Wrinkled his nose at it.

A small television played in the background; sound all the way down. Newsreaders gave way to weather forecasters. Local, then national. Not a bad day for the time of year, tomorrow, if the man in the suit's gesticulations were to be believed.

'Appreciate that,' Frank said, clearing away the plates.

'No problem.'

'You don't mind, do you?' Frank had his pipe in his hand.

'It's your place. Want a hand with the dishes?'

'No need. I'll let them soak. I do the washing-up once a day. In the morning, after my shave. Saves on hot water that way.'

Matlock nodded. He wasn't sure if Frank's thinking was one based on economy or on some other bit of caravan-life arcana. We all have our routines.

The dog stirred itself; came over for a fuss. Matlock tousled its fur. A name tag dangled from its collar. 'Lumpkin.'

'Family tradition,' Frank said, as though that explained everything. 'Isn't that right, girl?' The dog looked up, perhaps hopeful for more of that fish.

*

Matlock left the caravan, after having made the vaguest promise to do something like this again before the weekend. He hadn't committed to anything, though, and he hoped already that he'd not sown some seed of hope for companionship. He couldn't see a way that he'd be free for fish and chips again soon.

There was still a light on in the campsite office. Matlock carried on past to the welcome signs at the entrance. The phone box was a couple of yards from a street light. There was a bench, too. The street light had a notice holder bolted to it. Bus times. There was no bus stop sign that he could see.

Matlock dialled the number on the message. Again it was picked up fast. This time though, no one rushed to speak. A careful 'Yes' instead.

'You left me a message.'

'You've got something of ours. We'd like to... trade... to get it back.' Tobacco Man, Matlock reckoned. He spoke carefully. He was measured. Delicate. Walking a tightrope.

'Go on.'

'Look. We understand. Hit the ground running. Best form of defence is attack. All that. Like I said, understandable.'

Let him talk.

'You there?'

'I'm listening,' Matlock said.

'We'd like to make this right. So, like I said, a trade.'

They hadn't informed the Mintons of the snatch yesterday. Or if they had, not that someone – a someone probably right at the top of the family shit-list – had helped himself to a pile of their cash. They were attempting a cover-up. Trying to make it right. Tobacco Man wanted to be the man who walked into the boss's office with both the problem and the solution in the same conversation.

Okay then. 'What kind of trade?'

'Information.'

'About what?'

'About your dad.'

'For what?'

'The money.'

A bus drove by; the double-decker was grey to the upper saloon with mud and windows misted with condensation. Matlock waited until its rumble receded.

'You there?'

'I'm still here. What do I get for the money?'

'Everything.'

'Everything?'

'Everything I know.'

'I don't have all the money. Expenses. You know.'

A breath. A hand went over the receiver at the other end of the line. A conversation; muffled. The timbre of two voices. A shuffling sound. The receiver being passed to another.

'How much do you have?' Joe Kayode.

'Most of it. Nearly all.'

'Good enough.'

'It needs to be tonight though.'

'The sooner the better. How about we m–'

'No. Car park opposite the cinema.' Like Matlock was going to give these two a free choice over when and where.

'When?'

'Eight.' Matlock hung up.

Armoury Street car park wasn't big. Thirty spaces, tops. But it was busy. A dance school to one side, the Town and County Club to the other. And the cinema opposite. A single-screen effort. Nightly shows at 7.30pm. Matinees at weekends at one and four. The auditorium was upstairs in the old circle. The stalls had long since been converted to bingo, but that had died in its time. The downstairs was now partitioned off. The local paper ran occasional stories about promises of the building's rejuvenation. They'd been ongoing for years.

The point was, though, that the car park would be likely full; folk parked up for their film. And it would stay that way until the film let out. Until way after nine. And this would only take a few minutes.

Matlock got there a touch after eight. The car park was a simple U-shaped route through marked-off spaces. Cars studded the outsides of the oval; others filled the centre. A single vehicle patrolled in circles. Onto the road, then back into the car park in slow loops.

Two men in the car. They were halfway around their circuit. Matlock pulled up onto the pavement where the kerb dropped to road height, blocking off their exit. He wound down the driver's side window. Waited for the car to stop.

It did. A window came down. Kayode – driving – stuck his head out. 'Now what?'

'Get out. Both of you. Empty hands.'

Kayode left his lights on. Wanted to show willing.

They got out. Hands up for an open-palmed moment. Tobacco spoke next. 'And you.'

Not that it meant anything. He could have had an arsenal stashed here. Nevertheless. 'See?'

They stood by his open window, like kids waiting for their ice creams. Kayode did the talking. 'The money?'

Matlock showed the cash. 'It's here.' He riffled through the notes to show it wasn't a wad of cut-up newspaper.

'Hand it over.' Tobacco Man held out a hand.

'Information.'

'Your father.'

'What about him?'

'We know where he's been kept.'

'Where?'

'The money.'

'Tell me. Everything.'

'A16 Eggs.'

'What about it?'

'There.'

'He alright?'

A shrug. 'Was fine last time I saw him.'

'When was that?'

'Sunday.'

Okay.

'Why?'

Another shrug. 'The Mintons don't tell us that kind of stuff. But it's got to be for leverage, hasn't it? To stop you doing anything stupid when you got out. Except you came barging around town like a tiger in a tearoom, didn't you? Didn't go straight round to your dad's. Didn't get the message you were meant to get. And now it's got all messy.'

'A16 Eggs.'

'There till Friday.'

'Why Friday?'

'You'll see. Or maybe you won't.'

'What does that mean?'

'Put it this way. This is what we're offering. Give us back the money. Then that's us square. If you want to do anything about your dad, do it before Friday. Grab him and go. Get out of town.'

'What if you're lying?'

'You've found us once. I daresay you can do it again.'

Matlock handed the money over.

Tobacco Guy counted, fast. Murmured a figure to Kayode, who nodded. Tobacco Guy went back to their car.

'We good?'

'As gold.'

Wednesday

Matlock had spent Tuesday night at Joe's house. Let himself in the back door. Ensured everything was locked as tight as it might be. With the radio on for background noise, he spent the evening going through Joe's things.

There's a point when time stops. Your clothes don't get renewed. The house stays the same. Meals become a weekly rotating ritual. Your life runs on tracks like a toy electric racing car. Butcher's on Monday. Pension on Tuesday. Bath on Wednesday and Sunday. Supermarket on Thursday. Joe had his routines. The imposition of order on his life. Reasons to go out every day.

The kitchen and bathroom were regimented. Easier to keep track of things. Like drawing an outline around tools hanging up in a workshop. Makes the putting back all the easier.

Joe's bookshelves were in sequence. Alphabetical by subject, and then by author. Where there was more than one book by the same writer, they were arranged by publication date. Books about the railways. Steam locomotion. Traction engines. Fairground organs. Books about the Wild West. Famous outlaws like Jesse James and Billy the Kid. Lawmen and showmen: Wyatt Earp and Buffalo Bill and Wild Bill Hickok. Militaria: maybe early 1930s through to early 1970s. The Spanish Civil War to Vietnam. Mostly non-fiction, but some novels. Charity shop finds, remaindered library stock. Broken spines and sun-bleached author names.

His clothes were hung up, squared away in drawers, folded neatly. Joe didn't iron these days, preferring simply to pull a jumper over his shirt, but again there was the echo of military routine put to good use. His bed had been made. There was maybe two days' washing in the clothes basket on top of the machine.

He might only have stepped out to the shops.

Matlock went through everywhere he could think.

There was nothing weird. Nothing strange. Nothing you might not expect to find. And nothing he would have expected not to find.

An ordinary house with an ordinary man living inside.
Except he wasn't there.

*

Matlock had slept in his old bed. He woke early; still dark outside.
Took his time having a bath. The first in over two years. Brushed his
teeth. Shaved. The milk was still okay, so he ate some cereal. There
was frost on the windscreen, but not so much that it needed scraping
off. The wiper blades dealt with it fine. Matlock ran the van's engine
for a while to let the cab heat up before he pulled away. Started out
towards the coast.

The A-road east is a zigzag trail. An indecisive snail across the landscape. West of Loweth, the Wolds; not quite a national park. East
of the town, and all compass points between east-northeast and east-
southeast, though, the territory is altogether other. Where the Wolds
is undulating grazing land, photogenic villages, long barrows and
points of niche historical interest, the flatlands east is a zone without a
past. A perpetual present; of course there's things from long ago, but
they're all a part of an ever-changing, slow-crumbling now. Where
the past thrums under the stout boots of Wolds' hikers on their weekend rambles, the floodplain has no equivalent, save a long last dying
exhalation.

The villages immediately to Loweth's east bear the final remains
of the Cold War: former air bases converted into council buildings,
hangars into grain silos. After five miles or so, this falls away too. A
ten-mile run of hamlets distinguished by minute variations on the
theme of decaying pub, shabby general store, closed petrol station and
rusting Methodist chapel gates.

The road narrows to little more than a single car's width in places,
the tarmac hemmed in by drainage ditches on both sides. The land
here is reclaimed from the sea; an ongoing leasehold arrangement
with nature. This means the soil is good, but it costs to work it. Time,
sweat, the loneliness of toiling in featureless fields. No hedgerows,
fences or drystone walls here to break up the landscape, to partition
property. The ditches do that work, an inversion of the usual laws of
farming division.

These roads used to be full of coaches. Matlock remembered sitting on his front step in shorts, counting the day trippers heading to the coast. That was a generation – or more – ago though; when working men's clubs arranged regular trips out for the community. Fleets of buses full of miners' kids from the Nottinghamshire coalfields. DH Lawrence made the same trip when a young 'un. Before flowers and sex and uncomfortable feelings about his mother had poached his mind. They'd done *Sons and Lovers* at school, the book chosen in part because there was a whiff of a local connection. Books weren't things that could only happen in London, their teacher, Doc – Matlock had no idea of his first name – Winterman, was keen to get across. The Doc was writing his own novel, a story about the imp who lived in Lincoln cathedral, and about the mischief he got up to when released from his stone prison. Sometimes he'd read them a passage of the work in progress. Matlock remembered liking it because it happened hereabouts. It made the magic and the monsters real.

The coaches didn't come any more. The economy had changed, and the old close-bound communities centred around industry simply weren't there. These days, though there were still day trippers and self-caterers renting flats for the week, the bulk of the holiday trade was residential of sorts. Caravanning, whether static or touring, was where the money was.

In America, Matlock had read, folk retired to Florida. From Essex they went to Spain. From the Midlands, though, and up into South Yorkshire, what you did was buy a caravan. Some ran them as second homes, staying over at weekends. Others moved in, going back to Derby or wherever only when they had to. Most of the sites were part residential, part holidaymaker. Residents came first; the unspoken but real class system of the campsite.

Matlock passed one such site now. Maybe five miles from the coast. A flurry of flags, a parade of hoardings advertising the superiority of this place over others. Fishing lakes; a nine-hole golf course. Live entertainment in the clubhouse. On-site supermarket. Bingo. Pitches to lease for the season. There was a run of static caravans for sale. Credit available. Easy, pleasy terms, a sign asserted, the last of the morning's frost making it shimmer.

Matlock squinted as a seam in the cloud cover moved across where the sun had been hiding. A crossroads ahead. Go left here, and you'd drive through Theddlesby: a gas terminal for the North Sea fields, a naturist section of beach. Maybe they liked the industrial look. Turn right, and the road would elide the boundaries of Mabo and Sutton, and would lead you down the coast a dozen miles or so to Skegthorpe. Skeg was where the main action was. The national chains of holiday camps, a working railway station, greyhound racing and stock-car action. A tarnished half-mile of arcades, candyfloss, all-day breakfasts and fortune-tellers. Skeg Vegas.

Up ahead, you had two choices: Mableton-on-Sea and Sutton-holme. Suttonholme traded in gentility. The kind of seaside village trapped in a permanent past of Agatha Christie novels, cream teas and bathing machines. By-laws prohibited gambling machines. Mableton was Skeg's little brother; it wanted to be brash, but it came across as whiny.

A tractor pulled into the road ahead of Matlock's van. He had plenty of time. The tractor driver indicated by hand signals that he was cross-ing to another field on the other side of the road a ways down. That he wouldn't hold him up for long. A wave back; three fingers off the steering wheel. No problem.

The driver was as good as his word. Fifty metres further and he drove off-road into an open-gated field. Another wave. A nod back.

And then Matlock passed the sign indicating that he was crossing into Mableton-on-Sea. A mermaid riding a dolphin side-saddle, both waving. Hand and flipper raised in greeting. Miles of sandy smiles were promised.

The main street was an uncurved spine leading eventually to the slipway to the promenade and beach. There was a matching ramp on the far side for the lifeboat crew. That was perhaps half a mile away. Roads branched off either side of the main drag. Matlock had stayed here for holidays as a kid. They'd rented places as close to the sea as they could afford that year. Joe's logic was that as long as it was sunny and there was a beach, then it didn't matter if you were in the Canary Islands or just down the road. It was all the same.

Out of season. The cafes and what Joe had always called shit shops at this end of the road wouldn't bother opening until later, if at all. 'Chip shops and shit shops,' Joe'd grin, gleeful at sharing a sly swear with his kid. Buckets and spades. Postcards. Plastic cricket sets. Insubstantial footballs. Cheap crap, all of it. Disposable tat for the tourists.

The closer Matlock got to the slipway, the bigger the shops got. Windows and doors gave way to roller-shutters. These were places forever open for business at all hours in the high season. Maybe they'd open a single shutter on a grey day like this. Achmed's Bazaar. Land O'Plenty. Pound Palace. Marje's Warehouse.

Then the arcades. Slots Of Fun. Million Dollar Dreams. End Of The Rainbow – complete with an unlit leprechaun, neon tubes itemising his dance steps around his cauldron of gold – and Royale Casino. There were other, smaller, offerings down the side streets. Up on the promenade too. But these were the main players. And each of them was owned by the Mintons.

There was no parking on the high street. Matlock followed the signs around the corner and found somewhere he didn't have to pay. He pulled the army surplus jacket off the passenger seat. Got out of the van. It complained as he exited. Let it.

It was cold enough to make having your hands in your pockets worthwhile. Not long after half-eight. Kids in school uniform in the distance, kicking a football between them. Matlock headed back to the main street. There'd be somewhere open.

Matlock found a newsagent's crammed between two of the arcades. Went in. Bought a chocolate bar and some chewing gum as a pretext for conversation.

'There a cafe open around here?'

The newsagent nodded. 'Most won't open till nine, but if you go up onto the prom there's one on the left. Taffy's Cabin. They're open from six. Dog walkers and the like. Joggers. Been known to stay open all night if there's a night-fishing contest on.'

'Makes sense. Cheers.'

Matlock ate the chocolate walking up the slipway. A Topic; the bars were always small compared to Mars and the others, which was why he'd never bought them as a child. This one was gone in two bites.

Still, the combination of a cocoa hit and the seaside air was something. Made Matlock feel like a kid on holiday again. Made him think about Joe. Not as the old man stuck in a room in the back of a battery farm, but as a dad. Trousers and an open-collar shirt rather than his perpetual overalls and work boots. Enjoying minor acts of spoiling; sneaking sweets and money to him. Faces behind Mum's back, before she got ill. Shared secrets, like Matlock's first penknife. The air rifle that had to be hid. Crumbs of knowledge about the outside adult world.

*

The slipway was surprisingly steep, and slippery underfoot with dry sand blown over from the beach. To the left, a noticeboard with tide times, information about the flag system warning when it was too dangerous to go into the sea. Fly-posted adverts for events long gone: Christmas markets, a New Year fireworks display. To the right, a new-built toilet block. Behind that, the funfair. Nothing so grand as Skegthorpe's offering, but it was the only one in town. Make the most of it, kids.

The promenade was wide, silted with more sand. Built in the 1950s when the dunes had proved inadequate against high spring tides. Local papers dined out on two events: flooding in Loweth in the 1920s, and the spring tide of '52 or '53, or whenever it was. Dozens had died. And the disaster had triggered government money to prevent the same happening again. So far, the concrete had stood strong. The sea defences ran maybe a mile north, up to Theddlesby, where the dunes were more substantial, and to the far side of Suttonholme to the south. It made for a decent walk. Five miles or so of wide raised promenade. Good views of the sea and the beach to one side, towns and countryside to the other. Much of the prom was populated by chalets. Some were privately owned, but most were let by the council, either by the season, the week or even the day. Simple structures to give you a shelter from squalls, a place to brew up and stash your stuff, somewhere to towel the kids dry. Some had been knocked together to make premises for small businesses. This is what had happened with Taffy's.

There wasn't much room for seating inside, so a bar with stools had been put up along the outward-facing windows. A cluster of tables and chairs: the moulded plastic sort you could buy in garden centres. Two rinsed-out ice-cream tubs. One half-full of sand for cigarette ends; the other full of water for dogs.

Matlock bought a coffee. Took it outside and leaned over the promenade wall. The tide was out. Hardly anyone on the beach; those there, Matlock assumed, were regulars taking their morning stroll. No one in the water that he could see. To the left, and further out, commercial shipping; they'd be waiting for the tide to turn so they could enter the Humber.

He sipped his coffee. It tasted of limescale in the water heater.

A shadow to Matlock's right. 'Not much of a day, is it?'

'Not really, Roy.'

'Saw you got yourself a drink. Bacon or sausage? There's one of each, and I'm happy with either.'

'Sausage. Cheers.'

Minton handed over a roll wrapped inside a paper napkin. 'Sauce? I've got a pocket full of those sachets.'

'I'm good, thanks.'

'Ketchup for me.' Roy Minton rested his bun on the promenade wall while he fiddled with a packet of sauce. Squirted Heinz over his bacon. Closed it up and took a bite. 'Always bugs me how the kids these days call it "red sauce".'

'They did the same in prison too.'

'Did they? That'd send some mad, knowing felons got condiments for their grub on the inside.'

'It's one way to tell it apart from brown sauce.'

'There is that. Red. Brown. But brown is the generic word for HP or Daddies Sauce. No such thing as red sauce. Ketchup. Red might be chilli sauce.'

'There's a practical joke in there somewhere.'

'You're right as well. Could bottle it and sell it in our shops next to the fart powder.'

Roy Minton was almost as tall as Matlock. Once-blond hair that had gone to grey. One of those guys who had picked a trendy hairstyle in his youth and had kept the faith for almost forty years. A cheery, open face. Always a smile. Cheeky. He was wearing a fleece jacket with a Slots Of Fun logo. The words were arranged into a banana-yellow grin.

'How's your sausage?' Minton said at last.

'Alright. Bacon okay?'

'Mmm. Better had be as well.'

'The place one of yours?'

Minton wiped his lips free of fat and sauce. 'That it is.'

'They could work on their coffee.'

'I'll mention it at the next board meeting. Always been a tea man myself. Never got into coffee at all. Will you take a walk with me along the promenade?'

Matlock poured the last of his drink away. Dropped the beaker into a bin. Dug his hands back into his pockets.

They headed southwards, towards Suttonholme. Matlock let Minton chat amiably about coastal life, about tourist trade and how it wasn't what it was. About a minor operation he'd had. About his knee and how he reckoned he had a bit of arthritis sneaking up on him. They walked past the funfair, the pleasure gardens with its play areas and miniature railroad. Past a council work crew doing roofing repairs to a run of chalets.

'Is it alright if we sit?' Minton indicated a bench.

'Sure.'

A dog danced on the beach ahead of them. Eventually, its owner caught up with the animal. Threw a ball using one of those plastic scoops. The dog raced off again; danced on the spot where the ball landed. This time the owner whistled, and the dog picked up the ball and trotted back.

'That's a good dog,' Matlock said.

'It is.'

'I want him back, Roy. He's nothing to do with any of this.'

A sigh. 'That's understandable. Family. Nothing more important, is there?'

'No.'

'And it's the same for me.'

94

'So?'

'So you know who I am.'

'I do.'

'And you know what that means.'

'Yes.'

'I could have done something. Something crude. Easy as that. Have had you visited in prison. You know the sort of thing.'

Razor blades melted into a toothbrush handle. Three or more, with gaps between to make the wound larger and to make holding or stitching up the mess nigh impossible. A slash across the guts or over the face for payback. If you wanted to be certain of a kill, go for the major arteries. The femoral: one man to hold you in the shower, another to carve your inner thighs. The carotid: two deep cuts, one either side of the neck. If you didn't get one of the blood vessels to the brain, you'd get the other. Though it had never happened in Lincoln while Matlock was there, it had gone on in the past. Older lags called it 'koshering'; younger ones 'halalling'.

'I wondered at first. When I was being held on remand. But after the sentencing it was clear that the chain of evidence would run straight back to you, and that there's no way you'd want the kind of spotlight that'd bring.'

'We like to keep our business in-house where we can. And there's limits to influence. It's best not to challenge them. Besides, you weren't going anywhere, were you?'

'And the waiting. Knowing, or at least hoping, that this was snagging on my mind?'

Minton shrugged. 'If it did, then that was a free extra. We knew when you'd be out, and that was enough. Besides, there were... associates, I reckon you'd call them, who had cause to stay over at HMP Lincoln on and off, so we got updates.'

'Always good to know you're being looked after.'

'Odd you should mention that.'

Matlock didn't prompt him to continue. Let Minton pick up his thread in his own time. The dog walker came back along the beach, more or less shadowing the footprints they'd left in the sand on their first traverse. The dog was now hard on their heels, snapping at the sky. It was being flicked snacks.

'Still,' Minton said. 'We'll come to that.'

'Let's talk about Joe.'

'Let's not. Not yet. We'll get to him in good time. Let's talk about young Anthony.'

*

A body, out of nowhere. The gap between the cars, impossible to resist. Then the realisation. Not Matlock's own; that had already happened. But in the face of Ant Corrigan. That it was inevitable.

Matlock's car cut him off right above the knees. Both legs broken. The trauma propelled Ant back against the side of his brother's car, then forwards onto the bonnet of Matlock's.

Ant was alive when his head smacked the metal. Dead by the time his body came down a second time. His mouth was open, but only blood came out. A liquid scream that pulsed once, twice. Blood was coughed across Matlock's windscreen; the impact had already caused the wiper blades to be triggered.

A shout from a passer-by. The smell of engineering: metal, oil, grease and petrol. And Matlock's left foot, pressed uselessly against the brake pedal until after the police came.

*

'Anthony,' Matlock said. 'You know it was an accident.'

'"It".'

'His death.'

'Should never have happened.'

'I know.'

'You're not going to apologise? Not going to say that you're sorry to my face?'

'No,' Matlock said. 'Like I said, it was an accident. He never should have put himself between the cars.'

'So no apology.'

'There's none needed. None that I can give that would be meaningful. Do I regret his death? Of course I do, Roy. Do I wish he

96

had never been involved? Absolutely. Would I take it back if I could reverse time? Yes. But I can't apologise. Apologies are for when you intentionally did something wrong. Which I didn't.'

'And you can't bite down on your pride to say sorry to an old man who's had his kin snatched from him?'

'I don't know if it's pride or not, Roy. But the word doesn't fit the occasion. It should never have happened. And like I said, I regret his death. Every day, I think of him. But an apology? The words would be meaningless.'

'Others wouldn't think so. I don't believe that I think so.'

'I can't help that, Roy.'

'Can you not, Daniel?'

'No.'

A line of people – they all looked to be male – were walking the breadth of the beach. Hi-vis jackets, rubbish bags. Metre-long tongs for picking up garbage. An overseer: forties, to the others teens and twenties. Occasional growled reprimands if one of them missed a washed-up bottle or crisp packet.

'Little acorns,' Matlock said.

'Little shits, more like.'

'Maybe so.'

'Should be you out there with a shiny tabard.'

'Community service? Is that your idea of justice, Roy? Painting park benches four hours a week till my debt's paid?'

'I don't think there's enough paint in the world to make my family whole again. Do you?'

Matlock didn't answer that. He watched the community service kids' progress. Wondered what they'd each done to end up on beach patrol. Eventually: 'Joe.'

'Joe,' Roy said.

'He's just an old boy. Got nothing to do with any of this.'

'As Anthony had nothing to do with Liam's... stupidity.'

'And yet.'

'And yet.'

'Let him go, Roy.'

'And in truth it wasn't my first idea, but it's got your focus. And attention is good. So we'll work with what we've got. He's a good man, Joe Matlock. A good man. Knows his subject. Even helped me out on a job or two.'

'Really?'

'I've put some work his way. Bit of a passion project. Do you want to see?'

Matlock shrugged. 'I've got all day.'

'Good man.' Minton stood. 'This won't take long. And then we'll finish our chat. Get this sorted out. Okay with you?'

Matlock nodded.

*

Matlock and Minton walked back along the promenade. The council lads had finished their roof repairs. The beach had got a little busier as the morning had gone on. A flock of birds at the low-water point, fussing over whatever the still-retreating water had exposed.

Minton stopped by a padlocked gate. The gate led into a high-fenced compound. Work sheds and stacks of pallets and old chipboard. The compound was screened by high evergreens on three sides. The fourth side let onto the funfair through another razor wire-topped gate. 'In here,' Roy said.

Minton unlocked the largest of the outbuildings. Ran his hand over what must have been a bank of switches. Clunks rather than clicks. An assortment of lights sputtered into use.

The shed was part workshop, part artist's study, part storeroom. Funfair signs and equipment in progress. A calliope horse, stripped back to the wood. Dodgems' pricing boards ready to be updated for the new season. 'Prize every time.' 'Scream if you want to go faster.' 'Keep your hands inside the car, always.' The heady feel of varnish and wood glue all about.

'Used to be about excitement,' Minton said. 'Now, it's nostalgia. Tradition. I don't mind that, getting older myself. It's good to go back sometimes.' He indicated a line of video-game carcasses. Galaxian. Tempest. Super Contra. 'Where's the fun in those anyway?'

Matlock was led to the rear of the shed. For the second time in as many days he was surprised by what he was brought to see. A fairground organ. Bare in places, its skeleton shining through. A work-in-progress, but nevertheless.

'Charles Marenghi,' Minton said. 'Built in Paris, 1914. Whether it's true or not, I don't know, but the family history has always been that it was the last of its type made by the company before the Great War broke out.'

'And you had Joe work on this.'

'It was Joe's idea.'

'How so?'

'He came to me. Took guts. The day after you went down. Felt he owed the family. Wanted to do something that would go towards making things a bit less wrong.'

'He never said.'

'You never let him. Don't visit, don't write. Those were your instructions.'

'I didn't want him to have to come to Lincoln and see me inside.'

'You won't be the last to play at being hard man. So, Joe came to me. Knew I had an interest in the old fair machines. Was likely to have more than one steam engine needing maintenance. And of course, we had her.'

'Her' was the machine. Matlock assumed there was a pet name for her. That in time it'd be painted on a panel in flowing travelling circus script.

'In bits, more or less. She'd been raided to keep other machines going. She runs off paper cards, you know. Like a player piano. Almost an early computer. It's always been a retirement plan of mine of sorts, to potter with her and get her back to her best.'

'But you're not the retiring sort, are you, Roy?'

Minton shook his head. 'I've no gift for complex mechanics. Electrics I'm alright with. Painting I'm not so bad at. Some of the stuff in here is mine. Those over there, for example.' He indicated a pair of boards advertising candyfloss and hot dogs. 'And it's no point asking the boys. If it's not internal combustion they've no clue.'

'Must have been like a gift from the gods.'

'It was unexpected. I'll give you that. Still, he felt we were owed, and this was a way that some acknowledgement of that debt could be made. That counts for a lot. So we worked here, what, a couple of days a week. That was about as much time as I could spare. You could say he apprenticed me. Learned a lot from your Joe, I have.'

'And now you're holding him on account of me.'

'As I said. Not my first idea. Still, we work with what materials we've got. Don't worry about Joe. He's both sound and safe. Comfortable. And he'll be returned by the weekend.'

'In exchange for what?'

'Come on. Got a couple of things to check on. Have to show my face or else they'll slacken off. That's the downside of employing family wherever you can. Entitlement. But there's no free rides in my funfair, Daniel.'

They went through to the amusement park proper. A couple of big rides: a vertical boost ride decked out in Spider-Man decals; a contraption called the Spinning Spider, with a car on each of its eight legs. 'Goes up, down, round about. Makes someone puke every day.' Much of the rest were scaled-down attractions for families with young children. A roller coaster in miniature, variations on the classic roundabout. Dodgems. Stalls for games of chance and skill. Rifle ranges, tombolas, ducks to be hooked. These were interspersed with food outlets, places to buy seaside tat, token booths. The rides didn't take money. Cash went to the tellers behind the perspex; fewer to have to trust. A ghost train. Something called the Wibbly-Wobbly Funhouse.

'In there,' Roy said. The funhouse.

'What is?'

'Not a "what". More of a who.'

'Not like you to play games, Roy.'

'No game. Remember that. You're safe as long as you do nothing stupid. Nothing rash. Nothing violent or impetuous. Consider this neutral territory. No-man's-land. Go on. In. I'll wait here for you. It'll only take a few minutes.'

The funhouse building was the width of a static caravan. It might have been one, repurposed. Or else something of similar size. Maybe a shipping container. Perhaps two; its exaggerated frontage made it impossible to determine how far back this thing went.

An entrance and an exit. Dancing clowns promised laughter and amusement. The way in was split down the middle, double-hinged. Like a full-length Western bar saloon door. There was a secondary door inside, something soft to keep the light out. Or the fun in.

It was built for kids; Matlock had to crouch to get in. It opened up inside enough for him to stand. The floor indeed both wibbled and wobbled. Then a maze led to a ball pool. Climbing nets around the outside. A hall of mirrors corridor. Through another partition into a blackout zone. Wispy bits of cotton wool were draped to mimic cobwebs. Grinning faces in luminescent paint popped out when triggered by staccato lighting. The floor zigged and zagged again. At one point the walls did too, until Matlock could barely fit through the gap. Then a maze of tubes to crawl through.

The tube work opened out into an indoor bouncy castle. Matlock didn't spot the change in flooring until it was too late. He sprawled forwards, bounced and rolled to the edge of the surface.

It took a minute to right himself. He was done with this place. Enough of Minton's petty amusements. Time to get this sorted.

Matlock oriented himself. Found the exit. He'd stick to the side of the inflated surface. Work his way out slow and careful. Find out the point of all of this.

Then he wasn't alone. That bit of the hunter–gatherer brain that tells you that you're being watched; that the room you're in isn't empty any more.

A shape blocked the exit.

Then the lights came up. An incandescent slap. Matlock blinked away the red-green sprites capering to the corners of his vision.

And Liam Corrigan was standing there. At the solid lip of the bouncy castle, in front of the exit.

Corrigan had changed. Gone was the London suit and the slicked-back hair. His head was shaved. A goatee; long enough to be no affectation. Tee shirt and oily jeans. Work boots. His body had altered too. He no longer had the softness of handling money and drinking from before noon. Muscle mass had developed. Arms and shoulders indicated either an exercise regime or else manual work and plenty of it. Maybe both. When he moved, he did so with a lightness that was at odds with his new build. Confidence had replaced cockiness.

'Two days,' Corrigan said. 'Been a long time coming.' He swung back, ducking out of the bouncy castle room. 'Oh. Your dad said it wasn't your fault.' And he was gone into the blackness beyond.

What the fuck?

There was no point going after him. It'd take too long to get out of this room.

This was what Minton had been working towards. Showing off Liam Corrigan, born-again hard. To what end? Matlock skirted the stupid wobbling surface, and got the hell out of the funhouse.

It ached to have Liam Corrigan even saying the word 'dad'. The kind of bleak throbbing you got from an amputated limb. Ghost pain. Wasn't his fault? What wasn't?

No. He was just fucking with you.

Wasn't he?

*

Minton was sitting at a trestle table. Two takeaway beakers, both lidded. Sugar sachets and stirrers. 'Sit down,' he purred. 'I've got you a tea. Doubtless you've got a head full of questions.'

That wasn't the half of it. 'Enough.'

'I agree. But first, tea.'

'So you've put Liam to work.'

Minton tore a sugar packet open. Opened his tea. Shook away the condensation from the underside of the lid. Tipped the contents in. Swirled with the plastic not-spoon. Blew. Sipped. 'Grand,' he said. 'And, in answer to your question, no. Do you not understand yet? People come to me with solutions. And I say yea or nay. Liam did just the same as your dad did. He felt the right responsibility for his actions, or for his part in the wider proceedings, before you give me any more of your prison philosophy about apologies or otherwise. And he took his medicine. Has been working off his debt.'

'Two days?'

'And in two days his account will be clear. Corrigans and Mintons: we don't forget, but we can forgive, and never more than when the appropriate penance has been done. Men's hearts – and women's as well I daresay, though the Good Lord knows that I'm no expert in matters as deep as those – know both what's right and what's wrong, and they know also what's to be done for the best to right those same wrongs. Liam's no saint. But he is an angel. And he knows which side he's fighting for, even if – as in the past – he goes either too far or acts unwisely on his own intuition. Many men... men such as you, Daniel... mistake gut instinct for foresight. Liam's made that error before, and he's spent two years doing what he can to rectify matters. Ever cut yourself, or been cut?' Minton sipped again, but didn't wait for an answer. 'Of course you have. We all have. We heal, but we scar also. Our scars are important. Like tattoos, but all the more so. They help us remember.'

'And you chide me on philosophy.'

'I bought the teas.'

No one spoke for a while.

'Friday,' Matlock said, eventually.

'Yes.'

'What about it?'

'That's when you'll fight Liam.'

'Oh?' That throbbing again. Down his arms. Into his hands. Like the aftermath of pins and needles. His fingers tingled. Wanted to make fists.

'And after the fight, you'll get back your dad and Liam'll have had the chance to take his brother's death out on you.'

'Before.'

'Before what?'

'Before the fight. You let Joe go before the fight. If you're holding him to make sure I turn up to this, then you don't need him once I'm there.'

'Immediately before. He'll be released, unharmed. He'll stay and watch; there's the outside chance he'll try to call the police or some such foolishness, and I'd rather not have that if it's all the same. But he'll not be hindered in any way. I'm more than happy for there to be someone there for him. As soon as our business is done, then he walks free, and you with him if that's possible. But it'll be you and Liam, bare-knuckled and stripped to the waist. And only one of you will walk away. It doesn't matter who. What matters is that debts will have been paid. It's just a shame that we've had to go to all of this trouble to hold you to account.'

'Where? And when?'

Minton smiled, and told him.

*

It was afternoon by the time Matlock got back to Loweth. The first market of the week was set up in the middle of the town. Market hours run early; stallholders would be setting up by seven, selling by eight and would look to be packing up by three at the latest. Earlier if there was nothing doing or if the weather had taken a turn towards foul. Occasional empty stalls indicated that some had already bailed on the day. Matlock bought some fruit – pears and apples – for something ordinary and mechanical to do. A simple transaction; no agenda. Found a low wall to perch on. Ate a Braeburn. Did not think about the possibility of a fight for his life and for that of his father in two days' time.

*

'Chris.'

'Still with us then.'

'For now.'

'And what's that mean?'

Matlock told her.

'Shit.'

'Why there?'

'You've been away, of course.' Heavy breathing from the far end of the phone call. 'Tell you what.'

'What.'

'Come for me after the school run. Nine.'

'Want a breakfast bringing?'

'No need. We'll eat there.'

'Thanks Chris.'

'Don't.'

'Don't what?'

'Thank me yet.'

'There's something else as well.'

'What's that.'

'A16 Eggs.'

'What about it?'

'What do you know about it?'

'What do you want to know?'

'Everything.'

Chris's breathing again. Out, in. Out, in. Lungs working a double shift. She'd always been big. Even at school. Sat on the low benches at the classroom end of the playground. Hand clamped around her Ventolin inhaler. Staying out of the skipping and the clapping games and the circles of girls playing jacks. Cards were her thing. And money. Even in primary school. Always had money to lend. Didn't charge interest, but made herself invaluable by fronting change for sweets on the way home. The cards were riskier, being frowned upon by teachers and could be confiscated by the deputy head if he was on the supervision rota.

Three-card brag was her game. Fast and vicious; both simple and complex at the same time. She taught Matlock the rules. Took him for all of his money. It wasn't much, but it was everything.

'Okay,' Chris said eventually. 'In the morning, though.'

'Perfect.'

'Dan?' She never used his first name. 'What are you up to?'

'Do you really want to know?'

'I'm not sure.'

'If you want to know, I'll tell you.'

'I'll sleep on it.'

'See you at nine.'

And she was gone.

*

Matlock went to the supermarket. Half-filled a basket with basics. Milk, tea, sugar, bread, cheese. Topped it up with relative luxuries. Biscuits that came in boxes, not packets. A good-looking coffee and walnut cake. A bottle of a creamy liqueur. Packed all of this into one of the more expensive carrier bags; the kind meant to last forever. Then he drove to a house he'd visited once before.

'Hi,' he said when the door opened to him. 'I don't suppose the lady next door has returned with her little one?'

That same impression: age and sickness. 'No,' the frail woman said. 'I think this time she's gone for good, love. Can't say that it's a surprise.'

'Do you have any idea where she might have gone? Sorry if I've asked before. It's just that I want to make sure that she's alright.'

'That's good of you, love. No. Never really had much to do with them. Signed for a couple of parcels, said hello over the back wall, that was about it. He's still there. I can hear him. Snores like a buffalo, he does. Still, it's better than the bawling that used to go on.'

'Oh?'

'I don't mind a bain crying; that's only to be expected. You can't do much about it when they're teething, can you? I struggled with both of mine. I shouldn't talk, but arguments. Shrieking and carrying on. Better that than the silence, mind.'

'Really?'

'He'd lash out. Then the quiet. I hope she's alright. Her and her little one.' Her face brightened. 'One minute.'

'What is it?'

'It was here somewhere. In that pile.' A heap of fliers and unopened post on a shelf above the hall radiator.

'Could I have a look?'

'Course. Pull out anything that's got the surname Fields on it. That's me. Anything else, you're welcome to. But there might well be something in there of use. Puzzled me at the time it did, but I never thought to raise it. And then, of course, she upped and went.'

Matlock riffled through the papers. Some bills, the local freesheet, takeaway leaflets and fliers for window cleaning and an ironing service. And a postcard. It had been redirected, a sticker with the fresh address overlaid over the original.

'That's it,' the woman said. 'No idea who it's from. I did wonder if it was for her.' The sticker had next door's address details on it.

'May I take it?'

'Course.'

'Thanks. Oh, and there's something else.'

'What's that, love?'

'This has been left for you.' Matlock placed the bag of shopping at the old lady's feet, and was gone before it could be refused.

*

Matlock turned the postcard over once, twice, three times. Didn't bother trying to peel the redirection sticker off from the handwritten address. He knew what was under there.

The photograph side of the card showed a beach, arcing away to a point where sky and ocean became a single point of blue. The image was taken from above. Maybe a high hotel balcony. Perhaps from a helicopter. Curving rows of loungers and parasols in the foreground, the sand becoming less densely populated as the picture retreated into its own background. No clue on this side as to the location.

The side left blank-ish for writing claimed – in the vertical lines separating message from address – that the image was of the Canary Islands. The handwriting was familiar to Matlock. The rounded uprights on the t's, the star above the sign off.

This was a thing Sarah always did. Send a postcard to herself from wherever she was when she was away. There'd been a stack of them, rubber-banded in a glittery red stretchy hair-bobble, going back to since she was old enough to be allowed to walk to a postbox on her own. The cards were more frayed the older they became in the bundle; a stuttering flick book of seaside holidays and weekends staying with relatives. The collection was now incomplete.

Matlock opened the glove compartment on the van's dashboard. Expected the usual clutter of someone else's work vehicle. Found it empty save for a plastic wallet containing an owner's manual, old insurance and roadworthiness test certificates. The van hadn't been serviced for three years. Was illegal in all kinds of ways.

Didn't matter. At least the last owner had kept it clean.

Matlock replaced the wallet. Laid the postcard on top. Tried not to summon spirits of the past.

*

'What'll it be?'

'Coffee, Woody.'

'Owt to eat with that?'

'I'm good, thanks.'

'Right you are.'

There was nothing prepared on the griddle. Surfaces had been wiped down. Only now, Matlock appreciated that the sauces had been cleared away.

'Not keeping you, am I?'

'No, mate. Been a bit quiet this afternoon. Was going to knock off soon and get to the cash and carry. Fill up on diesel. Get some eggs. Then get out to the allotment.'

Matlock had never understood allotments. But there were those who swore by them. A sliver of England. Lines of runner beans; a few new early potatoes. A shed made of salvage. Furniture scrounged from skips. 'Spend much time up there?'

'Not half enough, I don't reckon. Pound, mate.'

Matlock handed over the right money.

'Much obliged.' Woody had cashed up, it seemed. The quid went into a pocket. Then the apron came off.

'I'll get out of your way.'

Woody left his trailer. Put the bin inside. Shuttered up. Adjusted whatever you called the stabilisers allowing the trailer to free-stand. It was hitched to a grubby tan Range Rover. An elderly model.

'You go to Tom Coton for your eggs?'

'No. I go to the same place I get my diesel. On the A16.' Woody had paused before saying the last sentence. Matlock got the hint.

'Cheers, Woody.'

'No problem at all.'

*

It was time to take a trip out.

Matlock headed north, following the main road out past the industrial estate. There were as many commercial premises as industrial ones these days. Agricultural machinery dealerships. Car showrooms. Tyre and exhaust places. Not quite retail, not quite industry. One of the newer units was a laundry: a sign advertised itself as a contractor to the hotel and catering trade. That enquiries from restaurateurs and B and B owners were always welcome; businesses large or small.

Then the countryside proper began. The A16 is the seam which joins the floodplain to the Wolds; hills to the west, and little troubling the horizon to the east save the raised sides of Wycham reservoir. An artificial pond maybe a quarter of a mile square, big enough to have its own yachting society, clubhouse and all. Scouts earned their kayaking- and dinghy-related badges on its waters.

A16 Eggs advertised itself as a traditional farm shop. There was a newish building where when Matlock had been a kid there'd been little more than a wheelbarrow full of jars of honey and boxed half-dozens of eggs. Behind the shop premises, a large detached house. Behind that, and glimpsed through a run of evergreens presumably planted as camouflage, a run of low battery hen buildings.

Batteries meant that this was a twenty-four-hour operation. A continual production line of eggs for the supermarkets, then spent chickens for animal feed. Doubtless there was an organic and a free-range element to the site, but the business here was in bulk, not in the friendly laying of happy chooks tended to by a rotund farmer's wife. No matter what the company logo might have you believe.

There she was now, a placid smile on her face, straw-laid wicker basket laden with farm bounty in hand. In the background, fat hens pecked at handfuls of grain. A cartoon wolf's wet dream.

Matlock parked up in one of the few spaces not marked out for disabled drivers and/or vehicles with young children on board. There was a petting zoo. A playground with an agricultural theme. Not big, but enough to keep the little ones quiet while you stocked up on premium conserves and artisan cheeses.

The evergreens here were a recent addition; not yet grown dense enough to fully shroud the industrial nature of the site from visitors' gazes. Three lorries in bays outside a warehouse. Movement of pallets with hand trucks and forklifts. Crates of shrink-wrapped goods making their onward journey.

Joe was here somewhere. Some storeroom with a camp bed and no window.

That urge again. To break something. Someone.

Fists in pockets, Matlock shouldered the farm shop door open.

Two kids running the place. A radio in a back office; dancey pop. The staff might have been brother and sister. They both had the same Nordic eyes, pale hair and skin. Matching checked shirts – logoed, so a uniform – completed the effect. Midwich cuckoos, working part-time jobs.

Friendly enough smiles, though, and enough sense or experience not to be too forward in asking if he wanted any help with anything. They'd get their share of browsers. Tourists. Weekend parents killing time while their charges scrambled over the plastic tractor outside.

The cafe was empty. Bland, new. Rural scenes in rustic frames. A pricey-looking coffee machine.

'Hi. Coffee to take out, please.'

The kid went through some options without thinking.

'Just black.'

'I'll do it.' The girl speaking. 'You sort out the rest of that mess in the kitchen.'

The boy disappeared into a back room. The music got a little louder. The girl busied herself with wiping down the rest of the coffee machine while the device made the espresso.

'Here you are.' She'd double-cupped the drink. This always seemed right to Matlock. Single cups – or worse, those little card belts slipped around the cup as a token defence against burning – were a sign of meanness. She even gestured to a bowl of complimentary caramelised biscuits instead of assuming he'd have one no matter what.

Matlock waved the offer away. 'Thanks.'

He paid for the drink. Looked out of the window, back to the farm-house.

'People still live in there, in the middle of all of this?'

'Oh no. It's all offices now. Well, storage, mostly. Mail order for the hampers.' She indicated a card advertising wicker baskets by post for all occasions. Tastes of Lincolnshire. Cheese, plum bread, sausages.

Smoked fish, ales, ciders, perries. Prices from the stark to the bewildering.

'Makes sense.'

'Used to be, though.'

'That's progress for you.'

Matlock went back out to the car park. Got back into the van – leaving the driver's door open – so it wouldn't be quite so obvious he was scoping the office building.

It was a house, when all was said, and so it had the issues that came with a house. Limited means of exit and entrance. A standardised layout. Kitchen, living and dining rooms downstairs. Three bedrooms upstairs. Bathroom and a second toilet somewhere. All standard enough. Double-glazed. Curtains in the windows, but there either as part of the farmhouse illusion or else simply left behind when this was converted from residential use.

No alarm box. Then again, if the place was staffed around the clock then there'd be a perpetual presence. And local thieves would be deterred by the family connections. Matlock guessed a deal of the security operated on reputation alone. No one would dare to rob one of the Mintons' places, surely? Not for a haul of Christmas puddings and farmhouse chutneys.

Maybe it was time to put that to the test.

Matlock turned the van around. Ignored that rumble in the cargo section. It took longer than he'd have credited to pull out into the main road; a steady flow of traffic. Commercial vehicles. Too many of them. Delivery lorries. A fuel tanker. Then a second.

Matlock wondered why.

Came up with an answer he liked the feel of.

*

'Diesel.'

'What about it?' Chris's voice crackled down the receiver. The phone tasted of wet cigarettes.

'You tell me.'

'That's part of this, isn't?'

'Part of what?'

'Of the Mintons. The Corrigans.'

'I don't follow you.'

'I was out on the A16, trying to get out of the egg place.'

'What were you doing there?'

'Having a look-see. You prompted the idea, remember.'

'And that was dumb of me.'

'And it was too busy.'

'It's a main road. About the only usable bit of highway that's been put down since the Romans buggered off.' That wasn't so far from the truth. The dual carriageway that led into Grimsby from the west, and which connected it eventually to the motorway system, was a concrete experimental road surface. Prefabricated, and thus quick to install, except the big idea the planners had did not work as intended. Run-off grooves, meant to improve the dispersal of rainwater from the driving surface, added little but percussion to the driving experience; the ten or so miles of grey cement were a vibrating nightmare.

'Still. Too much traffic. Too many trucks. Got me to thinking.'

'About what?'

The phone started bleeping. Matlock put money in until he ran out of coins that would be accepted.

'About the diesel. About the Mintons.'

'You've lost me.'

'A16 is a farm, right? And I'd bet that the Mintons own other farms in the county.'

'I'm sure they do.'

'And what do farms run their vehicles on?'

'Diesel, I suppose.'

'There you go. What kind?'

Matlock scooped the rejected change from the hinged hopper in the phone box while Chris replied. 'Cherry juice,' she said.

'What?'

'That's what it's called. Red diesel. Cherry red. Thirty-five seconds.' Something to do with viscosity. Domestic heating oil was called 'Twenty-eight seconds' – there was a test with a ball bearing of a particular diameter falling through a tube of the stuff. Road diesel was thicker; the ball bearing dropped more slowly. Hence 'Thirty-five seconds'.

'That's part of what the Mintons are up to. One of their sources of income. It's why they need to launder their money; some of it, anyway.'

Red diesel is taxed at a different rate to the kind bought at the pumps. It's a lot cheaper. Cheap enough to sell on at a profit and for that to be worth both the buyer's while and the risk attached. Sell enough of it and you need to disguise the source of the money. That's why it's dyed; so roadside checks can differentiate it from the ordinary sort.

'There you go,' Chris said. 'Always wondered why the Mintons owned those launderettes.'

Launderettes, like amusement arcades, are ideal fronts for money laundering on a modest scale. They deal almost exclusively in cash, in everyday forgettable transactions. It's straightforward – as long as you're not too greedy – to introduce money from other sources into the banked receipts of the legitimate business. Be consistent, run the front as an otherwise clean enterprise, and you're home and dry.

That was the source of the cash Matlock had snatched on Monday. He was sure of it now.

'I'm still not entirely sure what this has got to do with you and your dad. Surely that's all straight revenge. Family honour. All of that.'

'Maybe it is. But maybe it isn't.'

'We got time for this cryptic approach?'

'I think we have.'

'Want me to call you back?'

'No need, Chris. Still got a bit of change to go.'

'Oh goody.'

'I'm working this out as I'm going.'

'Never.'

'It's this. Minton can't help himself. He's got to have an edge. A hundred little fiddles. Money saved here, tax dodged there. Tourists ripped off elsewhere. And you know what they say about tourists.'

'"Fuck 'em."'

'Precisely.'

'So.'

'So there's more. And it's precarious. A domino rally of scams. And you upset one, you upset them all.'

'You sure you're not just a fly in their butter?'

'That's not the question to be asking.'

A huff down the phone. 'Then what is?'

'I'll tell you over breakfast,' Matlock said.

He tried to hang up fast, but still caught Chris murmur 'Twat' down the line.

Thursday

Matlock picked up Chris after her kids had left for school. She'd dressed for the occasion. A scuffed Barbour jacket. Wellingtons. She didn't say anything clambering into the van.

'Morning.'

The suspension grunted. Rust and springs.

'I just remembered how much I don't like going out.'

Chris didn't. Really didn't. After what had happened to her happened, defence mechanisms had activated deep in her psyche. Weight gain. Agoraphobia. The sawn-off. There was every chance the damn thing was tucked in her wellies.

'You don't have to.'

'Yeah, I do. Besides, there was a promise of breakfast.'

Matlock started up the engine.

'Better be a good one. That's all.' Chris coughed. 'This thing smells. You been sleeping in it?'

'Cheek. Anyway, thought you set this up with Mark out at Welton Motors.'

'Told him you'd be likely as not calling in with a fresh-nicked car. And where else around here do you take of one of those?'

'Fair point.' The place had a reputation.

'Even fronted a few hundred quid. Didn't expect you'd get something quite so roomy.'

'Yeah, well he took me for another two hundred.'

'Plus the car you came in with?'

'Yep.'

'Not bad for five minutes' work. Still smells though.'

Chris was right. It wasn't the freshest. It didn't matter though. He'd only need it for another couple of days, tops.

'Where do you want me to park?'

'Remember where the pig pens used to be?'

'Take it that they've gone.'

'That's progress for you.'

Time was when there were two beast markets a week. Everyone referred to it as the cattle market, but the place dealt in auctions of cows, lambs and pigs. There was even a special livestock market at Christmas, where farmers would offload the turkeys too big for the supermarkets' requirements. If you didn't mind plucking your own bird you could get a bargain. There had been markets on Wednesdays and Fridays; the fruit and veg style of market grew up as a counterpoint to the livestock sales. But the market was dwindling, business-wise. There were other ways to buy animals. Much of the trade was done over the phone, like as not in advance. Two hundred head wanted in twelve months for such and such a pound. That kind of thing.

The market had condensed, both temporally and physically. A single beast market ran on Thursdays. A new central auction building was built, and some of the old outdoor pens were dismantled. The council converted the now-excess land into car parking. This included what had been pig pens. An area the size of four tennis courts. When Matlock was a kid, this had been a corrugated iron-roofed labyrinth of enclosures and gates. The location for a hundred chasing games. A favourite was to come down on Wednesday or Friday evenings after the sales were concluded, and lob handfuls of straw and pigshit at passing cars and at the council workers paid overtime to sluice the crap away.

Even now it felt odd. A bland asphalted space where there had once been a place dark, fell and fascinating. Matlock bought a ticket from the inevitable machine. Stuck in in the van window to appease the parking gods.

The council wanted to sell the land. All of it. Get rid of the cattle market; convert the acreage to retail. Bring in the big stores. Corporate fantasies of a Tesco, an ASDA. Brands that might otherwise have no reason to mess with a small market town. That in itself was a thumb in the soup. The town, as pub bores would tell you, had a covenant requiring a beast market to be held. The law went back to King John, one of the earlier Henries or an Edward depending on the teller. Point was, the council was stuck with it.

Being stuck with the cattle market meant being saddled also with the pub that came with it. The Bull's Head had been on the site of the market since the eighteenth century. Wags reckoned the same carpet was still down from its opening day. The Bull's – never The Bull – had a licence dispensation to open early on market days. Another archaic annoyance for the council. That meant they were serving drink from seven on Thursday mornings, which meant often as not that there were pissed farmers scattered across the market by ten.

But they did reasonable grub. Never a menu, but there was food. Fish and chips on Friday. Roast beef on Sunday. And breakfast on Thursdays.

Matlock pushed through to find a free table. The Bull's had three rooms: the main bar, a side room which led out to the market and, on the far side of the bar, a snug which was used only by local societies having their meetings. Young Farmers, Friends of Loweth Hospital Radio, St Herefrith's Bell-ringers. Darts was big in the Bull's; Tuesday was league night.

The place was busy. All were drinking; a fair few eating. Empties at the next table indicated that the pair of farmhands there were on their fourth pints already.

'Want anything to drink?'

'Tea.' Chris glowered. It must have taken guts to come out in public. To sit in a crowded, noisy place.

Matlock realised he'd perhaps been tough on her. To think she'd go against what was in his best interests. Maybe they had differences of opinion about what was best for him, but she was looking out for him in her own way. Being here was evidence enough of that.

That was the only true test of character. Behaviour over time.

You are what you do.

'Tea,' Matlock repeated. 'One sec.'

A lull at the bar. The woman serving was gulping from a mug. Matlock took the place in. Optics with brands he didn't recognise. Fridges half-full under the back wall. Only two bitters on tap; beer mats over the other hand-pulls. A box of Caramac bars. Someone had a sweet tooth. Next to Matlock, a plastic jar, the kind you sold loose boiled sweets from, a quarter-full of coins. Mostly coppers. A couple of notes. A handwritten sign Sellotaped to the jar said the collection was for the county Air Ambulance. More tape around the screw-top lid; a slot had been cut into the plastic for donations to be posted.

'Yes love. Sorry.'

'No rush. Two full Englishes. A tea and a coffee.'

'Where you sat, love?'

Matlock said where, and paid. 'Hang on and I'll get your brews.' The mugs came with knives and forks wrapped in paper napkins. 'There's sauces on the tables.'

'Gotcha. Ta.'

Matlock carried the drinks back. Chris didn't look any happier to be here. The guys at the next table were loud. Some bullshit conversation about their boss.

There wasn't any sauce at Matlock and Chris's table. A grey-brown plastic tub, moulded to look like it was woven, sat on the next table over. Ketchup, brown, salt, pepper. A pot of mustard, excess crusting around the lid.

'You bring me to all the best places.'

'Thought it only right you got the lie of the land. We'll get some food in us and I'll show you what to expect.'

Two plates came quick. Double egg, sausage, bacon. Mushrooms, grilled tomatoes, black pudding. They were soon followed up with side plates of toasted white sliced. Butter, yellow and soft for spreading, in a bowl.

Chris focused on her food. She ate quick, but not fast. Zoning out the room, Matlock reckoned.

Matlock took his time. Lifted the slices of black pudding off his plate and slid them onto Chris's. He'd never been a fan. Chris raised her knife in thanks. Pointed to her remaining sausage. Exchange? No.

The banter from the next table rankled. Matlock leaned over. 'Pass us the mustard, mate.'

'I'm not your mate. Mate.'

'Give him the mustard.'

'Fuck you, telling me what to do.'

'Fuck you. Someone's got to tell you what to do. Have to tell you to take your cock out else you'd piss your trousers.'

'Just the mustard. Mate.'

The louder of the two grabbed the yellow jar. 'This?'

Of course, that.

Chris was paying attention now. Kept eating, but was watching, wary.

'If you would.'

'Hand it over. Don't be a dick all your life.' Even his mate was tired of this guy.

The man with the jar of mustard stood. His chair wobbled backwards under the force of his movement. A shade over six foot. Dirty jeans and Doc Martens. Steel toe caps, by the look of them. Several layers of tees and overshirts. Fit and fat at the same time; his belly hung over the belt, but there was working strength in his shoulders. 'Get two more in. I'm off for a piss. And as for you, you can wait.' The last words were for Matlock. The mustard disappeared into the shirts.

The gents' loos weren't even in the Bull's. There was a ladies' toilet, but the men had to go out of a side door into a courtyard beyond. Time was there was a tin shed, little more than a trough with a roof, with an outside lavvy at one end. Now the arrangement was slightly updated. The council had built a toilet block; the Bull's male customers shared that with car-parkers and – on Thursdays – with the cattle market clientele. Back when day trips to the coast were still a thing, the Bull's had been a stop-off point. Last piss before the seaside.

Chris didn't smile. Nodded over to another table where there was more mustard.

Bollocks to that.

Mustard Fella's mate mumbled a half-arsed apology. Went to get two more pints. Even took some of the empties back with him.

Matlock made his way out of the room and through to the outside.

Cattle noises: lowing, the scuffle of hooves, heavy breaths. Men shouting, cajoling beasts into or out of lorries and pens. Different kinds of dung smell hovered in the air. Other smells: frying onions from a tea van. Sweat. The antiseptic taint of a public lavatory.

Matlock went into the gents'.

Mustard Guy had his back to Matlock. Urine streamed between

his legs. He was chasing a yellow block of cleaning stuff down the drainage channel.

Two cubicles. Both occupied. Belts being unbuckled. Splashes and strains.

The guy shook; zipped himself up. Turned away from where the sinks and paper towels were, making ready to leave.

Matlock was about three feet away.

The guy reacted. Puzzlement, then a grin. This twat wanted a fight after all. Opened his mouth to say something.

Matlock's fist was already travelling. A left, arcing to the temple. The guy was big. Head shot. Disorientate. It connected hard, side-swiping the man and knocking him off balance.

Good. He looked like a brawler. A kicker. Would try to smother you, bring you down. Leather you with his size tens.

A right to the face. This blow didn't have the same power. Not enough to do real damage. Still, he was turning into it from the previous wallop.

A third punch, this from the left. Matlock adjusted his stance, moving forwards and to the right. This one landed where his jaw hinged under his ear. It bloody hurt to hit him.

'Fu–'

Now, one to the gut. His belly was soft on top, but there was a solid-enough core beyond it. But a stomach full of liquid will always react the same way to a punch delivered with force. The guy exhaled: beer and bile. He didn't puke, but there was a dribble of something wetting his lips.

A shadow behind, soon gone. Someone had walked in, clocked the fight, had scarpered.

The guy was doubling over now. Stringy drool fell from his mouth. Time to end this.

Matlock brought both hands over the guy's head. Cradled it from above. Pressed down with his hands, and then brought his left knee up. Full in the face. Now his nose gave way. Cartilage cracked like chicken bone. Matlock pulled his hands away, stepping back. The guy slumped over onto one side. He convulsed once, and then he vomited.

Beery puke spread across the damp tiles towards the urinal. Matlock shifted to have the fallen man be a barrier between him and the piss-and-vomit soup. Patted him down as best he could. A rubber-banded roll of banknotes. Keys. No cards or ID. No wallet. The mustard, undamaged.

Matlock thought about it. Took two tenners from the roll and chucked the money and the keys into the urinal trough.

The guy was okay. He'd stink, but live. Matlock put his hands under the guy's armpits and dragged him to a sitting position, propped up by the bin next to the sink. Left him to it. As he exited the lavatory, he heard both cubicles gingerly unlock.

*

Chris had finished her food. 'Better now?'

'Much.'

The other guy finished his pint quick when Matlock put the mustard on the table. Left his buddy's full one to go flat. Went off out towards the toilets.

'That your answer to everything these days?'

'Says the woman who sent her pet gorilla to beat some sense into me with one of my torn-off arms.' Matlock smeared mustard on his sausage. Ate. 'I'm getting the prison out of me. That's all.'

'You'll be getting the prison all around you again if you keep that crap up.'

'You can't take me anywhere.'

'So it seems.'

Matlock ate fast. No reason to dally. And there was the slightest chance he'd get himself involved in a full-on bar fight if he wasn't careful. But the two men didn't come back. No hue and cry from other patrons. Another one of those Thursday morning things. The bloke's an arsehole. Every week he gets pissed and ends up in a fight. And you can't win them all.

'All done?'

'Yep.'

'Come on then. We'd better go the long way round just in case.' They could have cut through the back – past the outside toilets – but

Chris led Matlock back through the main bar. Matlock paused long enough to put twenty quid in the collection jar for the Air Ambulance.

*

'Question.'

'Go on,' Chris said, as they made their way over to the main auction building.

'Where does a drunk oaf get a fat roll of cash from?'

'Maybe he just got paid. Sold a car. Hundred possibilities.'

'But he knows he's an arsehole. That he'll get drunk and like as not lose it, spend it or stick it on a lame greyhound.'

'So maybe he just got paid.'

'You already said that.'

Chris said the phrase a third time. Now she put more emphasis on the word 'just'.

The place was busy. Even out on the asphalt, halfway between the pub and the auction area. Movement of men and livestock. The hum of deals. Money changing hands. 'Here?'

'Best place for it. Plain sight. Farmers work with cash whenever they can. No reason why not. Debts being settled, wages being paid. All in notes.'

'So what would someone like him have been given a wad of tenners for?'

'Farmhand, you reckon?'

Matlock nodded. Then remembered something. Keys. The fella had a roll of money the thickness of a cigar tube. And he had a set of keys. Nothing unusual in that. There was a fob on the keyring. Like a small medal against a leather teardrop. It had a Scania logo. 'HGV driver. Goods vehicle.'

There were lorries everywhere. Those not actively involved in backing up to or pulling off from the loading points by the auction area were parked up in a separate section. That was full to overflowing, though, so drivers had found spare spaces wherever, and had trusted to luck that they wouldn't get called on it.

'So he's transporting animals. What's that got to do with his money?' Chris knew already, Matlock guessed. Was enjoying having him work towards the solution.

'One, it's wages. But if he's a known arsehole, then his boss wouldn't pay him off in the morning, because he'd like as not piss it up against the wall. Like he did just now.'

'So?'

'So it's not pay. Not for driving anyway.'

'Makes you wonder what the money's for.'

'Some scam he's got running. Him and his mate. A deal on the side. Something his boss doesn't know about or turns a blind eye towards. Maybe the money's not all his, and he's taking it back somewhere.'

'Didn't look the trustworthy type.'

'No.'

'I'd have chosen his mate. He seemed the more level-headed of the two.'

'There you go.'

'So he's up to something. And he's got paid off for it.'

'Didn't seem to be especially excited.'

'So it's a regular thing.'

'Makes you wonder.'

'Yeah.' They were outside the auction house now. A barn of a place, built on the cheap. Like two stands of a football ground sandwiched together. Breeze blocks and metal cladding up to a roof that was made of corrugated panels; two-thirds of them plastic, a third of them aluminium.

Chris led Matlock in. Office, trade stalls. Animal feeds and nutritional supplements. Tractor spares. Agricultural clothing. Farmers' Union. A place to get teas and bacon buns.

Rows of pens, roiling with animals to be sold. The building echoed with beast noises, banter, shouting, laughter. Jacketed stewards with white gauze trilbies, marshalling men and animals. Livestock came in through the goods inward doors; were allocated places in the pens. In their turn they were led through into the auction ring. Small lots – a couple of pigs maybe – went through to the ring complete. Larger lots were sampled; farmers and stewards quibbling over which of the stock was the most representative. A separate channel funnelled the sold animals onwards and out; to their new homes. To the abattoir.

The auction ring was in a separate enclosure. From his position by the main entrance, Matlock couldn't see inside it. He and Chris had to walk around to find an access point.

'So where's the money coming from?'

'It's a pay-off,' Matlock concluded.

'For what?'

'For whatever operation he wasn't the brains of. It was a chunk of money. He's a piston ring at best, not an engine.'

'Getting warmer.'

'Tease.'

Now, the loudest sound was the gabble of the auctioneer. A delay on the sound system meant there were two sets of echoes: one organic, one electric. The latest announcement was that they were taking a mid-morning break. Fifteen minutes.

Matlock and Chris stepped back out of the way. The auction ring area emptied out; maybe fifty, almost universally middle-aged, grey-haired, either in outdoor working gear or else the smarter farmer's uniform of tweed jacket, brown trousers and shoes and checked tattersall shirt. Two dozen variations on a clothing theme.

'Come on,' Chris said.

The auction ring was horseshoe-shaped. The central enclosure where the beasts were paraded was at ground level. Maybe twenty foot square. Big enough to walk a couple of cows around in, but not much more. The ring was surrounded by high-sided steel sheeting. On three sides there were ranked tiers of stadium standing. Concrete steps up with steel barriers every couple of sets to allow for leaning and pointing at the beasts. You could get two or three hundred people in here, easy.

The fourth side had tall gates for animals in and out. Behind and above that there was a platform supporting a windowed office. Microphones and chalkboards. Three people inside the office, each dressed like the stewards Matlock had seen earlier. A metal staircase down from the office, leading out into the auction house beyond.

Chris stopped by a leaning post with a decent view of the ring. A steward summoned a flunkey. The guy, in waders that stretched over his belly, came through with a hosepipe. Started to sluice down the ring area clean of droppings.

'Made for the job,' Matlock said.

'It's a good choice. Doubtless Roy Minton will make sure that they've got uninterrupted access tomorrow night. Plenty of space for spectators if it's going to be that kind of thing. You and the Corrigan lad as the main event.'

You'd never risk an illegal dogfight here. Too close to the town centre, for one thing. The last thing you'd want would be to have some do-gooders or the RSPCA turn up. But as a one-off, an event you'd had up to two years to think on, then it could work. Bouncers on the door. Moonlighting cops from out of town if you had any sense. You could sell tickets.

Maybe they had.

The fight wasn't the issue. It was getting out afterwards.

The steel sides to the ring area were maybe five feet high. They'd be nigh impossible to scale. The two entrances to the ring had industrial bolts to keep the animals inside. The tunnels in and out of the ring to the gates were covered with sturdy grilles. There'd be another gate at the far end of each: an airlock system for the efficient management of livestock.

There was another possibility. The auctioneers' office on the raised platform. There was more of the smooth steel from the ground up; above that there was what looked like ordinary-enough scaffolding holding the office in the air.

The man in the ring jetted water into the corners of the auction area. The surface wasn't flat. Each side slanted downwards enough to allow water and faeces to be swept to a central drainage point. A slotted cover allowed the foul-smelling gruel to be washed away.

'Not many ways out,' Chris said.

'Let's walk around.'

Matlock went first this time, out of the stadium and around to where the livestock was introduced onto the selling floor. Channels of metal tubing filtered beasts in to be sold, then out for their onward journey. A gantry behind the auctioneers' podium allowed for standing and pointing down at the cattle below. The staircase down included a walkway over the two lanes of sales traffic, then safe to ground level. Where the stairwell came to earth, another office shack. Here was where bills were settled. Cash swapped for receipts. Handshakes between parties. Instructions barked from the new owner to whomever was responsible for loading their new purchases into the animal transporters.

The pens were filling up on the sale side again; sheep were being introduced into the airlock system ready for the first auction after the interval.

Matlock followed the route out to a loading area. More lorries. Articulated trucks to horseboxes. All sizes in-between. If you only had a single sow to sell you could shift it in the back of a pickup. Hell, a good-sized estate car might do the trick.

The smaller vehicles carried no logos. The purpose-built units did. For two sets of reasons. Either you were a major producer with thousands of head of animals for milk or meat. Then you'd have the wherewithal and the pride to have your name on the cab of the tractor unit of your vehicles, and the resources behind your business to make owning the haulage and employing drivers a necessity. Or else you were a haulage company yourself, and you were advertising your trucking wares.

An itch of an idea in the base of Matlock's skull. Under that bony lump where the back of the head meets the top of the neck. The occipital bone. There.

Matlock sped up. He didn't mean to, but he left Chris wheezing behind. She'd catch up. Or he'd go back. The latter. Chris knew, after all, what some of this was all about.

Matlock got to the first of the parked trucks. Haulage company name and telephone number on the side. Between the wheels and the fuel tanks.

Tanks.

Two of them.

It was a good job but the work of a skilled amateur rather than a trained professional. The outward-facing tank was a ruse, remade to look like it was bigger than it was. It butted up to an auxiliary tank.

Welding, paint and deliberately left grease and dirt did a reasonable camouflage job, but any disguise only works when it's not expected. The second tank was large. Not a backup; not some jury-rigged measure to prevent being caught on a B-road with the fuel gauge hard against the back end of the red line. A deliberate conversion.

Heavy goods vehicles run on diesel. Road diesel costs; but the bulk of that cost is tax. And big rigs are thirsty. Fuel's a much bigger cost than labour. So what if you had your trucks modified? Agricultural red diesel. In comparison, untaxed. Cheap. But detectable at a roadside inspection. Hence the outward tank for show.

Matlock walked around a second, similar haulier-owned lorry. A third. A fourth, to be certain. Three of them had similar modifications made.

And these were trucks on farming-related business. You could argue the toss on that one. A decent brief might muddy the law sufficiently to make the Crown Prosecution Service decide it wasn't worth the bother.

Get caught with a wagon full of plastics, say, and it was a different matter altogether.

That was why Mean Mr Mustard was walking around with a tube of cash like a roll of Extra Strong Mints. Either cash for red diesel, or else payment for his part in the other end of the transaction.

Matlock made his way back to Chris. 'Crafty bastards,' he said.

'Crafty? Hardly. This is serious money we're talking about.'

Everything industrial moves by road at some point in its journey. Maybe the whole way. And the machines doing the moving are invariably diesel-fuelled. You buy that diesel for a fraction of its supposed cost from a friendly farmer, and your margin goes from slim to positively girthy. Enough meat on the bone to cut everyone a steak and have plenty left over to treat the dog.

'And serious money demands serious consideration. Vested interests. Payments for cataracts from whomever. Police. Council planning department. Customs and Excise. Inland Revenue.'

'Grease the wheels.'

'Keeps the money machine turning.'

Red diesel fraud was nothing new. But criminals tend to be, by their nature or through circumstance, either desperate, short-sighted or stupid. Any combination of the above. If the feature held, a line of all three.

Two years in prison teaches you that you're maybe one of those. And if you don't learn the lesson, then there's plenty more jail time waiting for you further on down the line.

'Roy Minton.'

Chris shrugged. 'Bigger picture.'

'Not for the next thirty-six hours.'

'Perhaps not.'

'But by Saturday?'

'You'll be a stain washed down into the sewer system, Ant Corrigan will have been avenged and his brother will have earned his way back into the family's good graces.'

'You think so?'

'I'll bet it's what Roy Minton's got in mind.'

'A shame. We had a good talk. He came across pretty fair, all things considered.'

'He can afford to be. He's got people to do the rough stuff for him. Always at a remove. Messages passed through two or three sets of hands. Nothing over the phone, because c'est la vie, say the old folks.'

'Goes to show, you never can tell.'

'Also,' Chris said. 'You know this. You've met him. He's getting old. North of sixty. Not ready for the nursing home yet, but he's slowed enough to see the trees for the forest. He likes being king.'

'Judge and jury.'

'And a reasonable court of appeal. He's the better for knowing. And you, like you said, have had that conversation with him.'

'You think I can trust him.'

'I think you can trust his word.'

'That might be all I've got going for me,' Matlock said.

'Might be.'

*

Matlock and Chris made their way back to the van. Got in.

'Want taking home?' Matlock asked.

'In a minute. Wait here a mo.' Chris was red-faced. Swept a paper tissue from a handy pack across her forehead. Wiped her eyes. Her mouth. Cranked the window down. Lost the tissue outside.

'You can get fined for that.'

'I can afford it.'

'Hardly the attitude.'

'Just wanted a reason to get some air into this death trap. I'm sure this thing stinks worse than it did this morning.'

'In case you hadn't noticed, look outside.' Cowshit everywhere.

Chris snorted. Pulled another tissue from the pack. 'Home, definitely.'

Matlock waited until he was back on the road before speaking again. 'There's something I've got to do,' he said. 'Tonight.'

'I'm not sure I want to know.'

'That's why I'm giving you a heads-up.'

'I'm not sure I want even that. You shouldn't have come back.'

'Turned out that I couldn't not.'

'Want me to come with you tomorrow?'

Matlock had thought about that. A second. A ring man. A backup, just in case. But then, there was the risk factor. If he actually went through with this, then having Chris there only put her in danger he didn't want and she didn't need. 'You're alright.'

'You're up to something, aren't you?'

'You probably don't want to know.'

'No, I probably don't.'

*

Mugs of tea back at Chris's. Hers: a chunky but nevertheless porcelain souvenir of a trip to Chatsworth House. His advertised the '77 Silver Jubilee. Elizabeth – with her Mona Lisa amused indifference to the street parties and the day off school for the kids – was superimposed over a blurry photo of the Tower of London. A packet of biscuits on the go: own-brand chocolate digestives from the cheapie shop. Chris took two, sandwiched them together. Took a bite. Dunked. Checked the consistency of the chocolate. Risked a second dip in the tea. Then ate again. 'You going to tell me what you're up to, then?'

'It's your fault.'

'Mm?' A mouthful of biscuit.

'Shouldn't have given me that lead about A16 Eggs.'

'Shouldn't have bothered trying to warn you off in the first place.'

'Never was much good at taking a hint.'

'Yeah, well.'

'Part of your half-arsed charm. And it makes you good when you're focused. Stickability. You keep with it.'

'I'm a dog with a stick.'

'Yeah. Not altogether in a bad way.'

'I know where they're holding Joe.'

'At A16?'

'Yeah.'

'Makes sense. Close to town, but out of it. Folk there all day every day. Big place though. Could be anywhere.'

'The farmhouse.'

'Thought that was offices.'

'So do the people working there.'

'Well then.'

'That's what I thought.'

'So the plan is what? Go in, grab Joe?'

'Yep.'

'Intricate. Then what?'

'Pop Joe in the caravan. Talk with Minton. Leave it there.'

'He'll not like that.'

'No.'

'Got any leverage?'

'All I want is Joe back. He's got no right to be mixed up in any of this.'

'You didn't answer the question.'

'I'll need a number for him. Something that'll get a quick response.'

Chris sighed. Took another digestive. Offered the packet to Matlock.

'I'm alright thanks.'

Chris twisted the packet more or less shut. 'Kids won't touch the cheap shit. If it's not branded and advertised on the telly they're not interested. Only way I can keep these to myself.' She ate her last biscuit. 'I can give you a number. No such thing as a direct line to him, but you make a strong case and Minton'll be back to you in ten, fifteen minutes tops. That good enough?'

'Perfect.'

Chris wrote down a number. No dialling code; somewhere local.

'Thanks.'

'Let me know how it all works out.'

'One way or the other, finding out about this'll be the last of anyone's problems.'

'You're a one-man ulcer machine.'

*

Matlock needed to check something out. He drove into town. Bought a few things in the hardware store. Went to a leather goods place. Felt conspicuous against the high-end handbags and wallets. Bought a good pair of gloves. Light, strong, soft. Black and bewilderingly expensive.

He turned up at the old people's home not long after two. He waited in the van until the first wave of afternoon visitors had been and gone. When the car park was empty save for the kinds of cars affordable on a nursing assistant's wage, he got himself buzzed in.

'Hey,' Lucy said.

'Hey yourself. Remind me again. What time's visiting open till?'

'Eight. But I'm gone by five-oh-one, so there's not much to see after then.'

'That true?'

'I'm not one to hang about.'

'Life's too short.'

'Something like that.'

Matlock smiled. 'I'll bear that in mind.'

'You should.'

'Be back down in a few minutes.'

'No hurry.'

131

Matlock waved a hand at the nurses' station. Went on down to room 112.

She was asleep. Might not have moved since last time Matlock had seen her. Her breathing was ephemeral. Stick arms and legs jutted out from under a sheet-and-blanket combination. The glycerine gloss of moisture on her lips.

A side table was untidy with the aftermath of an unsuccessful feeding attempt. Tissues. A Tetra Pak of meal supplement. Strawberry-flavoured. A needleless syringe with traces of the same bright pink goo. Matlock sniffed the drink. It smelled like a sweetshop. An open pack of mouth swabs.

There was a bin under a handbasin. Matlock poured the rest of the strawberry gunk down the plughole. Ran the tap until the sink was clean. Swept all but the swabs into the same bin.

She didn't have long. This might simply have been a bad day, but if this was kept up, then she'd be lucky to see the weekend out. Taking no water will do that to you.

Someone had visited. Fresh flowers. More cards than previous. Matlock wasn't sure, but there might have been another family photo to join the throng on the chest of drawers. We busy ourselves with details while our world turns to ash.

The room was well appointed. TV, radio, phone. Might have been in a hotel but for the high-sided bed and the wipe-clean cover on the mattress. That, and the institutional tang of bleach and broccoli.

He left her to it. Whatever it was.

A cart in the hallway. An orderly, doing room observations. Ticks on a clipboard. There was a dispensing Thermos for hot water on the trolley; tea bags, instant coffee, sugar. Plastic mugs. Sippy cups. The woman gave a tired smile of welcome. Put her head around the nearest door, continuing her checks.

Snatches of television from some of the rooms. There was a lounge by the nurses' station, but he had not seen anyone use it as yet. A larger TV set, sound down to zero, subtitles scrolling, blinked down at empty chairs arranged in a slack arc.

A woman behind the desk in the nurses' station. The desk was placed so that, if you wanted to, you went undisturbed, but a crook to the right and you had an unimpeded view along the length of the corridor. All the better to see you with, my dear. The nurse bent her head, smiled. Put a steadying hand out to support her rising.

'Hi.'

'Hi, petal. Don't mind me having a word, do you?' A name tag: J. Pearce. The upside-down fob watch. Charity pins. A badge for blood donation achievements.

'No, not at all.'

'It's just that, well, she's very tired these days. I appreciate that it's always a difficult thing to consider, but the family really has to prepare itself for some bad news.'

'I thought so,' Matlock said.

'I'm afraid that she's not very responsive much of the time. A few hours in the mornings, usually, but that's becoming less. She's really not taking in what she needs in the way of fluids.'

'I know it's one of those piece-of-string questions...'

'A week. Maybe a little less. If there's other family members who need to pay their respects while they can, it might be an idea to have them visit sooner rather than later.'

'I see. Thank you.'

'That's no problem at all, petal.' Nurse Pearce was kind, but efficient. Long used to death in all its guises. She had a novel on the go alongside the usual administrative paperwork. The book's cover showed a land girl, hair wrapped in a kerchief, driving an ancient tractor while a Hurricane – or a Spitfire; Matlock couldn't remember the difference between the two – flew above. The paperback was covered in the wipe-clean plastic binding you got with library books. 'When their time is coming, it's no problem at all to stay later. Some like to be there. You know.'

'Yes. Thank you. I might. Over the weekend, maybe.'

'Have we got your contact details in the book?'

'Yes. I'm sure it's all there in the file.'

'It's good to check. What with her being in here so long, people move house. Change their numbers sometimes. Not everything gets updated.'

'How long has it been now?'

'Let's see.' The nurse took down a file. Flipped the pages. 'Four years, as near as. Two in the main house, and two here.'

Matlock assumed that 'the main house' referred to the residential care part of the site. This was a nursing ward. The main house was all afternoon bingo, craft sessions and getting about under your own steam. Here, it was hourly room checks and a GP making twice-weekly visits. The only way out of here was in an anonymous white van with an extractor fan.

'Thanks for your time.'

'My pleasure…' She let the sentence fade so that Matlock could fill it with his name by way of belated introduction.

'Mine too,' Matlock said, deliberately misreading the cue.

*

'Here he is.' Back at reception.

'Here you are.'

'Thought you'd never come back.'

'Wondered about checking in myself. Bed, breakfast, evening meal. Can't be all bad.'

'I've got the forms if you want to give it a try.'

'You think of everything.'

'I'm an efficient kinda gal.'

'That was my first impression.'

'Was it now? Whatever does he see in me, I wondered to myself. That's it. Efficiency.'

'It's an undervalued characteristic.'

'Is it now?'

'So I'm told.'

'I bet Mrs Efficient is very pleased with her catch.'

'So efficient, that she found someone better a long time ago.' The postcard.

'That's the downside of efficiency. Always looking to make improvements.'

Matlock shrugged. 'Tell me about it.'

'When?'

'What about tomorrow?'

'Any time after five and I'm yours.'

'What about lunchtime?'

'Classy. One till two. Sandwiches and a yoghurt in the canteen.'

'Maybe we can do better than that.'

'Well, it is Valentine's Day.'

'So it is.'

'I'll see you at one, then.'

*

Maybe Chris was right. The van didn't smell so great. Stale water, maybe. There was probably something growing in the engine bay. Maybe a bird's nest, full of dead eggs, wedged between the pipework. Who knew how long the vehicle had been standing being shat on by sparrows until it was handed over to Matlock?

He was parked up in a country lane. The road bordered the land occupied by A16 Eggs. The van was in a passing place, the asphalt not wide enough to allow two cars to pass each other otherwise.

His purchases from earlier were in a small backpack by his side. A heavy torch. Tape. A retractable knife: the sort for opening boxes.

The gun. Matlock wondered about the wisdom of bringing the Ruger with him. Guns were trouble. Pistols were worse. Too easy to fire in panic or frustration. Too easy to have it knocked out of your hand; then you've lost your advantage, or worse, someone stoops and picks it up.

In and out. No confrontation.

Find Joe, get him out of there. Make sure he was okay. Stash him in the caravan. Get some food into him. Then ring Minton. Tell him his payback fight was off.

Then?

Take the B-roads over the Wolds out of the county. Worry about the details later.

No. That was the old plan. The prison scheme. And like all jail-born ideas, it didn't stand up on the outside.

No point getting too far ahead.

One thing at a time.

Matlock ate. Petrol station savouries. Jail had given him a taste for stodge. Porridge. Potatoes. Overcooked pasta. Damp white sliced. New routine as of Saturday. Back to the old ways. Convert fat back into muscle. He liked the stabby thoughts; slivers of a possible future.

He turned his attention back to the tall leylandii that screened the egg place from the curious. Might have been a planning requirement. Might have been design. The trees meant there wasn't much detail to see, but there were impressions of movement, and there was light. It was five; dusk. The yard beyond the trees was lit by fierce fluorescence. Shadows were cast: forklift trucks, pallets of whatnot, lorries back and forth.

Some of the trucks were squared-off. Some of them were rounded. Curves on the trailers. Tankers, not box wagons.

Cars came down the lane infrequently. There wasn't much down here to go to or to come from. A lattice of narrow strips of tarmac linking hamlets to farms to the main road.

Matlock got out of the cab. The air was fresher, both in scent and in temperature. It was still early enough in the year to threaten a frost. Clear skies. Dark enough, despite the paler purple to the west, for there to be stars visible.

Let your eyes acclimatise to the gloaming. Then you see your first star. Once the initial adjustment has been made, other stars come easy.

Two years and more since he'd last paid attention to the twilight sky. Joe had taught him some. He'd told Matlock about more, but only fragments of the knowledge remained. Memories of the memory weren't the same as the real thing.

The five stars making the W of Cassiopeia. The bent line of Orion's belt. Ursa Major; the Big Dipper if you preferred. Simple to make out. Others, not so much. The patterns fragmented; the connections made by the ancients hadn't held for him.

Joe knew them all. The same way that he knew what leaves came from which trees, which feathers had fallen from what bird. Latin names for plants. Hymns Ancient and Modern. The Book of Common Prayer. Joe had it memorised; hammered into him through repetition and the hard-edged slap of the classroom's yard-long wooden ruler back when that was how information was transferred.

Hercules. Above it in the sky, Draco. To the south, Ophiuchus. To the east, the Corona Borealis. A subtle arcing slash of points of light. It was meant to reflect the crown worn by Ariadne, the daughter of Cretan king Minos, who had the labyrinth. The crown was a gift from the god Dionysus; set in the sky as a reminder either to commemorate his marriage to Ariadne, or else as a monument to Theseus using the light from the crown to escape the labyrinth after killing the minotaur. Joe had told different versions. All as true as each other, he had said.

Joe was only a field away.

The distant thump of a heavy lever. Shutters rattling downwards. The light through the trees from A16 Eggs halved; alternate bulbs extinguished. The illumination was now an assertion of a security presence, where it had until recently been a proclamation of industry.

Cars. Headlights tracking towards the main road. The feeling of a place that had been shut down for the night.

Matlock gave it an hour.

*

He'd done seven hundred-odd days inside. He supposed that Joe could have stuck out four. And an old back bedroom was better than a cell. There was something trite about the true prison being the mind-set, not the bars.

No way to treat an old man, though.

There had been old men in the jail, too. Not so many as you might have thought; they tend to get released eventually, or transferred to open prisons and then to halfway houses, then to wherever. The real bastards – the ones who deserved to die inside – were in secure units, high-security psychiatric wards. Places with names like Rampton and Broadmoor. Lincoln jail had been aglow with the reflected glory of lifers who'd done some time alongside the truly notorious. The serial killers, the East End villains, old-school terrorists from the Irish days.

Joe had better be perfect.

That tingling feeling. Not quite goosebumps, not quite the after-math of cramp. The anticipation of a fight. The impulse to curl his hands into fists and to bludgeon whomever was there.

Matlock drove to the main road; turned towards the egg place. Pulled into the car park. There was no barrier preventing entry; the way in was too wide. A sign in homely wood, saying that they were closed. No cars in the car park. The shop and cafe windows were dark.

Matlock idled up to the house. Killed the engine, and allowed the van to trundle. Eventually, it stopped.

No movement. No exterior noise save the sporadic swish of traffic on the A16. What passed for rush hour for commuters back to Loweth from Grimsby was over. Thursday. Jacket potato and beans in front of the telly. Regional news programming, then the soaps.

Outside the van, Matlock shouldered the bag. He'd taken the torch out first. Its heft was welcome.

Silence from the house. Lights around the back, but not at the front; they'd only attract potential customers. The lighting was a security deterrent only, Matlock reckoned. Make the place look more industrious than it was. Maybe there'd be some human presence in the factory area. Maybe not. He supposed they worked all hours. You'd not know from the front of the premises. Perhaps they'd put in a freight entrance around the back somewhere.

Matlock went around the house, taking the far side from the cafe and farm shop. A slim gap between a high fence and the wall. Barely enough room to bring your bins out. The passageway led to a courtyard, marked out for parking. The yellow lines were faded, cracked, intermittent. Across the courtyard, a building that might once have been stables. The old brick wall had been retained, but the rest of the building was standard cladded warehousing. Floodlights illuminated the periphery of the building; only every other light was on.

From here, there was quiet. The voiceless tone of electricity aside, no sounds. The farmhouse masked any traffic noise from the A16.

No cars in the courtyard. Matlock crossed to the warehouse. Took a look down the length of the building. The warehouse led in turn to two lower buildings, their rooves maybe only eight feet off the ground. Battery runs for egg farming. No movement; no cars.

Okay then.

Matlock went back to the farmhouse.

No lights on inside.

He didn't like that. If you were holding someone, then you'd have guards there, surely. They wouldn't have locked Joe in a windowless room overnight. Or would they?

Matlock opened his rucksack. Took out the tape. Tore off lengths, sticking them to a windowpane. All but covered the glass.

There was an alarm box up high. A blinking red light asserted its functionality. Didn't matter. Out here, the alarm response time would be in the tens of minutes. He'd be long gone.

They'd be long gone.

Matlock put the torch to the taped window. Butted it with the heel of his palm. The glass cracked. Matlock pushed on through, and the window gave way. It sounded loud.

Matlock waited. No response. He leaned into the empty space; found the catch. Pushed the window up. Threw the bag inside, and scrambled in after.

A kitchen, long converted to canteen use. Microwave. Health and safety posters. Noticeboard with a cleaning rota. Mugs upended on the draining board. Catering drums of instant coffee, whitener, tea bags. Ceramic tub marked for sugar. Bread bin and biscuit tin.

Matlock turned the light on. The room faced back; the light wouldn't be visible from the road.

Okay. In and out.

No sounds of movement. The back door had been replaced for fire safety purposes. A simple push of the bar across its midriff would open it. No one had padlocked it up.

Matlock swept through the ground-floor rooms. Storerooms, toilet and an office. Looked like they did a decent mail-order business with hampers, gift baskets and the like.

Stairs up. Nothing moved. The house had that empty feeling.

Matlock's guts tensed.

Upstairs. Landing. Bathroom. Still had the bath with shower over. The big bedroom at the front was a makeshift boardroom. Flowery wallpaper and ordinary corporate furniture. Bedroom two was more storage. Old stock. Christmas remainders.

Bedroom three. 'Joe?'

Nothing.

Matlock tried the door. Locked. 'Joe?'

No sound.

The door gave in on the second kick.

A single bedroom. A camp bed, folded out for use. Sleeping bag. The curtains had been drawn, and then sheets of plywood had been screwed into place behind. It'd look like an ordinary enough room from the outside.

A mug, plate, some crumbs. Sandwich and a brew at some point. Several days earlier. The remains of the tea told the tale.

Joe wasn't here. Hadn't been here for days.

He'd been lied to.

But Joe had been here. Or someone had. Then moved.

What to do?

This was the only lead he had. Joe was here somewhere. Put here over the weekend, when the offices were not being used, then shifted again before Monday morning. Further away from curious eyes.

Where?

Somewhere onsite. Had to be.

Okay then.

Matlock went back downstairs. Opened the fire door. Crossed the courtyard and ran along the warehouse wall. Went to the first of the roller-shutters. A space big enough to back in an articulated lorry. A side door. A safety-glass window; hatched with wires to prevent it blowing in or out. The wood surrounding the window was old. Layers of green gloss covering the signs of rot.

Matlock used the butt of the torch. He attacked the frame around the window. It buckled, then gave way. Matlock pushed the window to make a gap big enough to get a hand through. Found a bolt. Drew it backwards.

Matlock held the torch down so that its beam wouldn't be cast too far.

It's not the light that draws the attention; it's the movement.

A loading area. A small office. Forklifts at their charging stations. A turntable for wrapping finished goods. Spindles of pallet-wrapping plastic film. A working area for warehousemen; job sheets, a nudie calendar from a tyre company. Miss February, nineteen, stared back down the camera lens.

Racking for pallets. Not much; space maybe for fifty. Then a stack of empty pallets, storage for other packaging materials. Cardboard sheets. Labels and marker pens. Boxes of parcel tape and dispenser guns.

The warehouse went on. Swing doors: scratched plastic above, rubberised material below. This was a finishing area. Goods onward only. The main warehouse was beyond.

Matlock checked this zone first. To be certain. Not only was Joe not there, there was nowhere where he could have been.

Work through the buildings. First this, then the battery farms. Rule out the possibilities. Work with what's left if that's what needs to be done.

Matlock tried to focus on the here. The now. He pushed the dividing doors apart. Cut through into the main warehouse.

Tankers. Two tanker trailer units. The kind used for fuel transportation. Spaces between them for vehicles to pull up. Tyre marks and fuel spillage stains leading to roller-shutters out.

The smell of diesel; not unpleasant.

The tankers were connected via hoses to pumps. You could pull up, fill your lorry, pull out.

Big business.

Discounted fuel for hauliers. Free money for those with a legitimate reason to buy virtually tax-free agricultural red diesel. Pay the right people off to deflect those wondering what an egg farm was doing with the thousands of gallons of fuel it was buying.

No one gets hurt except the taxman, right?

Your only problem was how to hide the money.

Amusement arcades. Takeaways. Launderettes. Betting shops. All the cash-intensive businesses you could think of. A set of books for the government, and a set to itemise the truth.

It took five minutes to check the corners. No hidey-holes, except for a lean-to acting as another office. It was unlocked. Paperwork. Fuel in and out. No mention of money. You wouldn't leave that lying around. Somewhere there was a ledger. It travelled in a bag with a lockbox. In the box, that day's takings. Bigger clients might have something more complex; a more formalised set-up. Invoices for fictitious goods. Hampers bought as corporate gifts, or whatever it might be.

But no Joe.

The battery farm was next.

Matlock's innards hadn't yet unclenched.

*

The door wasn't even locked. A latch held it shut, like it was the entry to a suburban greenhouse.

Matlock was expecting hard lighting, heat, the din of thousands of pecking and squawking birds. Racks of cages. The ammonia stink of industrial quantities of guano. Maybe the rattle of conveyor belts: feed being brought to imprisoned hens, eggs trundling down a line to be packed.

Nothing. Like the house, the shed felt empty.

It had been a battery farm. Once. Perhaps years ago. There were cages and walkways, runs of lights and hoppers for feed. But no chickens. No industry.

Nothing.

The farmhouse and the shop were set dressing. At some point in the past, a little diesel swindle had taken root; had made the need to farm eggs redundant.

Matlock found a bank of switches. Turned enough of the lights on to illuminate the length of the space.

He checked. Nothing and no one.

It was the same with the second battery building. A ghost of a farm. There were signs of some recent activity: part of the old cage system housing the birds had been removed and the scrap metal had been sorted into different skips. The cleared area had been swept out. Some fresh electrical work was in evidence. They'd found a new use for this place. Maybe the plan was to extend the diesel scam.

What there wasn't was anywhere that could have held a man, let alone evidence that someone had been kept here.

Matlock exited.

He walked back the length of the site to the courtyard. A vehicle was parked there.

A black estate car, the rear windows tinted dark. A discreet security firm logo on the front door. On the tinted-out rear opening.

Voices from inside the farmhouse-cum-office. Two males. Laughter; workmates at ease.

If they were deep enough inside the offices, then Matlock would be able to get to his van before they got out.

He took out the knife. Pushed the button forwards that exposed the blade, locking it into position.

Keeping low, Matlock got to the car. Cut deep into the passenger side front tyre. He sawed a curve in the rubber mimicking the arc of the wheel alloys. Did the same to the passenger side rear tyre. The rubber sighed. The car sagged.

Now, Matlock ran round the building – this time taking the other way around past the shop, children's play area and tea rooms – to his van.

He didn't see the second car until it was too late.

A Range Rover. Black, again. Personalised plates. Parked by Matlock's van on the driver side, so on the far side, away from the house. Three numbers, then two initials. An L and a C.

Liam Corrigan.

Corrigan stepped out from the dark side of the van. Something in his hand. Something heavy-looking, which was already being swung.

*

It felt as though only seconds had passed. Matlock was on the ground. He was cold. Three men standing around him. Red and green sprites danced when he blinked.

Liam Corrigan and two he didn't know.

'He with us?'

'Yeah.' Corrigan got down on his haunches. 'I'm amazed. Amazed you've not found him yet.'

Matlock tried to speak, but his jaw wasn't working properly.

'Shh. Save it. Can't have you too damaged before tomorrow.'

Matlock tried to get up, but Corrigan swept his arm away with the thing he'd used as a club. It looked like a hockey stick, only shorter.

'See you at the cattle market. And sort out those wheels of yours. Your van stinks.' A sound more like a bark than a laugh. Corrigan kicked Matlock in the side; just a distraction. Matlock didn't see the thing that wasn't quite a hockey stick come down on him again.

And again.

There might have been a fourth time.

Matlock might have dreamed it.

*

Maybe twenty minutes had passed. It could have been forever since he'd last been upright.

Matlock got up. Swept gravel from his palms. Felt his chin. His jawline. There didn't seem to be any blood. But his head felt odd; like he'd been held underwater. Ears clogged, refusing to pop.

That stick Corrigan had used on him. Short and vicious. Surprisingly heavy. Wide at the business end.

Matlock had seen them before. Maybe on television. It'd come to him.

No sign of the Range Rover. He assumed the black estate was back in the courtyard.

He felt alone.

What was it that Corrigan had said? Something about the van. About being amazed.

Matlock picked up the rucksack. It was open; had been searched but left behind. He had nothing of interest to them.

It was not even half past seven, Thursday night.

Matlock got back into the cab. The step up to the driver's seat stretched him in ways he didn't like. His intestines were still twisted from their anticipation of finding or not finding Joe.

Breathe. Sit there. Red and green flecks still wobbled at the reaches of his vision. Give it five minutes. Close your eyes. Head back. You've been beaten up before. It'll pass.

Five more minutes.

That smell.

Jesus, no.

Some vans allow the driver or passenger to peer over their seats to the back. Sometimes there's nothing behind at all, in other models, there's a partition, often as not with a small window. This van had neither. A metal bulkhead between cab and cargo. Matlock got out of the van. Took the keys out of the ignition. One started the engine. The other didn't. This was the key now between Matlock's thumb and index finger.

He put the key into the lock. Turned. Pulled the handle to unlatch the mechanism. The door cracked open. That smell followed.

A scent like damp, but not. Autumnal, like wet leaf mulch and wild mushrooms. Rotten timbers, stagnant water.

Roadkill.

A bundle to the right-hand side of the cargo area. One end by the wheel arch. Five and a bit feet long. Maybe a foot and a bit diameter. Swaddled. Wrapped in who knew how many layers of plastic.

The rational part of Matlock's brain told him there was no need to rush.

He got the retractable knife from the rucksack. The interior lights in the cargo compartment weren't up to much.

He fetched the torch too.

Flies. Little ones. Fruit flies. Or not.

Matlock put the tools down. Reached in. As gently as he could, he pulled the bundle towards the van opening.

A cocoon. The static adhesion of pallet wrap. There were two kinds. Shrink wrap went around the goods; you heated it up with a gun attached to a gas bottle to get the plastic to retract to size. The other sort – this kind – was simply an industrial variant of the stuff used for covering leftovers for the fridge.

The plastic was wrapped in enough layers to make the package look off-white.

You know what this is.

This is merely a confirmation.

No surprises.

Matlock – with care – cut a line down the length of the chrysalis as far as he dared. Peeled the plastic back. Saw what he had to see. Then he folded the shrink wrap back into place. Moved the body enough to be certain that it wouldn't be struck by the closing door.

It.

He.

Joe.

Matlock locked the van up.

Got back into the cab.

Didn't drive off.

*

It took time for the shakes to dissipate. For his ear to clear. Only when he was confident of being able to operate the van again did Matlock get moving.

That rational bit of his head had been working. A pathway became clear. A to-do list presented itself.

*

Joe had been dead maybe four days. Rigor mortis had been and gone. What was left was readying itself for decomposition. New life – the insect kind – was beginning to thrive. Pink foam at the mouth. Swelling in the torso indicating that gases were building up. The second law of thermodynamics doing its thing.

Only the shrink wrap was holding Joe together.

Matlock didn't think that Joe had suffered. The head had flopped; his neck had been broken. Some bruising indicated that the injury wasn't post mortem. Someone strong had taken him, and had put the old man in a headlock. Had twisted. And then had dragged the body to get wrapped.

*

Matlock found himself outside a phone box. One of a pair: one was out of order, the other engaged. The occupant – a man in a dinner jacket – was gabbling, their half of the conversation running against their lack of change. They got cut off. Tried to exit the cubicle with anger but the weight of the phone box door prevented that. He grunted something anyway towards Matlock.

Matlock didn't hear what he said.

He dialled Chris. The pickup took forever.

'The van,' Matlock said.

'What van?'

'My van.'

'What about it?'

'Whose idea was the van?'

'Not mine. I didn't think I'd given Mark enough for anything more than the most basic wheels.'

'When was that?'

'When was what?'

'When you spoke with Mark.'

'You alright? You sound off.'

'When was it?'

'Saturday. Matlock–'

The phone had already been replaced on its cradle.

*

Matlock drove out to Welton. The garage site was dark. A light on in the living accommodation over what had once been the filling station shop.

Matlock parked by the rusting pumps. Took the torch with him.

The lights went off upstairs.

The shop door was flimsy. But obvious. Matlock went around the side that didn't have the compound full of pallets and used cars.

A workshop; shuttered and padlocked. There'd be a way in around here somewhere. And a way out too.

A door, opening. The sound was low but distinct. Someone attempting stealth.

Matlock waited in the dark.

Movement; someone coming closer. Matlock brought the torch up to shoulder height.

The sound of motion ceased. Breathing; a smoker's huffing. Matlock readied himself for the inevitable rush.

Mark stepped sideways from around the corner of the building. Something hefty held in two hands.

There are options for dealing with a long gun. One is to step inside the radius of the weapon. Two, to deflect the barrel. Down or up are riskier than left or right if you're on your own; you're taller than you're wide. Besides. Most people expect a rifle or shotgun to kick, so they're braced for upward movement. Lateral, not so much.

Matlock swept sideways, knocking the barrel towards the wall. Then he stepped in.

The gun went off. One barrel. Light and smoke and brick chippings. Matlock brought his arm back. The torch connected. Mark's head went with it. The gun fell.

The second blow was harder than the first. It came down on the back of the neck. Mark grunted. Wobbled forwards.

Matlock put his foot down on the stock of the gun. Didn't want that getting picked up.

'Alright,' Mark grunted. He held his hands up, palms out. 'Alright.'

'Try anything and I'll finish the job.'

'I said alright, didn't I?'

Matlock picked up the gun. Pushed Mark back the way he'd come. 'Inside. Try something. Do it.'

'Fuck that.'

Matlock shoved the mechanic inside. A storeroom, racked out with shelving. Dusty boxes of old car parts. Tins of paint. Most of a lawnmower. A pull-cord for a light; greasy to the touch. A strip light buzzed. Spasmed. Kicked into life.

There was a single chair. A stool, with a swivel seat. A machineminder had perched here. Had watched the production line, shifting only when there was an interruption to the throughput.

Matlock gestured with the barrel.

Mark did what he was told.

A desk adjacent to the stool. Pads for writing out invoices. Stained mugs. An upturned hubcap serving as an ashtray. Flecks of loose baccy.

Matlock checked the desk drawers while Mark sat there. Filched stationery. A ball of rubber bands. Foreign coins. Unopened mail. Handkerchiefs. A hairbrush. Trophies taken from a dozen repair jobs. Something from the glove compartment for his trouble.

Nothing to worry about.

Matlock put the mouth of the shotgun to the back of Mark's head.

'Shit. Fuck. Fuck, man. Stop it!'

Wait.

'Jesus. I mean it. I only did what I was told.'

Matlock shifted the gun. Nuzzled the curly hairs at the top of Mark's neck. The pellets would pass through his spinal cord, vomiting out the other side, taking his teeth with them.

All it would take was a squeeze.

Matlock tightened on the trigger.

The tension must have translated down the barrel. 'They came. Not long after I'd got back from Big Chris's. Saturday, teatime-ish. Maybe a bit later. Told me what to do. Give you the keys. That was it. Make sure you got the white van.'

'Did you see what they put in it?'

'No. I didn't. Didn't even know they had put anything in there. Three of them. Held me up in here. One watched me while the others went out into the yard. Came back for the keys. To check it was a runner, they said. In and out in ten minutes. Hundred quid in my hand for my trouble and a promise to burn the fucking place down if I shitted up their present for you.'

'"Present."'

'That's what he called it.'

A nudge with the gun. Say the name.

Resigned. 'Liam Corrigan.'

There were a dozen different types of cable the mechanic could have been tied up with. 'Hands behind your back.'

'What are you going to do?'

'Shut up a minute.' Matlock looped electrical cable around the wrists. Tied it tight.

'Fuck.'

Then Matlock took a roll of duct tape. Swathed the cable. Already,

Mark's hands were pink where his circulation had been impeded. 'Onto the floor. Kneel.'

If he was going to try something stupid, it would be now. Make a run for the exit. Charge the other way, into the building. Find a way to cut himself free. Or else he'd go for the headlong approach. Try to headbutt him, knock the gun away. Kick him to the ground. Matlock stepped back. Kept the gun aimed at the man's head.

Mark slid off the stool. Stood. Bent his knees. Tried to sell his submission.

Except why would he get onto the ground? It was all over if he went to the floor. There was nothing to lose in giving something a try.

Matlock was ready when the movement came. Mark lashed out with his right boot. Aiming for Matlock's shins. Upset him enough to give a chance at bundling him over.

Matlock stepped back again. The boot flashed past. The disconnect put Mark off balance. Having his hands tied didn't help. Matlock stabbed the gun into his gut.

Mark folded. Matlock brought the barrel up sharp into his jaw. Mark grunted. Wobbled. A third blow: a sideswipe with the gun across the face. Something broke. Mark toppled.

Matlock put the gun out of reach. Went through the man's pockets. Took the keys he found there. Chucked the detritus – rolling papers, a lighter, a stump of chewy mints – away.

Mark's stubble was smeared with blood. Ooze from mouth and nose. A welt across the cheek already forming.

'Stay down.'

Matlock used cable and tape to secure Mark's ankles. Then he linked the wrists and ankles together with more cable. Tied that off, bringing his feet up behind his body.

'Which one of these opens the compound?'

'Fuck you.'

That earned a foot over the face. Matlock shifted his weight. Allowed Mark to scream.

'Which one?'

'He'll kill you.'

'Which?' Stamp. 'One?'

'Fuck. Blue tag. The blue one! Where are you going? Fucking–'

Matlock grabbed his torch on the way out. Circled around to the padlocked yard. Opened up. Swung the gates wide.

Stacks of pallets arranged by size, by quality. A separate section where damaged stock was being cannibalised for repair or to make whole ones from bits of old. A corrugated shack; a workshop. Base of operations. Then a run of cars. Cheap runabouts mostly. Easy to steal. Easy to fix. Easy to sell on. And what Matlock was looking for. That had to be here somewhere.

He had options. A low-loader, big enough for the job. A smaller truck with a winch. Matlock went for the low-loader. Keys were on the same ring as the padlock for the compound. He started up, moved the low-loader forwards. Drove it out onto the forecourt, and parked it away from the van.

Then back into the compound. The same car he'd taken from Lincoln. A key was in a new ignition system. The window had been replaced. The plates looked different, but Matlock couldn't remember what they had been first time around. He drove this out of the yard too.

Mark had been busy. Had shuffled against one of the runs of shelving in the storeroom. Got himself to a seated position. His face was a mess. One eye socket might have been broken. What had been an impact bruise from the gun had spread across half of his face. Like he had been stung by something huge and septic.

His breathing was shallow, fast. Moving had been a struggle. 'Now what?'

'Phone.'

'Through there.' Into the shop in the front. Matlock found the telephone. Followed the wire to its socket. Took the stock of the shotgun to it. Four strikes were enough. Plastic and wires, corrupted. Matlock checked the receiver anyway. There was no dial tone.

*

Back in the storeroom. Among the car parts and old stock there were flammables. Turpentine substitute. Paint thinners. An old paraffin dispenser, maybe a third full. Matlock kicked the container over. It had a pink cartoon character on its front. The contraption leaked its contents, darkening the floor.

Matlock looked about. Found the lighter. Made sure it sparked okay. It did.

'What you doing?' A thickness to Mark's voice now. Maybe he'd bitten his tongue. Perhaps his jaw didn't work right.

'Making good on a promise. To burn the fucking place down.'

Matlock unscrewed the paint thinners. Threw the liquid over Mark. Mark stumbled back against the racking. Something fell from a top shelf. Glass shattered. Bulbs maybe.

Mark roared. Head down, he tried to charge Matlock. Had forgotten he was tied. Flailing, he hit the ground. 'Uh.'

Matlock stood over. Emptied the bottle onto the man. Let it fall.

'Please.'

Matlock opened the turps substitute. A strong, clean scent. It would purge.

He had everything he needed.

Almost.

He found a bit of rag. Stained with a lifetime of solvents. Tore it in two. Matlock lit one half. Dropped it at the edge of the pool of paraffin.

He took the shotgun, the turps substitute and the rest of the cloth with him. Closed the door behind. Tuned the shouting out.

Matlock got into the car and drove it off the forecourt. Went down the road towards Loweth. After about two hundred yards, there was a gated access to a field. Matlock unhooked the rope keeping the gate closed, and drove the car off the road. Parked it behind the hedge. It was well hidden enough. And far enough from the garage.

He walked back to the old filling station. The ground floor was alight. With the fire at the back of the building, the glow through the old shop windows looked almost homely.

Matlock went into the compound. Stuffed the torn rag into the turps bottle. Wedged the bottle into a tower of pallets. Lit the fabric wick. By the time he'd shut the gates, the resin smell of wood burning was around him.

Keep going. Don't think; do. There'll be time later.

He dropped the ramp on the low-loader. Gentle as he could – it was, after all, a hearse now – Matlock drove the van onto the loader. Secured it into place. Started the loader up. Drove away, a bonfire at his back.

*

He was back maybe an hour later. It wasn't yet eight. Ahead, there were fire engines. There was a fire.

Matlock parked the now empty low-loader in the field. Wiped down the surfaces he'd touched, on the inside and the out. Took the gun and put it in the car. After backing out of the field and closing the gate behind him, Matlock pulled out onto the road. He turned right so he would drive past Mark's place. Or what was left of it.

Three fire engines. Lights. A police car. An ambulance. Paramedics. A handful of the curious. A copper urging lollygagging motorists on.

The fire in the house was all but out. The compound burned like a castle at the end of a siege.

The policeman waved Matlock by, so he shifted past, then took the back roads into Loweth.

*

The caravan site was quiet. Nothing going on in the office block. A handful of lights in different caravans. Curtains closed. Telly flicker.

Matlock cleared the caravan out of anything personal. Not much left. He supposed it was the bottle of Scotch that he wanted. He took a glass too. A stubby thing like a rinsed-out chocolate spread jar.

Keep moving. Forward momentum.

Do it till it's done.

Yapping. The dog from next door. An old man's chuntering.

Matlock got out of there. This was no time for a neighbourly conversation.

*

Matlock parked up. His hands were spasming. His face felt red with fury and with withheld tears.

He got out of the car. He found himself on the far side of the industrial estate. A junction leading to a road that hadn't been built yet. Signs said there were options for units of all sizes.

He wanted to scream, but nothing came.

Wanted to cry, but it was like his ducts were blocked.

Wanted the crushing grip around his chest to shatter his ribs and spear his heart a dozen times.

He wanted.

Joe.

The mechanic, screaming.

Joe.

Hot fuel, igniting.

The stale smell of flesh, corrupt. Of life denied.

He must have cried. Because after, his face was crisp with dried residue, two men's deaths smeared on his hands.

*

It took a while for someone to answer the door at the nursing home. Matlock propped the gun he'd taken from the garage out of sight. Eventually, an orderly showed. Pressed a switch behind the desk. The lock clicked.

Matlock went straight for the signing-in book. Kept his head down. Wasn't sure how he looked. 'Thanks.'

The orderly was already leaving. Raised a hand in acknowledgement. Disappeared between double doors into another part of the premises.

Alone in the reception area. Matlock used the signing-in pen and a pad by the telephone to write a message. There were pigeonholes on the wall behind the desk for post. Most had room numbers. These would be for residents. The bottom row was marked for different departments. Kitchen. Accounts. Management. Reception. The note went in the last of these slots.

Matlock went back to the front door and opened it. Reached around and fetched out the shotgun. Went to pay a visit.

*

Business as usual down the corridor. Another orderly with a trolley. Matlock kept the gun under his jacket. It poked out down his leg, but people saw what they expected to see. Eye contact, a smile. Keep them looking at your face. Upset relatives would be ordinary here.

He might as well not have bothered. An alarm was sounding from the far end of the hallway. The reflection of a flashing red light in pictures down the corridor. Someone had pressed their panic button. The orderly went off, saying loudly – not shouting – that they were coming. Exasperation as much as concern.

Old Mrs Minton was asleep in her room. Looked better than the day before. Fuller in the face, less dry skin on the lips. She'd been awake, taken fluids. There were two empty cartons of mocha flavour food supplement milkshake in the bin. Today's newspaper. The local one from Grimsby. Loweth's only came out weekly. The crossword had been attempted. The quick clues, not the cryptic ones. The puzzle had been left abandoned.

A jug of orange cordial, half-full. Matlock was suddenly thirsty. Poured a beaker of the stuff. Drank. It wasn't bad. None of the synthetic sweet-then-bitter tang of what they'd served inside. He refilled the cup.

The cord on the phone was long enough for it to be brought over to the chair. Matlock rang the number he had got from Chris. Waited for the call to be picked up.

The orange was a childhood flavour. Gulped glasses of Quosh or Kia-Ora between halves of football. His boots were from Woolworths. Moulded plastic studs, not the metallic screw-in sort you got on the branded ones from the sports shop.

He'd got big young, so as often as not he played in goal. An old pair of keepers' gloves. Light blue, with Velcro at the wrists to keep them tight. They were padded with the same rubbery material that covered table tennis bats. It stung every time he caught the ball.

'Hello?' The voice was rough. Male. Not young. Pitched between curious and surly.

'Put Roy on the phone.'

'No Roy here. You've got the wrong number.' Noises in the background. Blokey chatter. A fruit machine. Ice on glass.

'Put him on.'

'Who is this?'

'Joe Matlock's son.'

A hand went over the receiver; sound cut out. Then: 'Give me a number he can ring you back on. Be a couple of minutes.'

Matlock read the digits off the label on the phone.

'Two minutes, yeah?'

Matlock hung up.

Quiet. The alarm had been cut off at some point. The old woman slept on.

The phone rang. Matlock let it. Picked it up on the fifth ring.

'Mister Matlock.'

'Mister Minton.'

'This isn't something that can wait until tomorrow, I take it?'

'No.'

'What is it then?'

'It's a conversation we should have face to face.'

'Alright. Where are you?'

Matlock told him.

Silence.

Eventually: 'How is she?'

'Asleep. Looks peaceful.'

'Let's keep it that way. Give me fifteen minutes. See if you can't rustle up a couple of brews in the meantime.'

Matlock stashed the shotgun in the wardrobe. Went back down the hall to the television lounge. There was a small kitchen set-up in the far corner. A sink and taps, a fridge. Kettle and microwave. It looked like the room doubled as a staff crash pad on quiet night shifts.

There was instant coffee and a catering pack of tea bags. Sugar and whitener. There was milk in the fridge too. Foil-wrapped butties. A collection tin for donations to the hot beverage fund. Matlock put some change in. Enough to cover the cost of two teas.

He took his time. Boiled a kettle. Made tea in two plain green mugs that looked institutional enough not to be any individual staff member's pride and joy. Couldn't remember if Minton had put sugar in his drink or not at the fairground. Put one spoonful in to be on the safe side. Carried the drinks back to the room.

Matlock went back to the lounge. Took a kitchen chair from under its table. Brought it to the room. He placed the chair where he wanted Minton to be sat.

There was a bag in the bottom of the wardrobe. The cupboard itself was all but empty. Someone had packed away most of the old woman's clothes.

There were no pairs of shoes in the room. Not even slippers.

Not a good set of signs.

Matlock sat in the chair by the bed. Leaned the shotgun against the raised side. Sipped his tea. On the whole, he preferred the orange.

*

Minton showed up ten minutes later. He knocked and entered, like he was going into his boss's office. His eyes went first to the bed. Then to Matlock. Then back to the bed. To its occupant. 'You better not have touched her,' he said, soft.

'Had a glass of her squash. That's all. She's been sleeping. Your tea's there. Sit down.'

'Why here?'

'How else to get your attention?'

A pause. Minton sampled his drink. It had cooled enough to take a mouthful. 'Okay. So you have it. What's all this about?'

'It's about Joe.'

'I've told you. He's as safe as. No harm other than a few days of not much walking, microwave food and telly-induced boredom. You did two years. He can handle a week.' Minton sipped more of his tea. 'Not bad, this.'

Matlock picked up the shotgun.

'Whoa.'

'I want you to get on the phone.'

'You brought a gun in here?'

'The phone.' The room wasn't that big. The shotgun pellets would pass through Minton like a single fat bullet.

Minton acted like this was what happened every Thursday. Maybe it was. 'Who am I ringing?'

'I want a proof of life.'

'Alright. I'm putting my tea down. Carefully.'

Matlock kept the gun on him. 'Pick up the phone.'

Minton did so. Then he dialled a number. There was no hesitation. One of thirty calls made a day. Matlock could hear the distant rattle of the unanswered phone coming down the line.

Minton shrugged. 'Give it a couple of minutes. We'll try again.' Reasonable, accommodating.

'Finish your tea.'

They drank. An orderly scuttled by. Apart from that, the corridor was quiet.

Matlock swallowed the last of his brew. Nodded to Minton. The phone was used to ring out again. It didn't get answered. Eventually, Minton cut the call off. Dialled another number. His expression had changed. He was no longer placatory. He was annoyed. A man who expected his calls to be answered, and who demanded that people were where they were supposed to be.

Nothing. Minton redialled; another different number. This time the phone was picked up almost immediately. 'Liam?'

Matlock only heard one side of the conversation.

'Who's watching Joe Matlock?'

Listening.

'When?'

Another pause for the response.

'That's not what I asked.'

A beat for a reply, soon cut off.

'Jesus.' A glance to Matlock. To the gun. Then attention back on the phone call. 'Jesus Christ. No. Do nothing. Go nowhere. Stay where you are. I'm coming to you. We need to talk. Christ, Liam.

Can't you–' Minton chopped the hand down on the cradle, killing the conversation before he said anything more.

Minton put the phone back with care. Breathed deep. Sat forward. Rubbed the bridge of his nose with index finger and thumb. Then sat back.

He re-established eye contact. Did not look at the gun. 'You were right to call me,' he said at last. 'And I know this will mean less than nothing to you, but I need to say it anyway. Hear me out. Joe... was a good man. Honourable. Decent. The way he came to me, to offer some service as a token of his... I don't want to use the word. But it was his word.'

'Say it.'

'Shame. He said he was ashamed. And he needed to do something. Something that had meaning. Not to work off your debt, but to deal with his own feelings. I don't know what you're like as a man. Heard some things. Asked some questions. The general opinion of you is that you're someone who does what they say they'll do. Predictable in a good sort of way. Joe, though. Said he couldn't live with himself knowing he'd brought someone into this world who'd taken another man's life. That was his debt. Not to pay for what you'd done. But for what he'd done. For having had you in the first place.

'Now, I don't know how you measure the worth of a man in those sort of terms. But Joe was insistent. Didn't rant or rave, didn't sob or clutch his cap in his hand. But he wouldn't say no. Took him time to get to me, and then more time to get through to me.

'He asked me what he could do. I asked him the same question. That got us to the fairground organ.

'All I asked was that he be held. In quiet and in comfort. Three meals a day. Telly and a book if that's what he wanted. And on Friday I'd have gladly let him go.

'Because he didn't owe me. You owed me, Daniel Matlock. You did then, and you do now.

'There'll be a reckoning. I don't care if you understand that I'm a man of my word in my own way or if you don't. But I tell you this. This will not go unpunished. But you have to let me deal with this.

'And,' Minton said, leaning forward again, hands on his thighs, 'like I said, I am sorry.'

The walls were closer than they had been. The ceiling had been lowered. The tiling somehow raised. The window – curtains still open, showing blackness outside – bulged inwards.

Matlock needed to get out of here.

'Put the firearm away, son. Pop the breech. There's no need for any nonsense going off here.'

Matlock's armpits fizzed with perspiration. His scalp writhed like he was infested. Ten thousand crawling, biting, burrowing, egg-laying things.

Keep it together.

Keep it together.

'I don't know if I can promise that, Roy.'

Almost a smile. Making the most of a sad inevitability. 'I know, lad. But you'll get your opportunity. Tomorrow.'

'Tomorrow.'

'In the auction ring in the beast market. Leave matters till then. It'll be you and Liam. Equally motivated, I suppose.'

'You think?'

A back-pedalling. Graceful, but cautious, nevertheless. 'Poor choice of words, maybe. Sorry. But you see what I mean. Just you and him. Take it out on each other. This has been a long time coming, and it can't be stopped.'

'I suppose not.'

'Beautiful, isn't she?' Roy was looking into the bed.

'Tell me about her.'

'My mother, long gone. Was never much of a… a homebody. Too busy trying to outpace the menfolk. Liked a drink. Loved a fight. Cared for us, but only as playthings. You know how people without kids of their own talk to children?'

'Like they're little adults.'

'That was us with her. Junior members of a gang. I'm not saying it wasn't fun, but there's more than good times when you're a little 'un. You need someone to wash you. Someone to tell you good and proper when you've done wrong or messed up. Someone to be there in the night when you can't sleep but for the monsters. That was where Nanna here stepped in.'

'She sounds special.'

'She was. Is, I suppose. But that person's gone. Bless her, she's a sack of sticks waiting for the rag and bone man to come calling. She's ninety-eight. Won't get her telegram though. She'd have liked that. Fond of the royals, she was. Is.'

'Soon, they reckon.'

'I should have visited more. It's hard, though. Not easy when there's no one to know you were even there any more. Might even have kept her longer in the other place, from back when she was with us. But there wasn't any point, except in flashing the money as though the extra cash spent meant that you cared more. Smart of you to think to meet me here. How did you know?'

'Prison talk.'

'There's not much else to do, is there?'

'Done some time yourself?'

Roy nodded. 'Handling stolen goods. A year. I hadn't done it, but by that time I'd done that much wrong that it only seemed fair taking a light tap on the chin. Besides, it meant that there was a favour owed.'

'And you were blooded.'

'That too. It counts for something. Taking your medicine. Not rolling over for a consideration.'

'It's nobody's business but ours.'

'Yeah,' Roy said. 'Cops are only for straight people.'

This was prison lore. 'Look out for each other. Look out for ourselves. Don't kick the rocks.' All kind of filth could come crawling out.

Matlock broke the shotgun open. Extracted the live cartridge. Pocketed it. Wiped the weapon down with tissues from a pack of moistened cloths left behind from mealtime clean-ups. Laid the gun on the floor. Stood.

'Daniel.' Roy held his hand out.

'Roy.' Minton's palm was dry, his grip secure. Two firm shakes, then he was let go.

'Don't leave. Wait. A moment.'

Matlock was in the doorway. The corridor was clear. Snoring. Telly sounds.

Minton had moved. He was standing over the old woman. 'Not long, they say?'

'Might stay the weekend, might not.'

Minton made a face. Deliberation; decision. 'I meant what I said about Joe. He should never have been treated with such disrespect. As I said, there'll be a reckoning. Whatever I do, though, I can't bring him back.'

Minton leaned into the adult-sized cot in which the old woman slept. With care, took the panic button by its cable and laid it well out of reach. He swept hair free from her forehead. Kissed her above the eyes. Then he smothered her mouth with one hand, pinching her nose with the other.

At first there was no response. Then, blood vessels flared under her linen skin. She convulsed. Spasmed a second time, her arms slapping against the raised sides of the hospital bed. One hand found purchase on a bedsheet, squeezing cloth through bony fingers like dough when kneading.

'Is this what you want?' Minton asked. 'An eye for an eye, after all.'

She tried to raise her head.

'No.'

What was left of her neck muscles strained.

'Hmm?'

'No, Roy.'

The instinct is always for life. Instinct isn't always enough.

'If you're sure.' Minton withdrew his hands.

She breathed. Light, dancing breaths. The tension in her neck faded. She let go of the bedding. The ghost of a handprint on her face; pressure marks rather than lividity.

Kissed her once more, this time on her temple. Her head lolled to one side. She breathed.

Minton looked to Matlock. Wiped his hands clean with another of the cloths. His eyes were dry. 'I'll see you tomorrow. Six. You'll be there. Won't you?'

The handprint was already fading.

'I'll be there.'

Minton sat. 'I'm going to stay a while.'

Matlock left him to it.

*

Matlock drove the car out to where he'd taken the van earlier. The viewing point was empty save for his vehicles. He got out, felt the wind, listened to the sea.

Saltfleet Nook was many things. A nature reserve, noted for its breeding colony of grey seals. The seals congregated here late in the year – October, November, into the final month also – to birth and to suckle their young. The sight of hundreds of pups brought crowds; more each year.

There were rare seagrasses here: a dozen different ferns and other plants found only in a handful of places along the coast. Birdwatching was good year-round. And the beach was also RAF property. Saltfleet Nook was designated an offshore bombing range: a place to see aircraft come in low over the sand chasing the tidelines, dropping ordnance into the sea. Here and there were other signs of military activity from the days when they dropped bombs on the dunes. The corroded masses of decommissioned tanks used for target practice. Concrete bunkers of various designs. Gun emplacements and observation points for exercise use; before that, as part of the defence network for the Humber estuary to the north. Other – odder – shapes persisted against the horizon: experimental reflective structures from echolocation and radar experiments. Matlock didn't know the details.

There was a slipway running downhill from the viewing-point car park to the beach. The sea defences proper started a few miles to the south, towards Mableton. Here, mounded sand and rare grass did what they could.

It was cold enough for Matlock to zip up the army jacket. He got into the van. Started up the engine. Edged towards the slipway. The wheels slipped on the dry sand coating the concrete ramp down through the dune. A bump where the manufactured surface didn't quite meet the beach.

The tide was far out. The beaches all down the east coast from the estuary to the other side of Skeg were wide; the resorts had clustered at the points where the walk to the water was the most manageable. Out here, it was maybe a mile to the water at its furthest-retreated point. There were villages out there. Two or three sites along the coast, where medieval reclamation attempts had been only temporarily successful. Towards Mabo at low tide you could see other evidence of the impermanence of the barrier between saltwater and soil: tree-stump remains of a petrified forest, a last echo of when you could walk from here to Denmark, canopied by the greenwood all the way.

The van shuddered. The engine complained about the softness of the sand. Wheels spun. Matlock rocked between reverse and first. Got it going onward again. He knew he wouldn't be able to get that far out. There was simply too much distance between the dry sand blown up the beach towards the dunes and the more solid matter worn into smooth grooves by the accordion tide. He had to try though.

The beach was empty. The seals had moved on for the year; birds were absent. Headlights made the sand more yellow than it was. Twin streaks of fresh-mixed mustard out into the distant nothing.

Lights ahead. Matlock cut the front beam. Found some comfortable going and let the engine idle. Let his pupils adjust to the fresh reality.

Stars. Intermittent because of partial cloud cover. Along the horizon line, evidence of mankind's working. Ships in the channel to and from the estuary. Gas rigs.

Matlock got out. Checked back to land. He could follow the tyre tracks back, even in the dark. Starlight would be sufficient, and he had that torch somewhere if need be. There was a breeze. Enough to stir loose sand, encouraging a shimmer over the surface.

Evidence of a once-impressive sandcastle to one side. A deep trough had been dug around a central mound. The kids who had made this had taken their design from the Anglo-Saxons. Motte and bailey. Keep the invading buggers out. Smaller piles indicated where plastic buckets had been used during the topping-out ceremony. Shells studded the sides of the mound. An arc indicated a main entrance.

This was good enough.

Matlock reached back into the cab. Took out his bag. Then

retrieved the pair of five-gallon canisters he'd bought earlier. He'd got them at the same time as the petrol inside them. Ten gallons was the most he was allowed to buy; the cashier had insisted. The containers were plastic. Pillar box red.

He took the retractable knife to the seat covers. Cut a length of fabric. Pulled out some foam. Stuck this in a pocket.

He'd taken the precaution also of filling up the fuel tank.

Matlock turned the headlights back on. Moved the stuff he wanted to keep to the far side of the sandcastle. He took the first of the canisters and soaked the cab. He poured petrol over the seats. Into the footwells. The door cards. In the space behind the seats. He didn't need all five gallons.

He took the full container to the back of the van. Doused the floor of the cargo section. Poured petrol over Joe's shrink-wrapped body. Said sorry as he did so. Then he walked around the van, sloshing fuel over each of the tyres. He splashed more up the sides. Over the windscreen.

Matlock opened the fuel cap.

He put the second fuel container – still about a quarter-full – in the back of the cargo bay. Pushed the door to, but did not close it.

With a heel, Matlock dragged a gutter in the sand from the van to where the children had been playing. Ran petrol down this new channel. Finished with a swirl of fuel around the moat. Then he threw the empty can back towards the van. It bounced off the sliding side door. Lay on the beach, dribbling out its last.

Matlock checked himself. Fire is capricious. It lives to burn. He was as sure as he could be that he didn't have petrol on him.

He found the Talisker. Opened the bottle. Took a swig. Held it in his mouth.

Two years.

Long time.

That clean taste. Astringent, antiseptic. Another of those childhood associations: Dettol or TCP on grazed knees. He swallowed.

The rush of the pure burn down the throat and into the gut. His eyes prickled. Now he sprinkled whisky on the fabric he'd torn off the seat. Put the bottle down safe in soft sand. Lit the wick he'd made.

Matlock dropped the burning cloth into the moat. Stepped back as it twisted downwards. It hit the wet sand. A circle of flame in an instant. Then a racing line conjured itself across the space to the van.

The tyres caught first. Individual spirals of grey-black smoke conjoined. Then the cab. The van was alive with flame. The smell of manufactured materials, burning. Plastic and nylon and rubberised compounds.

Matlock drank.

Flames jumped from wheel arches to the cargo section. First, a glow from inside the boxy van, then a single flat clap. The petrol canister exploding.

Whisky, again.

Then the van caught. Like the end of a match viewed close up. From spark to single flame in a moment.

Single malt was the only appropriate accompaniment.

The windscreen buckled in the heat, half melting, half falling into the cab. The engine cut out; flames must have severed some part of the fuel supply. In the same breath, the headlights died and the fuel tank gave way.

Matlock felt the force of the burning. Stood against it. Tears dried on his cheeks as the van was consumed.

Joe, mixed with engine oil, petrol, diesel and brake fluid, rose in yellow and blue-grey corkscrews.

Friday

It must have rained; the sand was freckled with darker splotches, turning it from an even brown to something more like camouflage.

It was light, though only just. Sunrise was perhaps half an hour away. Still patchy cloud. Still a breeze.

Matlock sat up. The bottle, beside him, held only dregs. The sand was damp here. Hard to tell how much, if any, of the stain was due to spillage. Or how much had been his drooling stupor.

A long-beaked bird pecked the beach, out towards the waterline. Foam marked the limit of the tide's reach. The water had come in, and was now on its return.

Six, maybe seven o'clock.

Matlock stood. The van was a black skeleton, dropped to its knees. The tyres had either blown out or melted, sinking the vehicle into the sand. The air tasted of rubber, of scorched metal. Of failed industry.

Matlock picked up his bag. He should have brought a bottle of water.

Seabirds swooped along the foreshore. It was still dark enough to have the gas rig lights stand out against the grey.

Matlock turned back to land. His joints were stiff. Lack of vitamin D. That's what the lifers in Lincoln reckoned. Poor diet and not enough sunlight does that to a man. Multivitamins were prized among those who'd dedicated themselves to making the most of prison. Otherwise, the lack of light and decent nutrition would play havoc with your knees.

The ache would walk off.

Matlock swept what sand he could from where he'd slept. He crossed the beach to what the wind had left of the tyre tracks, and followed them back to the viewing point. Somewhere, a horn sounded. Something maritime. There were still ships out in the estuary shipping channel.

A line of red lights jutted over the dunes. A vertical scar. It took ten paces through soft sand for Matlock to work out what it was. The television mast. Melmarsh. Maybe twenty miles away, twenty-five, as the gull might fly when there was a storm over the water.

Matlock walked towards the lights.

*

There was one other car parked up at the viewing point. A chunky Scandinavian estate. Perhaps twenty years old. The back of the car roiled with dogs.

A woman got out of the car. Something in her hand. One of those cups that screws into the top of a Thermos. It was cool enough for steam to be visible. As she exited, there was a din from the dogs, soon cut off with the door closing behind her. 'Morning,' she said.

'Morning.'

'Usually it's only me up here at this time of day. Coffee?'

'Um. Yeah.' Matlock gathered himself. 'Yes. Thanks.'

The woman smiled. Went back into the estate and fetched out a flask and a second cup. A beaker that fitted inside the one she was using for her own drink. 'White, no sugar is all I've got, I'm afraid.'

'Anything's good.'

The woman poured Matlock a cup. The flask was old enough for its tartan pattern to have worn away where it had been held. The woman – zipped-up fleece inside open wax jacket, jeans inside green Hunters, hair tied back, maybe sixty – held out the drink.

'Thanks.'

'Pleasure.' She moved around to the bonnet. Perched on the end of the car. Matlock put down his bag. Joined the woman.

Black specks along the fresh-exposed sand, still dark from the water's touch.

'Dunlins,' the woman said. 'The smaller ones. The larger ones are godwits. There'll be two breeds out there. Black-tailed and bar-tailed. That's how you tell them apart: by the plumage.'

'I don't know much about seabirds.'

'Me neither. Least, I don't know as much as I ought. Coming here every day, I thought it best to learn a little. I started with the signs over there. Took it up with books from that point.' A run of tourist information boards, angled like low pulpits, stood nearby. One for seagrasses, one for birds, one for butterflies. 'There's a pair of binoculars in the wagon.'

Matlock didn't know what to say.

'Two years now. More or less. That's when I moved here. My husband died. Testicular. At first. I'd been on at him to go to the GP, but he said that it was just work and he was tired, that was all. But sometimes you know, don't you? I think we both did. Three months from diagnosis to funeral. He always was organised. Anyway, this was in London. What with the insurance and his work pension, and what there was to come out of the house, there was more than enough to move away. Somewhere quiet. Somewhere where the streets weren't paved. The idea was to write a book. I've got a dozen first few pages. By that time I'd got my first. Sasha. Japanese akita. Rescue dog. We'd come out here this time of day. The idea was that an hour of walking and playing fetch would get the ideas rolling downhill. Turned out that all it made me want to do was walk dogs and play fetch. So that's what we do. Near as I can make it, morning, noon and night. An hour this time of day, then back for scrambled eggs on toast. A bowl of soup one-ish, and then out here again. And back between six and seven. Maybe earlier in the winter, later in the summer. Try to catch a sunrise or a sunset every day.' She paused. Offered a refill. Matlock nodded.

'Is that your van?'

'Kind of.'

'Shame. It's made a mess. Still, I daresay you had your reasons.'

'People always have. For the things they do.'

Matlock sipped the refilled coffee. It tasted of hot water and the taint of the flask.

'You sleep on the beach?'

Matlock nodded.

'Must have got cold. Once the fire died down.'

'I suppose.'

'And the Scotch won't have helped.'

'The smell that bad, is it?'

'It's not great.'

Matlock swilled the next mouthful around. The liquid motion

stirred up the dregs of last night's drinking. He winced, and swallowed. He balanced the beaker on the bonnet. Four large dogs watched from through the windscreen. Patient, expectant. 'Thanks. I should be going.'

'Anywhere's a long walk from here.'

'That's my car.' Matlock was grateful that no more questions were asked.

'You sure you're alright to drive?'

'I'll be fine, thanks.'

'Famous last words.'

Matlock put his bag on the back seat of the car. Held a hand up as the woman unloaded her dogs from the tailgate of her estate. She did the same in return. Her hand had a ball in it. Then the ball was thrown down the slipway, the dogs charged after it and the woman turned to close up her car. Matlock was out of the viewing area car park and around the corner on the narrow sandy track that led back to the tarmacked world.

*

There was time to kill. Matlock intended to make use of it. First, though, he stopped to refuel.

The car was low on juice. Matlock went to the station in Saltfleet. Serve yourself hadn't penetrated this far. A kid filled the tank. Ran a squeegee over the windscreen. Matlock asked if there was anywhere open he could get some breakfast. He didn't feel like eating, but that was part of the hangover process. Get it over with. Avoid food now and the hangover would get a second wind mid-afternoon. Hit you like a spanner to the back of the neck and another to the solar plexus simultaneously about three. That was no preparation for a fight.

No, there was nowhere open. Not here. You'd need to go into Mabo.

Paracetamol at least. Aspirin.

Matlock bought two bottles of water and a blister pack of pills. Sluiced down half a strip with most of a pint of water. Took the road south, skirted Mabo and found himself in Sutton.

The cafes didn't open until nine. Matlock went into a newsagent's. Bought a local paper and some bars of chocolate.

The paper was the coastal version of the one that came out weekly in Loweth. The guts of the thing were identical. All that was different was the wraparound layer: the first and last two pages. Feel-good stories about locals' dalliances with national media. A school that might have to close or merge with another if pupil numbers didn't pick up. Rumours about the council cutting funding for that year's illuminations and summer parade.

A train of kids being led to school. A yellow-jacketed lollipop fella. An uptick in traffic. Sutton was little more than a main road snaking around a central play area. Paddling pool. Retro chalets. Tennis courts and coin-operated electric go-karts. By-laws prevented electronic amusements. Cream teas were prized over fish and chips here. Still, there was always breakfast, even if it cost a quid more, came on a square plate and was altogether too formally presented.

Matlock gave it ninety seconds before the first place to open swung its sign over from closed. He ordered and reread the paper while his food was prepared. Double sausage, double bacon, double egg. Toast, grilled tomatoes, mushrooms, black pudding.

No, he didn't want beans.

No, he didn't want the hash browns. And yes, he understood that they didn't do substitutions.

Coffee and orange juice.

The coffee was good, even if it came in a teacup.

When Matlock had been small – six, maybe – Joe had taken him on the bus to Cleethorpes. Cleethorpes is where Grimsby mutates from a fishing port into a seaside resort. Neither big and brash like Skeg, nor punch-drunk like Mabo, nor even with delusions of middle-class respectability like Sutton, Cleethorpes does its own thing, servicing the needs of South Yorkshire in the way that Lincolnshire does for Nottinghamshire and Hookland.

It had been Matlock's birthday, or near enough. He'd spent half his present money in Woolworths. A cowboy cap gun. The small one; the Firecat. He didn't have enough for the big one, and wasn't brave enough to ask for the rest of the money. Besides, he wanted change for the slot machines. Not the bandits, but the horse and car racing ones, where you bet on the outcomes of toys sprinting around mechanical tracks.

By the time they'd got from Grimsby to Cleethorpes, it had started raining. Drizzle had emptied the promenade, but it had ensured that the arcades throbbed with people. An hour on the machines, thumbing coin after coin into the games, and Joe'd had enough. 'You hungry?'

No. Not really. Lunch had been a burger in the Wimpy in Grimsby's shopping centre and then a doughnut served with a piped spiral of soft ice cream. 'Yeah,' Matlock had said. 'Let's go.'

They scurried out of the arcade and along the covered walkway sheltering the kiddie rides from the worst of the weather. Skipped the first of the chippies; too busy because it was the one closest to the seafront. Stopped under the awning over the entrance to the second.

A menu; the usual. And a sign. Black marker pen, in small but firm capitals. NO EXTRA PLATES.

'What's that mean?'

'It means that if four of you go in and only have enough money for three lots of fish and chips, then you can't ask for another plate to share the food out so everyone gets something.'

'Right.'

'Also, it means the owners are arseholes. Let's find somewhere else.'

The thrill of being complicit in his dad's swearing.

There were plenty of other chippies to choose from. They went into one a couple of streets back from the seafront. Big windows clouded with condensation. Another handwritten sign: Frying Skate.

'This'll do,' Joe said.

It was clammy inside. Busy with families and chunky staff with trays of pies and chips. They sat. The tablecloth was under a sheet of glass. Salt, vinegar. A bottle of brown sauce and a squeezy tomato with a dried scab of ketchup at its nozzle.

A waitress came over. 'What'll you have, boys?'

Pot of tea for two. Steak pie and chips; sausage and chips. With beans. Bread and butter.

The tea was another grown-up thing. Other kids in here had fat cups of squash. The bread and butter came out with the drink. White sliced and thick marge. 'Order'll only be a couple of minutes.'

They talked about football. Cars. The rain. About how piers were built, and about the railways that brought the day trippers from Sheffield and Doncaster.

Matlock had watched, enthralled, at how a couple managed with their plates of fried skate wings. He ate his sausage; found he didn't care for the batter so picked most of it off.

'Any puds?'

Good question. 'Can you manage anything?'

Matlock had looked past the waitress. A girl with a bowl of ice cream; a wide slab of Neapolitan. She'd eaten the vanilla strip and was working on the chocolate. Saving the strawberry for last. A man in overalls, an upended sponge pudding in front of him. He was struggling to keep his custard on his plate.

'No thanks. I think I'm full.'

'I'm not surprised neither.'

Joe checked the order slip the waitress had left. Put the right money down, then a bit more. Saw the young Matlock's puzzlement. 'It's what you do,' he said.

They went out. The rain had stopped not long since. Shopfronts ticked with dripping water. They caught a bus back into Grimsby, then killed a half-hour for the connection back to Loweth by wandering around the indoor market. It was late; stallholders don't hang about at the end of the day. A council worker piled discarded boxes. Another swept away soil from under greengrocers' stalls, where loose potatoes had been sold by the pound.

Joe picked up a couple of pieces of fruit: a pear and an apple. 'These look alright to you?'

They looked fine. 'Yeah.'

'They do to me too.' Joe hid them away. 'Come on. Let's get that bus.'

They ate the fruit on the bus on the way back. Matlock had the pear, Joe the apple.

The pear was what Matlock remembered most. It had been a perfect piece of fruit. Sweet, full of juice. Not woody or bland, the way pears too often are. That pear had ruined the fruit for him; he found that they never matched up to that one, stolen from a pile of discards after a wet day by the Humber.

Now.

Matlock found that he had finished his breakfast. Had emptied his drink. The cafe had filled up a bit. At some point, the woman who had served him had left a bill; a scribbled note with a number below the tear-off line.

Matlock couldn't remember eating the food.

He put the right money on the bill. Added a bit extra. And left.

*

Some things to do. Then rest. Then whatever the evening would bring.

Matlock cut through the marsh villages on his way west, then north-west. He shaded Loweth to the north, coming out on the A16 not far from Tom Coton's place. This was where he was going.

Tom was in his yard. When he saw Matlock getting out of his car, he put the tools he was carrying down. Went to a standpipe, and rinsed his hands under the water. Wiped them dry on his overalls.

Matlock stayed by the car.

The honesty box had toppled over. Matlock righted it. There wasn't much on sale today. A few half-dozens of eggs. Three jars of gooseberry jam.

'I should really restock, shouldn't I?'

'I suppose.'

Tom shook the box. It sounded like there were only a few coins inside. He pursed his lips. 'Pickle thieves,' he said. 'The county's full of them.'

'Hi Tom.'

'Dan.'

Matlock's look must have said more than he'd intended it to communicate.

'I'm sorry. I am. I think I knew. The stories they tell about that Corrigan boy. I don't know what to say.'

Matlock shook his head. 'Nothing to say.'

'Come on in out of the cold. There's a kettle needs putting on.'

*

Tom Coton had brewed a pot. Arranged some plum bread on a chopping board. He sat down opposite Matlock, and buttered a slice. 'You should try it.'

'Your niece's?'

'Shop-bought.'

Matlock didn't feel like eating, but it was good to have something other than shaking for his right hand to do. Again, that fizzing feeling of stored-up tension. Like an overcharged battery, desperate to power something. He buttered and ate. Tom was right; it was good. Almost a fruit cake; it smelled Christmassy.

Tom talked for a while. The slow shift of the seasons. Jobs for the spring on the smallholding. Traffic levels on the main road. A problem he was having with a neighbour: nothing bad, just niggling bits of disagreement about whose job it was to cut the grass on which bits of verge and when.

Matlock was grateful for the appreciation from Tom that he didn't have to contribute to the soundtrack. He let Tom go on, until he was out of not much to say.

'What's next, lad?'

Matlock told him.

'And will that be an end of it?'

'It should be. I've had assurances.'

'From Minton himself?'

'Yes.'

'Should be, then. It'll depend, though.'

'On?'

'On what Liam Corrigan's got to say about it.'

'I don't intend him being able to say much about anything.'

'There's a gap between what you want and what you end up with.'

'Yeah.'

'There's no way the two of you can walk away from this.'

'I know.'

'It's not simply a matter of putting the man down. It's keeping him down. You've found Corrigan's not one to follow instructions.'

'No.'

'So you've got to put him down.'

'Yes.'

'There's other options. Not good, but they exist. It's only fair someone should say them out loud. So you can hear what they sound like outside.'

'I'm not going to run.'

'But it's a path open to you. Not one I'd thought you'd take. Nevertheless.'

'What else?'

'Make a phone call. There's precious little our boys in blue do around here except run speeding campaigns up and down the A16 and visit schools to pretend to the kids that they're on their side. I don't doubt that they've been bought off to turn blind to Minton or Corrigan doings. But there's some things that can't be ignored once they're made plain. Perhaps this is one of those.'

'Maybe.' The less contact between officialdom and Matlock, the better. If he hadn't come to that point of view already, then two years inside would have done that for him.

'I didn't think so either, but it still has to be said.'

'No.' But all the police in Lincolnshire, all the judges, all the prisons weren't enough. None of them would right the wrong. Would repay the debt now due for Joe.

'So what's the big plan?'

'There isn't one, Tom. I'll be there for six, and take it as it comes.'

'Brute force and ignorance.'

'Something like that.'

'If there's something I can do, you tell me. I owe Joe that much.'

'Thanks, but no.'

'If you're sure.' Tom looked disappointed. But what use would an old man be there? There was no sense in having another in the way of the worst kind of trouble.

'I am, Tom. But thanks.'

'You'll need to organise something. For Joe. He was liked. There's people – some of whom you don't know – who'd want to pay their respects.'

'I will.' After the weekend. If he was still standing to do so.

'That's something at least.'

Matlock stood. Held out a hand to shake. 'Thanks, Tom.'

Tom rose as well. Came round the table. Took Matlock's hand and shook it. Moved in closer and, still shaking his right, embraced him with his left. 'You do what's right. Joe's owed. You make sure the price is paid in full.'

*

It was lunchtime by the time Matlock got back into town. The Friday market was trading in the town centre. Kids in school uniform with trays of chips mingled with shoppers. He cut through town, and headed over to the cattle market.

The hardstanding outside the auction buildings was half-full of cars. Overflow parking for busy days. It wasn't much of a walk back into the town centre, and free parking was precious. The double doors into the auction area were open. Two council vehicles were nearby. Clean-up crew. A worker in hi-vis carried two refuse sacks out of the building and chucked them into the cage on the back of one of the council-liveried flatbeds.

Matlock took what he needed from the car and headed in. Nine-tenths of everything is confidence. Not necessarily in having it, but in being able to communicate it to others.

The place stank of cow piss and fried onions. Matlock made his way around to the auction ring. Council workers were occupied in the animal pens, hosing down the concrete and sweeping away the matted-straw-and-dung residue. Someone had brought a radio with them. The echoey rattle of music Matlock didn't recognise. With the right speaker set-up it might have been an all-pervasive thumping. In a chamber of this size, it sounded underwhelming. A kids' disco in a chill school hall.

One of the clean-up gang – the one who had been outside by the truck – was busy emptying black plastic dustbins that had been fixed into place with twisted wire at different points. He pulled the bin-liner he was now working on carefully; it sagged with half-drunk dis-carded teas. Then he replaced the liner, securing it with bungee cords in place for that purpose. He caught Matlock watching. 'Help you, mate?'

'Lost some keys yesterday. Think they might be here. If you see any, let me know. Tenner for you if you do.'

'Righto. Not found anything like that. Lost property goes to the auctioneers. We pile it up by their office, then take it down after. Brollies usually. Walking sticks. God knows how you lose a walking stick, but someone manages it every week.'

'Mind if I have a look round?'

'Not too hard. A tenner's a tenner, after all.'

'Yeah.'

The man went back to his bins. Matlock carried on round to the auction ring. On the way, he found something he thought he'd find. Something he should have picked up the day before. Copies of the lots for auction. Typed-up and photocopied lists. Lot number, breed, amount, similar details.

He checked to be sure he had the entire listings. Saw what he thought he might see.

There was a gap in the numerical run of lots. Up to the break in proceedings when he and Chris had been here, then continuing after-wards. A bunch of numbers were missing.

This is how he reckoned it worked. The gap in numbers was delib-erate. The auctioneers, though, had a fuller list. The missing lots were cover for transactions. Big ones. They'd be recorded as sales of non-existent animals. Money changed hands; was laundered by the process. The auctioneers would take their commission as a banking fee. Maybe there was an occasional stuffed envelope on top: Christ-mas bonuses for all. This was how you could make trade deals on huge quantities of red diesel. There was only so much you could run through the books by inflating the takings of cash businesses.

There'd be other scams too. Not just the diesel. But that was where the money was. Easy profit, and no one gets hurt but the taxman.

The Mintons had come a long way from running the arcades.

This was business worth defending.

Matlock folded the sheets of paper away. It was good to know, but it didn't change anything. This was about blood, not fuel.

He was at the auction ring now. A concrete amphitheatre; high steel barriers to keep the beasts corralled. The auctioneers' platform above. In the centre of the ring, the grille to help sluice the filth away.

The area had been cleaned already. Matlock checked about; no one in sight. He hid what he had brought, and then got out of there. He'd be back soon enough.

He took his keys out, and slid the metal loop over his little finger. Back outside the auction ring, he checked for exits. The main double doors. The loading areas. Two of these; goods – animals – in and out. Two sets of ordinary fire doors. The kind with a push bar to unlock. One at each end of the building. Green emergency exit lights above each. Okay; at least there were options.

Always have an out.

The council worker he'd spoken to earlier was back outside. Matlock held up his hand. Both a farewell and a display. Keys. You see them?

The bloke nodded back. Shrugged; ah well, that's a potential tenner lost. He went back to sorting out the bagged-up rubbish in the cage.

Loop closed. An explanation offered. Don't leave questions. Answers fade the memory. Matlock went to his car, and thought about where he'd park that evening.

Here, there was a single exit out to the road. There was a second option. Matlock bore that in mind. Dismissed it, but it came back at him. Okay then. Whether it would be viable would depend on later. He'd see tonight.

*

There wasn't much else to do.

Matlock rang Chris, but there was no answer.

He killed the call. The phone box chugged out his change.

A thought. Matlock put the money back in. Dialled a different number.

'Ashburn House. Good morning. Sorry, good afternoon.'

Matlock recognised Lucy's voice. 'Soon be time for your lunch.'

'I got your note. Sorry about your relative.'

'Sorry about not being outside at five.'

'It was hardly a date date. And besides, bad time for the family.'

'Yes.'

'So,' her voice brightened. 'To what do I owe the pleasure?'

'What are you doing tonight?'

'There's forward.'

'I don't know how else to say this. I'm fighting a man tonight. In a strange place. I might come out of it... pretty badly.'

'Hardly candles and soft music, is this?'

'No.'

'And is this a regular thing for you?'

'No.'

'Where and when?'

Matlock told her.

'I'm not promising anything.'

'No need to.'

'And I don't know what you expect.'

'Me neither.'

'Well then.'

Matlock wasn't sure what to say. Wasn't sure why he'd rung. 'Yes.'

'If I'm there, I'm there. How about that?'

'More than fair enough.'

'I think so too. Maybe see you later.' And then she was gone.

*

Matlock checked the car over. Tyres, oil, water, screenwash, fuel. He ran it through the car wash. The cheap option. Rotating brushes scraped over the car. Dirty water ran off the corners. He pulled out of the contraption, swished the wipers on and off. Soap suds, wet redness, clarity. Then he went back to the caravan.

All quiet. Not even the little dog yapping next door. Nor the inquisitive Frank. Matlock took his boots off. Shook out the sand from the beach. Sorted some clothes out.

There was enough water to have a wash. Matlock scrubbed himself down all over, and put on clean boxers and a tee shirt. He lay on the sofa. Fell asleep.

Prison trains you to sleep light and to a schedule. He woke at five. Dusky outside. A light rain falling. Matlock got fully dressed: army surplus fatigue trousers, an unbuttoned overshirt, flak jacket. Laced his boots up. Put the retractable knife in a coat pocket so there'd be something to find. Went out.

Lights were on in Frank's caravan. The caravan park office was silent, dark.

Maggots stirred in Matlock's guts. Electric eels sparked in him. He got onto the road.

Matlock turned right, going out of town, rather than take the direct route to the left. This way took him around the south of the town, up past the cemetery on the way back in, and towards the cattle market site from its far side.

The pub by the cattle market looked open. Lights on inside, the windows misted by smoke or condensation. Movement inside; multiple bodies. A sign on the door.

Matlock pulled up. To be certain. The front door was shut. He didn't try it, but he knew it would be locked. 'Closed for private function,' the sign said. Pub noise from around the back. From the exit that connected the pub to the gents' toilets, and onto the market itself.

The event was licenced.

Busy.

The next turning on the right led to the cattle market; the entrance was by where the pig pens had once stood. Two blokes under a golf umbrella on the gates. Kayode. Tobacco Man. Kayode made a wind-down-your-windows sign. 'There's a few in there don't think you're going to show.'

'That include you?'

'No. You've made me a few quid already. Been told to escort you in. So no one gets ahead of themselves.'

'Roy's orders.'

'He's been waiting a long time for tonight.'

Matlock reached over and popped the button to open the passenger door. Hefted his bag onto the back seat to allow the man to sit.

Tobacco Man stuffed his hands into his jacket. Shuffled his feet. He was thin; the scrawny always feel the cold.

Matlock pointed the car across the tarmac. There were perhaps twenty vehicles there. Dented runabouts to fierce-looking black Range Rovers. A trickle of men between the pub and the auction block. Beer in plastic pint glasses. One man held a small wrapped package. A burger or a sausage bap in a fold of kitchen towel.

Kayode gave off cologne. Nothing that Matlock could identify.

Matlock parked. Where he wanted to. If there were instructions issued, then they didn't extend to where Mr Matlock was to leave his vehicle.

Good. Partial thinking. Windows in the plan. If there even was a plan other than get him to the ring unmolested.

'Hold here a couple of minutes,' Kayode said. 'Gonna be a bear pit in there. Best for all concerned that you're in there as late as you can make it.'

'How long has the bar been open?'

'An hour.'

That was plenty long enough for someone to lose control at a word out of place. Okay then.

Kayode got out. Matlock followed, fetching his bag. He didn't lock his door. Let the car keys slide into the footwell by the pedals. A safe-guard against them being confiscated. Just in case.

'I'm supposed to search you.'

'Better do it where the light's better.' They were in the middle of the hardstanding.

'Come on. Stick close.'

Kayode walked Matlock to the far side of the double-doored main entrance. There was enough artificial light to make a pat-down meaningful, and not get hassled by arrivals in the doing so. The rain looked worse under the illumination than it was.

'Bag first.'

Matlock dropped it at his feet.

'Arsehole.' Kayode tried it for weight. Opened it with one hand. Checked the contents out. 'Okay then. Now you. Against the wall. Hands up, palms open.'

Matlock did as he was told.

Kayode didn't know what he was doing. He'd learned his technique from the telly. His hands were too heavy. He found the knife like he was meant to. 'Turn around.' A second check down the front. Nothing. 'Alright then. You're good.' He opened and closed the blade mechanism. 'I'll be keeping this though.'

'Do I get it back?'

'Sure. Yeah. See me after.'

Kayode tried to grab Matlock by the shoulder and pull him to the doors. Hadn't reckoned on resistance. Matlock didn't shift. Barely wobbled.

'Move yourself, tough guy.'

The auction building had been full of farmers' chunter and beast noises the day before. It had been warmer in here the day before too; the beasts gave off heat. It now resounded with the racket of men. Laughter, swearing, stamping against the worst of the cold compared to the comfort of the pub. Matlock walked ahead, Kayode keeping a hand on his arm like he was pushing him forward.

'Where are we going?'

'Office.' The whitewashed breeze-block structure where bills were settled. Kayode opened the door. Turned the light on. A basic working set-up: desks, chairs, filing cabinets. Calculators and pens. A safe, open to show that it was empty. No telephone. 'Wait here. Won't be long.'

The door was locked behind him. Matlock switched the light off; too much like a shop-window display with it on. There was a bottle of water in the bag. Matlock took a swig. Took off the flak jacket and the overshirt. Put them in the bag. Put the water bottle on top. Left the bag unzipped.

He sat on one of the chairs; the swivel one. Turned away from the window. The sound of banter; of men being jostled along. Occasional shrieks; beer being spilled. Pranks being pulled. Someone banged on the glass and shouted something as they passed, but Matlock tuned the words out. They were hurried along by their mates.

Two years.

Ant Corrigan's face. A smear of red. The sirens; eventually.

Joe. The shrink-wrapped mummy of a body. Broken-necked and bruised. Left dead in the back of a van planted for him to pick up.

Roy Minton's big idea for payback undermined.

The way Joe had bloated after death. Blood-tainted foam from his eyes, nose, mouth.

The van, burning.

A man, burning. Two men. One of whom Matlock was responsible for. If he'd died.

He couldn't not have done.

Shit. Blind fury or not, was there any excuse for that?

The rain must have got worse. You could hear it bouncing off the corrugated roof of the auction block. Echoing in the all-but-empty hall.

Matlock rubbed his eyes.

The van, disembowelled by fire. Metal ticking as it cooled on the scorched February sand.

That electric sensation was no longer confined to his belly. Matlock's torso surged with it. His arms pulsed with the need to strike out. His head buzzed with violent static.

A key in the door. The light spluttered, fighting to engage.

Kayode. 'It's time.'

*

Maybe forty men and a dozen women were assembled in the stands around the auction ring. Matlock was walked through to the ring via the channel meant for beasts on their way from sale to new homes or slaughter. He was caught in a holding pen. The walkway to and from the auctioneers' platform was above him. High-sided steel to each side. Bolted gates in front and behind. He still had his bag with him. Kayode was in there with him. The man led him forwards so the spectators could see who was in the pen.

Stacks of plastic empties. Wine bottles. At least one bottle of dark spirits being passed around.

Hard-faced men and women. Late teens to seventies. Workwear to weekend smart casual. A good half of them with the same face. The family didn't extend that far in genetic terms.

The arena settled. Still a buzz, but one of expectation, not of the vague thrill of fun to be had in the future. Anticipation was sharpening focus. Sobering people up. Acting as a reminder that this was as much business as pleasure.

A sliding, grating sound. Matlock turned to see Kayode exit himself from the holding pen. He stayed on the far side of the gate. Knocked the bolt back into its keep. Waited.

Back to face the crowd. People were still filing in. Those already there shuffled to accommodate the new arrivals. Some clung to their leaning posts, jealous of the spot they'd reserved through being early.

Crackling; the PA system being turned on. A splash of feedback, then sound levels being adjusted. 'Lock the doors.' The microphone clicked off.

There were still more new arrivals turning up. Laughing off a downpour. Steaming from the run across the yard from the pub. The gaps in the rows of terraces were filling. The sound of large doors on wheels being pulled together. The movement of people slowed, then all but ceased.

Rain beat down. Military drumming on the clear perspex panels in the roof intended to let some light in.

Matlock was standing in shadow. They couldn't see him. Nor, he supposed, Liam Corrigan, who must be somewhere near. In the corresponding pen on the other side of the ring, surely.

The mic was re-engaged. 'Thanks for coming.' Roy Minton. Twice. His natural voice, coming from above, and the electrified version being broadcast around the speakers. The crowd shushed itself. 'Justice needs to be seen to be done. You're here as witnesses. As jury. To some extent. Two years and more since young Ant was taken from us. Not by illness, not by old age. By being in the wrong place at the wrong time. With the wrong man at the wheel of a car.'

The crowd held its peace. 'Two years. A long time. And not long enough neither. Not long enough to pay for a life. Two years is no sentence at all. So back then I put out the word. That we'd wait. That the man responsible would be left alone. That there'd be restitution made in a time and in a place and in a manner of my choosing.

'Here. And now. And with bare knuckles. Until it's clear to us all that the price of a life has been paid.'

Minton paused. Took a drink. The echo of a loudspeaker slurp. That hard rain, a rhythmic undertone. He kept his voice low. Used his own quiet control to demand the same from the others assembled. 'So let's get on with this. Open the first gate.'

Matlock expected to be sent into the beast ring first. To be held there for inspection and for insult from the throng. To be spat on and to have threats hurled from the safety of the barriers. But it was the other gate that was opened.

Liam Corrigan strode into the auction arena. He was bare to the waist; jogging pants and trainers below. Tattoos worked to accentuate the body work he'd done in the last two years. He must have been three, maybe four stone heavier than he'd been the day his brother had died. Muscle mass had been piled on. There was not much of the over-definition of bodybuilding for competitions' sake. This was power developed with purpose.

Two years of training. Two years of sparring. Two years of steroids, he guessed, to develop that muscle mass.

Now the crowd let loose. Cheering, applause. Wolf whistles. Someone shouted, 'Fuck him up!'

The bolt behind Matlock slid back. Kayode ducked into the pen. Went to the gate leading into the auction ring. He grinned.

The mic stuttered into life again. One word: 'Catch.'

Corrigan caught the mic as it was thrown, cable trailing, out into the ring. The movement encouraged the crowd. Cheers, more wolf whistles.

Corrigan waited until they settled themselves again. When he spoke, his voice was deeper than Matlock remembered it. Another side effect of the steroids. 'You all know I've got a lot to thank Uncle Roy for. I was a dumb kid. Thought I knew it all. Full of spunk and piss and vinegar. And it was cockiness like that what got me into trouble. Trouble I thought I was clever enough to pull myself out of. There's a time to turn to family, and a time to manage your own busi-ness, and I forgot the difference between the two.

'After Ant... was killed–' a pause for effect '–I thought that I deserved everything that came with that. I'd already turned my back on family, and now the family had every right to turn its back on me. Worse, to take its time with me, and to teach me the rights of my wrongs. But that was when Uncle Roy stepped in. He saw how I was hurting. He gave me a place. A new start. Six months to lick my scars, then he gave me a new purpose.

'That purpose is tonight. To have the man who took our Ant's life from us brought before us. And to be able to pay him back the only way that means anything. With bare fists.

'Eighteen months I've trained. You've seen me. The raw eggs and the powder and the lifting. The sparring sessions. To you, Niall, whose nose I broke twice. To you, Des, whose tooth I knocked out. To you, Uncle Roy. Who gave me not only a second chance, but a third and a fourth. And who gave me – and us – this chance too. Thank you, most of all.'

He sounded genuine. The cocky little wine-bar shit wasn't there. This was a man transformed. Broken, then remade.

Matlock had it all wrong.

Liam wasn't behind all this. Wasn't the man responsible for Joe's killing.

Corrigan continued: 'And this is for Nanna Minton, who passed last night, with Uncle Roy looking over her, like she looked over him and you all from his generation. Like he's looked over us all.'

Fuck.

'But most of all, this is for our Ant. For two years I've wanted to be nowhere than standing in his place when he was hit by that fucker in the car. But not tonight. Here is where I want to be. This is for you, brother.'

Corrigan knelt. He put the microphone down. Crossed himself. The mic was reeled back up into the air.

The rain was louder. Someone swore on the terraces; the crowd shuffled away from where the roof was now leaking. A waterfall out of nowhere fed by the corrugated channels.

Minton again. 'Stand back, Liam. Out of the way. Nothing happens except for by my word.' Corrigan stepped to his side of the auction ring. 'Open the pen.'

'Cheerio, fucker,' Kayode murmured, as the gate was swung open. Matlock walked out.

Jeers, catcalls. Phlegm in the air. Matlock moved to the centre of the ring. He stood on the drainage grate. Let them scream all they wanted. The area was too wide for any of the gobbets of spit to reach him.

Matlock faced Minton. White shirt; chunky necklace showing through. Leather jacket over. Suit jacket, not biker-style. His face was pink with exertion, drink, heightened blood pressure. His hair was damp: sweat. Scotch too, perhaps. He had a drink in his hand. Something brown in the bottom of a clear plastic cup.

Glass broke somewhere behind him. A can, crushed, was thrown. It missed, bouncing to one side of the ring. It lay, leaking out its last. Laughter at the miss.

Stand there. Let it pass.

Matlock didn't have to engage with Corrigan. Hate was radiating off him; he shuffled his feet, flexed his fists then let them go. He thrilled with nervous energy.

Minton found eye contact with Matlock; he reflected impassivity. Eventually, he drank.

Minton then raised his cup; the crowd calmed itself.

'Alright. Listen up.' Silence. 'Better. Rules, the lot of you. This ends tonight. No referee. No gloves. No stoppages. No rounds. No mandatory standing eight count. No bells.

'Dan Matlock has come here tonight because, and I'll remind you all to keep your peace, he knows there's a debt to be paid. A reckoning that two years in Lincoln doesn't scratch the paint off, let alone dent. And for that understanding, there's respect. Liam Corrigan is in the ring tonight because he too knows there's a debt to be paid. Not only for the accumulation of his indiscretions of the past, but because he was his brother's keeper. A task in which he failed us all. Ant was a good kid. A decent kid. Not like you bunch of rogues and thieves and worse.' A pause for laughter. It came, but with caution. 'He deserved better. He deserved to live. And we all deserved to see the man he might have become. The father he may have been. The children he might have brought into this world. The loss of him echoes in me every day. Some of us have it coming. I know I do. Some of us deserve nothing of the sort. Ant was that sort of person. And that, too, needs redress.'

He had to speak louder. The amplification was struggling to rise above the rainfall hammering to get in from above.

'So mark this. This ends tonight. This ends in the ring. Both of these man have an account due. Due to all of us. Due to me. There'll be no interference. No quarter to be asked or given. They fight, and they fight until there's no fight left in them, or until one of them lies still and the other stands over him. And then that man may leave, and go out into the world, their account paid in full.'

Minton tasted his whisky. Then drank deeper, before resuming. 'Are we all clear on this?' Yes, the crowd was. 'And are you two clear on this?' Matlock waited until Minton's attention switched from Corrigan to him. He kept focus on Minton while he moved across the auction ring, back towards the gate he'd entered through. He took in the crowd. Waiting, expectant. Hands around drinks or else clenched on the crush barriers interspersed around the stepped levels of the standing area.

Then he saw Big Chris. To the left, on the near side of the viewing gallery. She must have been among the last to enter. Her usual shapeless clothes; an oversize fleece with Arctic wolves the topmost layer.

Corrigan must have nodded his assent. Noise levels rose. An incoming tide. Matlock gauged the distance between him and his opponent. Four yards. Maybe five. Plenty.

Minton crooked his neck. Quizzical. Playful.

That was when the elements fused together. That was when Matlock knew for sure. He nodded.

'Fight.'

The command was all the crowd needed. A sonic eruption.

Corrigan was halfway across the ring already.

Matlock's opponent was right-handed. The right was being held back, potential energy being stored to unleash at Matlock. He would step right, then left, then swing. A hook intended to connect on the side of Matlock's head. Take him clattering to the ground in one blow.

Matlock got ready to move. Anticipated the shift.

Corrigan swung like he was supposed to, grunting with effort as he let his right fist go. Even without the vocals telegraphing the move, he would have been easy to read. Matlock sidestepped to the right, robbing Corrigan of reach.

The right swept past.

Matlock let go with a right of his own. Low into his opponent's gut. It met a wall of solid muscle. Corrigan made no reaction; as though he felt nothing. Matlock stepped backwards. Another step. And a third. Corrigan followed.

The steel wall of the auction ring prevented Corrigan using his right like he wanted to. He threw a left. Matlock took it on the shoulder.

The impact played well; enthusiastic yelps from around the arena. The blow hurt. Corrigan had power. A well-placed right would do damage. The left, not so much, but pain could accumulate.

Corrigan tried a right, but could do little other than poke forwards. Matlock stepped back again, careful to keep out of its range.

They were below the auctioneers' perch. Halfway across the pen. Matlock counted how many steps he had left.

Corrigan still hadn't caught on yet. Kept coming forward. Someone had taught him the rudiments of boxing. An orthodox stance. The importance of keeping your guard up. But he wasn't so bright as to apply the new knowledge to his surroundings or to his context. This wasn't a boxing ring, and he wasn't in a boxing match. Corrigan loosed a left jab. Matlock dodged it, and kicked Corrigan on the shin.

The impact had an immediate effect, both with Matlock's opponent and on the crowd. Corrigan yelped – a yappy dog's bark – and pulled the leg back out of the way of further kicks, putting him off balance. The crowd yelled foul; a bottle was thrown.

Fight rules. Are there any? Matlock didn't think so, except one. Finish it.

Put the man down. End him on the ground.

He didn't hear the impact – the shouting and the demanding rainfall were too much – but there was now broken glass on the cement surface.

Corrigan swung, but he still hadn't recovered his poise from having pulled his leg away. He didn't make contact. Matlock stepped inside his opponent's reach; hit him in the face. The blow contacted on Corrigan's left cheekbone. Not hard enough to break either facial or knuckle bones, but smart enough a strike to tear the skin on both.

With Matlock still within his fighting reach, Corrigan tried to grab his man. Matlock saw the move; responded by ducking and stepping in fast. He brought his head up onto Corrigan's chin. Corrigan grunted. Still inside, Matlock dropped a low blow. No point going for a body shot. Left into the bollocks. Quick, a second. Pointed jabs into the crotch.

Corrigan slumped. He didn't fall, but he wasn't far off. He hit the steel wall. A second bottle had flown; diamond-sharp studs of glass exploded by Matlock's head, the remnants of the bottle ricocheting off the same metal partition Corrigan was still leaning against.

The impact empowered Corrigan somehow. Matlock thought he had him, but it was as though Corrigan had bounced off the wall. His left arm swept out, cuffing Matlock on the side of the head. His fist might only have been half formed but the impact still hurt. Matlock's ear stung; instantly, it felt hot, thick, swollen. He assumed that it was bleeding.

Corrigan must have seen something in Matlock's expression. He launched a right. A good one. Matlock tried to duck, but only succeeded in having the fist smash into his forehead rather than his face. Better than nothing. Corrigan's hand came away bloodied. Matlock was not sure whose gore it was.

He stepped back, to the centre of the arena. Trod on broken glass; it crunched, harmless, underfoot. There was liquid on the glass falling from above. A second leak. Matlock was breathing heavier than he'd have liked; he put his hand to his forehead and it came back both sweaty and bloody.

Corrigan was lumbering too, though. Those hits in the balls were taking their toll. His cheek was cut, a welt rising under his left eye.

Okay. Use the space now. Dominate the area. Have him circle anticlockwise. That would mean that he was exposing his left flank and, with it, any restriction to his vision brought by the bulge on that side of his face. The downside was that it gave scope for his more powerful right arm. Two good blows would ruin Matlock; a perfect one might snap his neck.

Neck.

The word conjured Joe. Dead and broken in the back of that van.

The fucker would pay.

Matlock shuffled back again. He was standing on the grate. Perfect.

Corrigan moved in fast. Matlock feinted with his left to get Corrigan moving in the direction he wanted. Corrigan obliged. Someone shouted something that cut through the din being made by the gathering. A warning. Whoever it was knew what was going on.

Corrigan shifted anticlockwise. Glass scattered. He wound back his right, cascading rain splashing across his face. Matlock got inside with another to the bruised cheek, cutting the angle for Corrigan's haymaker. Corrigan's face squirted; a blood blister under the skin gave way. He reacted, pulling his head away. Blood and rainwater arced.

It looked worse than it was, but it looked pretty bad.

Corrigan groaned; a tennis player unloading a two-handed backhand. A second time, he tried to swamp Matlock. Arms wide, smothering.

Matlock butted Corrigan in the face. A damp slap. Cartilage squeaked, then cracked. Matlock slipped Corrigan's grasp, then charged forward, head down. Two, three steps in, like an American footballer slamming into a tackling sled. He drove his man back. More glass; underfoot and in the air. Corrigan slipped, rotating backwards. He fell. Matlock fell with him.

Matlock put his hand out to brace the fall, like a fool. He caught his right hand on a spur of glass. Fuck. It dug itself deep into the meat of Matlock's palm. Into the drumstick of muscle that articulated the thumb.

Matlock squirmed; rolled his hand over to see the damage done. The cut was already overflowing with blood.

Corrigan was on his back. He was scrambling to get upright, twisting so he could get on his knees. He wasn't thinking of what he might have landed on. Shards stuck from his back like stegosaurus plates.

Rainwater bounced around him. The drumming from above, somehow louder, faster, more fevered.

Matlock's opponent had bulk, but not flexibility. He struggled to his knees. Worse, he was facing away from Matlock. Who was now standing over him.

The first kick went into the ribs. The second, delivered as Corrigan was still groaning from the first, went into the groin. Corrigan was now against the wall. The steel resounded with the impact. A third kick: right boot over the heart. Ribs cracked.

Spittle, flecked with red, appeared at Corrigan's mouth.

Someone pushed their way out of the gallery. They'd seen enough.

Minton threw something that landed in the periphery of Matlock's eyeline. It clattered. Not a bottle. Something metallic.

Whatever had been thrown energised the crowd.

Feral faces, screaming for their man to get up. Howling for justice.

Corrigan's face, bloodied. Swollen. A hand raised, perhaps for support, perhaps for some form of mercy.

A glance aside; a blade. Maybe seven inches long. Thin through being sharpened a thousand times. A fish filleter's knife.

Refocus. Minton, impassive. Drink in hand.

Back to Corrigan. Too-red lips, turning to purple. Still fight in his eyes.

Matlock leaned over him. Grabbed the top of the steel retaining wall separating the auction floor from the viewing gallery.

This is for the two years I spent inside. The two years spent waiting. He kicked. The boot impacted on Corrigan's face.

This is for the last five days. For making me kill a man. A further kick again to the head. Corrigan's skull whipped back, clanging against the upright barrier.

And this is for Joe. The boot slammed into its target. The noise a chicken carcass makes when being torn by a hungry dog.

Matlock did not look down to see what he had done.

The crowd was now quiet. Rainwater streamed from four, five places, where the seals between the perspex and the other roofing panels had failed. The roof throbbed with the downpour.

Matlock's hand pulsed. He raised it to quell the bleeding. Picked the shark's tooth of glass from his hand. He licked the wound; Joe had always said that there was stuff in saliva that promoted healing. That was why it never bled for long when you bit your tongue. He folded his fingers over to hold the two sides of the slice together; maybe it would clot, and maybe that would keep it together until he could get some stitches into it.

Minton. His glass was empty. He was expressionless. Didn't speak. Eventually, he held his hand up.

The low chatter around the ring ceased. Chris didn't return eye contact.

Matlock hadn't realised he'd been holding his breathing in.

Corrigan shifted. Christ, but he was powerful. Or simply too dumb to quit. Matlock willed him to stay down.

Don't make me.

Don't make me what?

Just... don't.

Corrigan was up on all fours. Began to crawl. Towards the knife. Rain cascaded around him.

Matlock stepped back. Gave the man a clear path towards the blade. It didn't matter any more.

Corrigan was blind to the glass scattered across the floor. That, or else his nerves were overloaded with pain; anything on top simply was not registering. He couldn't support his weight; Corrigan slumped to his forearms. Left over right. Right over left. Each shift got him a matter of inches forward. His mouth hung open, loose. A cocktail of sweat, saliva and blood drooled onto the concrete. A dying snail's trail.

Some urged him on. But not many. And not for long.

He coughed. Red matter leaped from him. A splash of gore.

Matlock took off his tee shirt with his one good hand. Wiped his forehead. Picked up the knife by the hilt.

Corrigan stopped crawling. Somehow, he pushed himself into an upright kneeling position. He rocked back; he could have toppled at any point. His hands fell to his sides. He might have been crying. It was hard to tell.

'Finish him,' Minton said.

It was unclear to whom he was speaking.

'Finish him. Isn't that what you want?'

Matlock shook his head.

'End this!'

Matlock dropped the knife into Corrigan's lap. 'No.'

The blade slid off Corrigan's knees onto the bloodied concrete.

Movement on the terraces. Some were sidling out. Heads down, sidestepping past their kin. Chris was still in her place by the entry point. One hand down to her side. The men around her had been coppiced. Only a few remained.

'Pick it up.' Minton grabbed the mic again. Pushed forward the switch to make it live. 'Pick the knife up, Liam.'

Corrigan raised his slumped head. Matted with blood and swollen with bruising, his left eye stayed shut. Some of the blood coating the rest of his face had dried. It crazed where his skin flexed under torsion. Head up, he stared back at Minton. He grinned.

'Pick it up.' Minton's voice was low. Cajoling. The bass in the words made the speakers rumble. 'Pick it up, lad. Show willing.'

Corrigan's teeth were black with gore. His lips were too bright. Made up with a natural, vivid red. His own.

More pushed past Chris. She shifted, letting the way clear widen. Those nearer her took the movement as invitation.

'That's it, lad. Don't let me down.' Still deep, still quiet. Still insistent. Thick with whisky. 'One more thing. Then your debt's done.'

Matlock did nothing. Let his body thrum with the aftermath of violence. With the prospect of more to be done. He breathed. He listened. He waited. And he watched.

He watched Corrigan try to reach for the knife. Watched him fail to grab the handle. Watched him have to prop himself up with one hand while leaning forwards. Fresh blood bubbled from Corrigan's mouth. He got the knife. Leaned back to fall back into a kneeling position. Pink bubbles made a goatee, then popped, spattering his chest with measles' spots.

'You can do this. One last thing.' The delay on the speakers bounced around the arena. Minton's voice carried enough to be heard by itself; a half-second later, its electric echo. 'Then it's over.' The amplification crackled; broadcasting the insistence of the rain.

Corrigan raised the knife. He closed his other eye. Levelled the pointed tip of the blade at throat height.

This was enough for those still remaining. The pretence of sneaking out was over; men and women made for the exit. The sound of the double doors being opened; a gasp of cold, wet air from outside.

Chris stood her ground. Hand still to her side; hovering over the side pocket in her coat.

Corrigan pushed the knife forwards. Found his skin. His neck yielded under pressure to the point of the blade.

Matlock could have kicked the weapon away. He didn't move.

'Go on, son.'

Corrigan pressed. He tried, but he didn't have the breath or the strength. The knife dropped out of his grip, leaving a pressure mark where he'd held it to his windpipe.

The mic clicked off. Footsteps across a metal gantry, then down stairs. Shouting, to a lurking bunch unsure of what to do for the best. For them to fuck off out of it. That the show was fucking over.

Minton came into the arena. He was flushed with exertion. With Scotch.

Corrigan slumped again, knelt forwards. Minton ignored Matlock. He got onto his haunches, careful not to tread on glass. He picked up the knife that Corrigan had dropped. When he spoke, though, he spoke to Matlock. 'I'm a man of my word.'

'You keep saying that.'

'And I meant it. This is over. Walk out of here and there's no more arguments between you and any of us. Job's done. Honour satisfied. Call it what you will. You've lost someone. I've lost someone. And I've got a mess to clean up.'

'If you say so.'

'I do. You killed one of his. He killed one of yours. Eye for an eye. Go and bury your dad. We've all got funerals to arrange.' Minton stroked the downy stubble on Corrigan's head. 'And there's tidying up to be done, like I said.'

Matlock checked his hand. Clotting blood was holding it together. He tugged apart his tee shirt where it had got stuck to itself. A

Rorschach pattern on the cloth. Two dogs lying down, back to back. He supposed a psychologist could have made something of that.

He went behind Minton. To the stanchions supporting the auctioneers' gallery. To where he'd hidden the gun.

Minton was still in front of Corrigan. He was saying something, but his voice didn't carry.

Matlock reached in with the tee shirt still in his hand. Found the gun. Swept the tee shirt over it. Turned to Minton. 'We're not done,' he said.

Minton didn't move. 'We're done. Get out of here.'

'Not until Joe's been honoured.'

Now Minton looked around. 'What are you talking about?'

'You shouldn't have done it.'

'"It"?'

'I believed it until just now.'

'Believed what?' Minton stood. He still had the knife in his hand.

The revolver was inside the tee shirt wadded around Matlock's hand. 'You, Roy. What you wanted me to believe.'

'And what was that?'

Matlock had to shout over the sound of the rain. 'That this was all a thing gone wrong. That Liam had stepped out of line like he'd done so many times before. Even when given this big chance to redeem himself. That he couldn't help himself. That a head full of ego and a body packed with whatever he'd been taking to help him bulk up had made it irresistible. That it was him that'd killed Joe. A "Fuck you" to you and your last chances. A "Fuck you" to me and the pissy little sentence I'd received. And damn the old man who was being held to make sure I'd play along.

'Is that what you wanted me to think, Roy?'

Roy glanced aside. He was checking the angles. The two exit points from the auction arena. Position relative to Matlock. To Corrigan. A check to see what Big Chris was up to.

Nothing. Just being there. In case.

'In case' meant she had her hand on the grip of her protector. The sawn-off. Not much good at this range; the gun was a close-quarters weapon. Something to repel boarders. It'd sting. Maybe you'd lose an eye if unlucky. Really unlucky. But that'd be the worst of it.

He could discount her.

Corrigan was still doubled over. Stinking of sweat and blood. Rust and piss.

That left Matlock.

'You're supposed to be the court of appeal, Roy. The man who your granddaughters' boyfriends have to present themselves to so they can ask to take them out. The fella who grants favours at family weddings. Who's supposed to keel over quietly in his garden when he's ninety.

'But you're not, are you?'

'You don't know anything about me, boy.'

'I know enough. Enough to know that all the fairground organs in the world won't be able to drown out your screaming by the time you're done with.' The wadded tee shirt concealing the Ruger was in his right. It would kick if he fired it; would tear the gash open again.

But Minton didn't know that. He knew Matlock was right-handed, and that was the one that was hurting.

It was important not to move first.

Retaliatory action; that was key.

It would make what he was going to do more bearable. Self-defence as self-justification.

'An old woman. Defenceless in her bed. After I left, because you could. Joe, a bloke who was trying to pay off a debt he didn't owe. A man who'd worked beside you for two years. What did you do? Come at him when he was asleep too? Put pills in his tea? Got him drunk and reassured him that this was all just for show, and that no real harm would come to him or me? The beating I deserved, nothing more. Was that it, you prick?'

The blade flickered under tension in Minton's grip. In time to the pounding on the roof.

It was working.

'Or was it something else? Is this what it takes to get any reaction out of you? All the money you need, a bunch of guys to boss around. Sex simply no fun now you can pay for it whenever you want. But to have your hands around someone's neck. That's life, isn't it? And this was your revenge all along. Having me mashed like a pan of boiled spuds was an extra. A life for a life, though. That was the thing. Working by Joe. Watching him machine new parts for your fairground attraction. Being close to him on a daily basis.

'That was when you got the idea. And to have that knowledge in you when you passed him a tea. When you took one of his custard creams. When you complimented him at the end of the day on a bloody good bit of engineering. Taking turns to buy each other lunch. That you would end up killing him. That there was no reason, not really. But because you could.'

'You don't know!'

'Don't I? Sixty years of being able to get away with anything, buy your way out of anything, convince people of anything. It's made you weak. You can't see the trouble you're in. Can't work out the consequences of your actions.'

Minton was shrill. 'Can't I?'

'It's why you let me be loose on Monday. Happy to get my petty bits of attacking as the best sort of defence out of my system. Laughing all the while because that van that'd been left for me was a hearse.'

Minton's knife hand quivered.

'Bet you had some grand reveal planned. Or else you were happy to let the river take its course. Maybe even go against your precious code and have someone ring the cops. Suggest a roadside search and turn up a body.

'Couldn't do it to my face, though.' Matlock dropped his right a touch. Left a gap for Minton to go for. 'Like I said. Weak.'

The knife trembled.

Matlock smiled. 'Take your useless nephew. And. Fuck. Off. Home. Roy. It's over.'

Minton snarled something; afterwards, Matlock could never remember what. He brought the knife up, swooping it in a serrated arc up at Matlock's face. He was going for the softer skin under the chin. A bladed uppercut through the jaw and up into the skull.

Matlock fired. The tee shirt erupted. It blossomed blood and flame. A metallic clang. Minton's bicep blew open. His hand spasmed; the blade fell.

You don't fall when you're shot. Not unless they take out a knee, or else they hit you with a cannonball.

Minton rocked, dumbfounded. His arm flopped, coughing red. Instinct brought his other hand across to protect, to stem the flow. Contact with the wound was the moment that the pain registered. Now Minton's cries had no form.

Minton retched. A mouthful of whisky puke splashed his open shirt. A roulette wheel of expressions. Fear. Surprise. Pain. Revulsion. And then, again, surprise.

Minton dropped to one knee.

And Matlock saw why. He moved back. From behind him, the cocking of a shotgun.

Liam Corrigan had got the knife in his hand. He'd already sliced across the back of Minton's legs at the top of the calves; that was why he'd gone to ground. Corrigan's face was warpaint.

Matlock didn't do anything.

The second cut came to the kidney. Minton having bought his arm up to staunch the gunshot wound had exposed his side. Corrigan stabbed deep. He twisted. He pulled the knife out, and Minton toppled over.

Corrigan leaned across the fallen man. He stabbed. Stabbed again. Minton became a robin. It was cold enough for the gashes in his torso to steam. The shot arm flinched one last time.

Corrigan moaned. He tried to pull the knife free, but it was stuck deep. Wedged between ribs. He fell forward on his uncle. He was breathing heavy. Then not so heavy. Then barely at all.

And then not again.

Jesus.

Matlock took a step back. Tried to think. Nothing came.

Jesus.

'Come on.' That was Chris. The uncocking of her gun.

Her voice helped. He got better hold of himself. 'One sec.' Matlock had to check.

Minton was going nowhere.

'Come on!'

Blood and rainwater trickled to the central drain.

He'd heard a metal sound. There was a dent in the steel wall behind where Minton had been standing. It was easy to spot the crushed bullet. Matlock picked it up.

'Okay. Yeah, I'm coming.'

'About fucking time too.'

The parking area was all but empty. Matlock's vehicle. One other: a Range Rover. The others had presumably retreated to what might be considered a safe distance. Shift the cars, get in the pub. Provide each other with a granite alibi.

From here, the pub looked busy. Yellow light and people moving around, the windows mottled with condensation.

So much for loyalty.

There was no waiting for the rain to ease.

'How did you get here?'

'Taxi. Can you drive?'

'No.'

'Come on then. Keys.'

'In the car.'

They crossed the hardstanding fast.

Matlock scooped the car keys out from where he'd left them. 'Here y'go.'

'Ta.'

There was a note under the driver's side wiper. Chris handed it over. Soaked, barely readable. But still intact. 'You got a coat or something?'

'Yep. Let's get out of here first.'

Chris shifted the seat back. Checked the pedals. Got out of there. There were sirens, but they could have been for anybody. Matlock didn't want to wait around to find out.

*

Matlock's hand was open on the workbench in Chris's shed. She'd cleaned the wound with an antiseptic Matlock remembered from when he was a kid. He was pretty sure there was a bottle with a rusty screw top in the medicine cabinet in Joe's bathroom.

'Stings?'

'Of course it bloody stings.'

'Good.' Chris pinched the two sides of the cut together. Then she dribbled contact adhesive over the edges. 'Wait for that to go off, then I'll pop a dressing over it. It'll keep it clean and it'll remind you not to flex it too much till it's properly healed. Okay?'

'Yeah.' Matlock sipped the brew that had been provided. Besides, if the cut started to play up he knew a tame doctor who'd stitch him up with no questions asked.

'Good as new,' Chris said, when she was done. The first-aid stuff went into an old gift tin that had once held crackers for cheese. 'Now what?'

'How do you mean?'

'What's next? You getting out of the shire?'

'No.'

'Oh?'

'Think I'll stay. Want to learn more about Joe.'

'What the world needs. Another railway enthusiast. Another fairground organ fanatic.'

'That's what I reckon.'

'You'll need a job.'

'Got any going?'

'Might have. But it'd be like the old days. Low-key. No muss, no fuss.'

'I hear you.'

'Good. You going to keep on with Joe's place?'

'No. I don't need a house. Keep it light. Keep it simple.'

'Prison rules?'

'Something like that.'

'Caravan's there if you want it. You'd need to pay rent though. I'm not running an orphanage.'

'Deal.'

'You want to stay over? Can clear the sofa for you.'

That was a big deal. Chris didn't let men into her house. Not ever. Matlock finished his tea. 'Best start as I mean to go on. Do me a favour though.'

'Another?'

'Another. Run me back, then pick me up in the morning. I'll drop you back off here after some breakfast at Woody's.'

'I can do that. It'll give that hand twelve hours rest at least.'

'Yeah.'

*

Chris dropped him off; Matlock struggled with the caravan key letting himself in. At least the rain had stopped.

He read the note that had been left under his wiper blade. A name and a home phone number. He'd ring Lucy on Monday; maybe pop into the nursing home, depending on how he looked after the weekend.

And then there was the postcard. Matlock read it through again. There was something to be going on with there.

A knock at the door. Tentative. One of those knocks that sounds ashamed of itself.

'Yes?'

Fumbling with the catch. 'Hello?'

Frank from next door. 'You there, Dan?'

'Yes Frank. Come on in.'

'Thanks.'

A couple of how-are-yous and would-you-like-a-brew and so on. Frank did his best not to stare at Matlock's beaten face or at his bandaged hand. They shared tea, which Frank insisted on making, and which Matlock was glad to have him make – supercharged with brandy from a flat half-bottle Frank magicked from his jacket – and then Frank got to it.

'I was looking for some advice,' Frank said.

'About what?'

'About finding someone. My daughter.' He told Matlock a story. It took two cups of tea and two slugs of brandy to get through it in full. 'Can you help?'

'First, why me?'

'Well, we're neighbours. And, you know, word gets around.'

'Does it?'

'That you're the kind of man who can be… convincing.'

'Oh?'

'I'd pay you for your trouble of course.' Frank had an envelope ready.

'Put your money away. Tell you what. I'll make some calls. First thing Monday. I still know some people. Hopefully they're still the people to ask. Is Monday quick enough?'

It was, thank Christ.

'Alright then. If I find something, and that leads to something, then we'll talk about expenses. Until then, you keep your pension. This can wait, like we've agreed. And I've had a long day.'

'You look like you have.'

Matlock imagined so. 'Lost a member of the family.'

'Oh, God. Sorry to hear that. Me bursting in, annoying you. You should have said something. Or ignored my knocking.'

Matlock shrugged the apology away. 'I'm glad of the distraction.'

'Maybe so. But pain's like good drink. Does it no good to be bottled up for too long.' Frank shared the last of the brandy into their cups.

'Is that right?'

'It is.'

'Cheers, Frank.'

They drank.

And as for wanting to talk about Joe, Matlock found – to his surprise – that yes, he did.

*

The End

Acknowledgements

Thanks first and foremost to Simon Spanton Walker, who saw something. This book wouldn't have existed without his initial interest, his guidance, his expertise and his enthusiasm throughout.

Thanks also to my brother Maxim Griffin and to John Ashbrook, for support in the crowdfunding period with specimen artworks and an audiobook sample, respectively. Cheers also to the M'Eating Point cafe in Llangollen, for first-draft writing space and for regular espressos (I recommend the falafel and hummus wrap, but the bacon bap's good too).

Thanks also to everyone who pitched in crowdfunding-wise with pledges, social media support and/or kind words along the way.

And to George Green and Lee Horsley, always.

Patrons

Eli Allison
Lulu Allison
Karen Attwood
Phil Austin
Liz Babb
Bobby Barker
Becky Barnes
Jackie Bates
Roy Bayfield
Darren Beels
Francesca Billings
Steve Birt
Stephanie Bretherton
Alex Brown
Simon Bryson
Gary Budden
Sean Carroll
Amoret Chaplin
Mark Ciccone
Alex Clare
Adrian Clark
Christine Clark
Sue Clark
Jo Clemmet
Wendy Cook
Nick Davey
Mary Delaney
Jamie Delano
Jo Dixon
Simon Drax
Alys Earl
James Ellis

Anna Emslie
Marie Fitzgerald
Hilary Gallo
Owen Garling
Amro Gebreel
John Giddins
Susan Godfrey
Caitlin Green
Diane Gregory
Maxim Griffin
Nikki Griffin
Carey Gustard
Elizabeth Gwiazdowska
Veronica Handover
Claire Handscombe
Andrea Harman
Lee Harrison
Grace Helmer
Bonny Hodge
G.P. Hyde
Oli Jacobs
Za'e Johnson
Sue Jones
Karen Keningale
Patrick Kincaid
Rosie Leak
Kirsty McKenzie
Peter Merrett
Adrian Mills
Kate Mitchell
Tony Morley
Susan Murray
Carlo Navato
Jamie Paradise
Sarah Parker
James Pierson

Emma Pusill (Plum Duff)
Gareth Rees
Louise Santa Ana
Bobby Seal
Dan Sloane
Jane Stephens
Tara Thomas-Hornsey
James Vella-Bardon
Paul Watson
Daniel Weir
Justine Whittern
Anjali Wierny
Sally Wright
Fiona Young

Coming soon, also by Eamonn Griffin

Canine Jubilee
the sequel to *East of England*

To be the first to hear about the *Canine Jubilee* crowdfunding campaign, visit the Unbound website at unbound.com, or follow @Unbound_Digital and @eamonngriffin on Twitter for the latest updates.

Read on for an exclusive extract from the new book…

Part One: Maundy Thursday

There was a knack to it, like there is to most things. Dan Matlock had picked it up in an hour or so. On the first day, the owner had let him struggle. See if he could work things out for himself; if he was savvy enough to ask for help if needed.

He pointed Matlock to a loaded pallet and asked him to handball half of them onto another.

Sacks of potatoes.

By the time the job was done, Matlock had the hang of it.

Dan Matlock had been out of jail a month. He was trying for a quiet life, not least since he had been involved – if not exactly responsible – for the death of two men in the week of his release. Since those two had been involved themselves in the murder of Matlock's father Joe, though, he wasn't getting any ulcers over worry about their souls. They'd been local gangsters. There might have been repercussions, but any threat of that seemed to have passed. Second-hand word had got back to Matlock that fair was fair, and no one had got what they didn't deserve.

Even so.

The closest thing Matlock had ever had until this week as a steady gig was debt collecting. Chris, a friend from way back, had come into money and had set herself up as a loan shark. Small-time stuff. Like running a catalogue, selling Avon. Near enough. And Matlock collected for her on debts overdue. But there wasn't much doing right now, and what with the last few weeks causing ructions, some time away from that line of work was no bad thing.

This was day four of the new job. Not quite halfway between Loweth and Grimsby on the eastern scarp of the Lincolnshire Wolds. You turn left off the main A16, and that takes you to Luthborough. Not much more than a passing place with a few houses. But there was a link road that'd take you north-west out of the county and towards the A1 north at Bawtry, and there was this place too. County Potatoes.

Truth was, they sold onions and carrots too, but spuds were the main business. A warehouse with three aisles: two for taters, the third shared by the other produce. All sold by the sack.

This is what Matlock learned on his first day. A sack of potatoes weighs fifty-six pounds. Half a hundredweight. Four stones. With one hundred and sixty stones in a ton, that meant you shifted a ton every time you clocked up another forty sacks.

You can move a fair few tons of King Edwards a day by hand.

That was the job. Potatoes came in either ready-bagged, or – just as likely – loose in pallet-sized wooden cubed hoppers. County Potatoes sold them on. Bulk stocks for greengrocers, chippies and hotel restaurants. Occasionally, a lorry-load for export out of the county, even overseas. A few times a day a sack of spuds got lifted into the boot of a car for domestic use, or for corner shops to sell on by the pound. They had a van for local deliveries. A forklift for unloading flatbed trucks and for pouring the crates of loose taters into the hopper above their bagging machine. There wasn't much to it.

Best of all, it was mostly outdoors work.

The agreement was that this short week – the long Easter weekend was coming so there were only four working days – was a trial. If it all worked out, then there'd be something more permanent arranged. Just so there'd be no concerns either way about being let down, the job was cash in hand, paid daily. Suited Matlock fine.

After two years inside, Matlock appreciated the flecks of rain in his face, the wind in his ears. The view, also: out front, the rise of the Wolds and the oncoming weather over the hills from the west; out back, the drop-off of the last of the slope to the floodplain, and – fifteen miles further out – the North Sea.

The fella who ran the place was Lol. Maybe sixty, balding, braces stretched over a gut barely held in place by his checked shirt. Blue factory trousers and rigger boots. Lol didn't do much except operate the forklift and take the money. He spent the rest of his time in the warehouse office. Taking orders, arranging for deliveries. Pencil in one hand and a ledger before him. Phone forever wedged between head and shoulder.

Lol was coming over. You didn't need to look to know. Boots clumping like he was Boris Karloff, wheezing like the thirty a day he smoked were catching up on him faster than Frankenstein's creature had ever shifted. Lol didn't smoke in his little cabin. Always came out at least as far as the warehouse doors, as though the fresh air counteracted the carcinogens.

Lol didn't talk much. A nod, then he'd light his cig, then he'd smoke it. Then he'd go inside.

All that was fine with Matlock too. What were they going to talk about, anyway? Football? Women? Telly? Lol was happy to stand in the mizzle, smoke his smoke, then get back to the phone before he got properly wet.

Not much was moving. No traffic. No wind to encourage the cloud.

'There,' Lol said.

'What's that?'

Lol held a finger up. 'There.'

A bird cry. Faint, but distinct nevertheless. It might have been a word. Curly. Split into two separate syllables. Cur-lee.

Matlock let Lol tell him.

'Curlew, that is. Don't often hear them this far inland. Should be on the beach, him, sticking for lugworms on the water's edge.'

They listened for a while, until the bird's call was lost to distance.

'Didn't know you were a birder,' Matlock said.

'Common knowledge. It was, once. We got taught birdsong at primary. Big old wind-up record player with a pile of seventy-eights. We all had notebooks. The idea was you kept a diary of what you'd heard and seen over the weekend, and make a little report in the class on Monday morning. Old Mr Lock'd then play us the calls of the birds we thought we'd seen. Show us slides of what they looked like.

'And not just birds neither. Leaves from trees, sketches of different grasses and sorts of bracken. Fish, if anyone'd been fishing. Small animals. All of it.'

'We didn't get any of that,' Matlock said.

'Shame.'

'Wide Range Readers. That's what we had. A load of story-books. Most of the stories were about the children of cavemen. And callig-

215

raphy. Our teachers were very into writing in italics with a fountain pen.'

'I've still got the notebooks,' Lol said. 'Mum kept them along with the school photographs and all that. I found them when we were clearing out her place after she left.'

'Better than having rusty penmanship.'

'I'd reckon.'

Lol lit another ciggie. Matlock pulled the hood on his waterproof over. Lol didn't seem to be minding the wet. No, it wasn't that. Something else. He wanted to say something. But he couldn't find a way to raise the subject.

He'd come round to it. If it was important, he'd say something. If not, not. He had all day, then they'd be shut over the long Easter weekend. Back open Tuesday, assuming Matlock had passed his four-day work trial. He couldn't think that he hadn't.

Then a van pulled into the yard. A bloke got out and asked for a couple of sacks of whatever was cheapest. Matlock loaded him up, Lol took the money, fetched him his change, then went back inside out of the weather, which was worsening. A few minutes later the phone rang, but it got picked up on the second ring.

*

Matlock heard the curlew again about three-thirty. It had brightened up, the asphalt yard had all but dried, and there'd been enough of a bank holiday weekend flurry of calls to have made the day speed past. He'd barely had time to eat his pack-up. Busy was best; not so much for the effect it had in speeding up time, but in the training. The thick end of a week shifting spuds had proved to be good for Matlock's body. He was getting stronger again. Leaner. He'd never been weighty, but the last couple of years of institutional food had taken its effect. He was feeling better.

And the birdsong helped too. Joe would have liked it. His Dad had been older than Lol but they had that same Lincolnshire thing. Country lads who'd been brought up in the expectation that they'd have a relationship with the land. Farmhand or engineer, it all came back to the soil. Lol was maybe the last generation of folk who knew what it was they saw, felt, heard, smelled, ate. Who understood they were part of something larger, and that there were responsibilities that came along with that.

Time for a last sweep of the yard.

Matlock ran a brush over the worst of the soil that'd accumulated through the day. Tidy enough. Knocking-off time was flexible here. The rule of thumb seemed to be if there'd been no customers – and no deliveries were expected – for half an hour at any time after four, then that was that. He assumed that folk would have made their bank holiday preparations stock-wise. That there'd be no more customers now. And there weren't any deliveries today. Today was a day to be headed back to base, not for venturing out.

The phone rang. Lol had a line set up so if there was no one in the office, another bell sounded that'd be heard clear across the yard. That bell was ringing now.

Usually it rang because Lol was out here smoking, or else he'd nipped to the lavvy that backed onto the office.

Usually, Matlock let it be. If it was important, they'd ring back. And besides, Lol was the office man. That was his work.

The bell kept ringing. In the background, the echo of its office buddy. There wasn't any way of shutting it off. Not unless you picked up the receiver in the office, or put it down at the other end when you got fed up of waiting on the line. Or if you went into the office and toggled the leccy from day to night mode. That shut everything down except the emergency lights and the alarm system. Not that there were many spud bandits roaming the county. The worst of it was checking the bait stations first thing each morning for any vermin, then going around if any had been caught to see if there'd been any stock spoilage.

The bell still hadn't stopped.

Okay then. Matlock went back into the warehouse. Timed a shout between the rings. 'Lol?'

Nothing.

Matlock went into the office. Picked up the receiver. 'Hello. County Potatoes?'

'Lawrence?' Male, local.

'He's not here right now. I can take a message.'

The line went dead. Cut off at the other end.

Matlock replaced the handset in the cradle. Glanced about. Found a notepad – a promotional giveaway from Skegthorpe Stadium – and a pencil. Lol was a chewer; teeth-marks under the ring of metal binding the eraser to the shaft of the pencil. He made a note. CALL REC'D 4PM. NO MESSAGE. You'd never tell he'd once been half-decent with a fountain pen. Left the notepad on top of the ledger Lol used to account for goods in and out. Stock cars and speedway bikes swirled on the logo on the paper.

Matlock checked the loo. Nope. He hadn't come out of the front of the warehouse. There was no way he'd have been able to have sneaked past.

Matlock went up and down the aisles of racking. Checked by the packaging and weighing machine. By the charger where the fork-lift was plugged in. Lol wasn't in the warehouse.

There was a back door. A concession to fire safety regulations, Matlock supposed. One of those push bars to open it. All this week it had been padlocked up, regs be damned. One less thing to have to check when locking up.

The padlock was on the floor, the chain used to secure the door coiled alongside.

Matlock pushed the fire door open. Out back there was more hard standing. Stacks of knackered pallets, for repair or for firewood. Some companies kept their broken ones to give to charity come November as Bonfire Night contributions. Then a hedge, and beyond that farmland. They were up on a bit of a ridge here. The land fell away to the A16.

There was a gap in the hedge where a man might get through. Enough of a desire line to show this was a semi-regular route. Some of the boot-prints looked fresh enough.

Okay. Maybe a bit weird. But okay. It was his business. Come and go as you please when you're the boss.

Matlock went back inside. Left the fire door ajar so Lol could get back in.

Then Matlock went to the office again.

First things. Top left-hand drawer of the desk. There was a cash box there. Matlock opened the drawer. The box was present. A set of keys also. The set looked complete: front shutters, office, toggle switch to go from day to night mode on the electrics. A smaller key that Matlock assumed would fit the fire door padlock. The keys weren't worn like a set used every day. Spares. Matlock took them.

He made a tea from the kettle in the office. Took the brew outside. Waited till five, then came back inside. There'd been no more customers, and Lol hadn't come back.

He didn't have a home number for Lol. Didn't know where he lived. Had met him here, and only here.

And he was owed a day's pay.

Matlock took his mug back inside, rinsed it out, and put it on the drainer by the sink in the office. He locked the fire door. Turned the electrics to their night settings. Brought the main warehouse shutters down and locked them the way Lol had shown him.

Lol came and went in the works van. Not quite a Transit. Didn't need to be. The vehicle stood there. If there was a spare set of keys then Matlock hadn't seen them. Nothing else for it. He'd have to leave it parked up. What was the alternative? Break a window and let the handbrake go, then ballachingly shunt it to the dark side of the roller shutters? Hardly.

If Lol was gone for the weekend he'd be lucky to have his wheels come Tuesday. Someone'd come along and have it, no problem.

Matlock gave it another few minutes just in case. Sat in his car until it felt like he'd done his duty and more. Then he set out to see Chris.

Matlock found a phone box first. Chris preferred her guests announced, if not dissuaded.

'Hey.'

'Got me any free spuds?'

'No.'

'Typical.'

'Got a question for you though.'

'Oh?'

'Lol.'

'What about him?'

'He bunked off early. Four-ish. Maybe earlier.'

'And?'

'And didn't come back. Sneaked out the back. Went without giving me a heads-up. Left his van.'

'So?'

'So I locked up.'

'Good man.' Pause. 'Okay, so what's the question?'

'I want to know where he lives. Man owes me a day's wage.'

'You need a sub?'

'I'm okay for cash. It's …'

'The principle of the thing?'

'Something like that.'

'One sec.' The sound of a phone being put down. Rustling. Then being picked up again. 'Tell you what. Pop over. Give me half an hour, though, cos I've got the kids' tea to sort out.'

'What they having?'

'Fish fingers and tater waffles.'

'See, you didn't need any spuds.'

'No harm in asking though. Half an hour, yeah?'

'Yeah.'

Near-silence down the line. The crackle of Chris working out how to say something. 'You reckon summat's up.'

'Yeah.'

'I'd warn you off sticking your beak in, but I know what you're like.'

Matlock sighed. 'Yeah.'